Praise for Jennifer O'Connell's Novels

The down-low on *Insider Dating*

"I'm crazy about Jennifer O'Connell's novels, and *Insider Dating* is another fun, smart, and insightful treat!"
—Melissa Senate, author of *See Jane Date* and *Love You to Death*

"Jennifer O'Connell is awesome! *Insider Dating* kept me glued to its pages as it told the story of Abby Dunn, a database I'd like to see in reality, and what happens when you not only expect the other shoe to drop—but kick it off yourself. A must read!"
—Megan Crane, author of *Frenemies* and *Everyone Else's Girl*

"What if a database could tell you everything you might need to know about someone, before you even met? *Insider Dating* asks just that with results that are both very funny and surprisingly heartfelt. I laughed out loud, I pondered, and I was ultimately thankful that such a database doesn't exist. Jennifer O'Connell's best book yet!"
—Alison Pace, author of *Pug Hill* and *If Andy Warhol Had a Girlfriend*

Everyone's top pick: *Bachelorette #1*

"Sarah's voice is fresh, occasionally sarcastic but always honest. . . . The result is a combination of insight and humor built on the foundation of an entertaining premise."
—*The Denver Post*

"A poolside page-turner. . . . If you long to be on a reality show, you'll love this behind-the-scenes peek."
—*Cosmopolitan*

"Hot book pick."
—*US Weekly*

"O'Connell's sassy novel is more fun than watching a reality dating show."
—*Women's Own*

continued . . .

insider dating

Jennifer O'Connell

NEW AMERICAN LIBRARY

New American Library
Published by New American Library, a division of
Penguin Group (USA) Inc., 375 Hudson Street,
New York, New York 10014, USA
Penguin Group (Canada), 90 Eglinton Avenue East, Suite 700, Toronto,
Ontario M4P 2Y3, Canada (a division of Pearson Penguin Canada Inc.)
Penguin Books Ltd., 80 Strand, London WC2R 0RL, England
Penguin Ireland, 25 St. Stephen's Green, Dublin 2,
Ireland (a division of Penguin Books Ltd.)
Penguin Group (Australia), 250 Camberwell Road, Camberwell, Victoria 3124,
Australia (a division of Pearson Australia Group Pty. Ltd.)
Penguin Books India Pvt. Ltd., 11 Community Centre, Panchsheel Park,
New Delhi - 110 017, India
Penguin Group (NZ), 67 Apollo Drive, Rosedale, North Shore,
Auckland 1311, New Zealand (a division of Pearson New Zealand Ltd.)
Penguin Books (South Africa) (Pty.) Ltd., 24 Sturdee Avenue,
Rosebank, Johannesburg 2196, South Africa

Penguin Books Ltd., Registered Offices:
80 Strand, London WC2R 0RL, England

First published by New American Library,
a division of Penguin Group (USA) Inc.

First Printing, May 2007
1 3 5 7 9 10 8 6 4 2

Copyright © Jennifer O'Connell, 2007

REGISTERED TRADEMARK—MARCA REGISTRADA

LIBRARY OF CONGRESS CATALOGING-IN-PUBLICATION DATA
O'Connell, Jennifer.
Insider dating / Jennifer O'Connell.
p. cm.
ISBN: 978-0-451-22116-2
1. Women bankers—Fiction.   2. Divorced women—Fiction.   3. Boston (Mass.)—Fiction.   4. Dating
(Social customs)—Fiction.   I. Title.
PS3615.C65I57 2007
813'.6—dc22   2006100308

Set in Centaur
Designed by Ginger Legato

Printed in the United States of America

For Vicki and Vangie, the best friends a girl could ever capsize with,

who, twenty years after the K's, still make me laugh . . .

and cringe . . . and do things I know I'll regret in the morning.

ACKNOWLEDGMENTS

Once again, thanks to Kara Cesare and Kristin Nelson
for their constant encouragement. And to my writer friends, who are
generous, honest, opinionated and so much fun.

"There is nothing so disastrous as a rational investment policy in an irrational world."

—John Maynard Keynes

"If past history was all there was to the game, the richest people would be librarians."

—Warren Buffet

prologue

Have you ever loved someone so much that you wish him happiness, even if it's not with you?

Good luck. Be happy. I hope you find what you're looking for. Those words sound so bittersweet, so achingly perfect when they're spoken over soft background music right before the final credits begin scrolling up an oversized screen.

That's the way it's supposed to be, right? When it's all over and his name is permanently deleted from your Palm Pilot, after you've divvied up the wok and all of the accessories you were supposed to use to re-create the sesame chicken from Ming Garden, and returned your now-favorite sleeping shirt to its rightful owner, you're supposed to wish him well. Because that's what grown-ups do.

And I thought I was a grown-up. I had all the accoutrements of an adult. I had a job that I couldn't blow off by pinching my nose shut and pretending to be sick while I left a message on my boss's voice mail. I had a mortgage that required proof of my dependability and ability to pay bills on time. And I had a reverence for my youth, including an on-going weakness for SweeTarts and the firmly held belief that pink Jellies sandals were the perfect complement to a pair of Jordache jeans with zippers at the ankle.

Adults forgive and then they forget. They bury the hatchet and let bygones be bygones. They learn that to err is human but to forgive is divine.

But what I learned was that I'm not that forgiving. I want answers. I want an explanation. I want penance.

And, once I finally admitted that, once I said it out loud, I learned something else.

I wasn't the only one.

They say that hell hath no fury like a woman scorned. But we weren't scorned; we were armed with experience. We had information, and information is power. In fact, there were enough of us around to form the biggest support group in history—if we wanted to sit and do nothing but cry into our cold mocha lattes and Krispy Kremes. But I'm not a crier. And I don't drink coffee. So I had a better idea. Instead, we could create a network that helped women look out for one another. A secret sisterhood. An underground information superhighway where women could find the dependable data they needed to avoid mistakes and shitty boyfriends didn't stand a chance.

And I was just the person to make it happen.

Score one for the girls.

chapter one

We're expected to remember our *firsts*. A first kiss. Our first day of school. The first time we considered the idea that maybe the presents under the Christmas tree had more to do with the locked closet in the basement than with a bearded man in a red suit. Firsts are supposed to open up a whole new world to us, to offer a sort of introduction to what lies ahead. In a way, they're the start of one thing and the beginning of the end for others. A first kiss eventually leads to sex. Kindergarten leads to college. And the realization that Santa Claus is more wishful thinking than Toys "R" Us gravy train sets us up for a lifetime of last-minute shopping and the Christmas Eve rationalization that a pair of one-size-fits-all gloves from the revolving rack beside the Stop & Shop checkout line is exactly the right gift, no matter who the recipient.

I do remember a lot of firsts, although I'm not sure they're the monumental occasions everyone expects. There was the first time I realized you should never jump on a trampoline if you have to pee. And the night I first discovered that the only thing worse than bed spins is experiencing the horizontal whirls at 2 a.m. In someone else's bed. On the top bunk, in a fraternity house where the bathroom doesn't seem nearly as convenient as simply leaning over the edge of the mattress. The poor guy on the bottom bunk also experienced a first that night. And I'm sure from then on he made it a point to never sleep below another freshman drunk on keg beer and peach Riunite.

But with all the firsts that have filled my life, the one first I never thought I'd be experiencing was the first anniversary of the end of my marriage.

Now, 365 days after I signed my name with the new Montblanc pen Maggie and Claudia bought me especially for the occasion, I was seated at Kingfish Hall for a celebratory lunch. Only the occasion I was celebrating had nothing to do with rejoicing in my ability to successfully navigate the legalities of marital dissolution and everything to do with the fact that I couldn't get out of celebrating my coworker's birthday.

Verity Financial wasn't some touchy-feely financial services firm, as if such a thing existed. There was no employee fitness facility, and we weren't encouraged to have a life outside the floor-to-ceiling glass windows of our Exchange Place headquarters. Birthday lunches were not the norm, nor were they as celebrated as beating the S&P 500 or landing an interview on CNBC. But when the birthday boy's portfolio is returning twenty percent for three years running, Verity ponies up. A seafood lunch isn't nearly as expensive as losing a top fund manager.

"How's the salad, Abby?" Jason asked me from across the table. Seven pairs of eyes waited for my answer, waited for me to admit that I should have tried the chowder as they'd all insisted.

"Great," I told them, and went back to picking the anchovies off my Greek salad. The dingy, limp strings now lying across my bread plate were my attempt to placate an entire table that couldn't understand how a woman who lived in Boston didn't eat seafood. To them I was the culinary version of Benedict Arnold, a midwestern transplant who swore off gifts from the sea after an early childhood being force-fed Gorton's fish sticks dipped in ketchup.

My coworkers smiled at me and went back to their lobster rolls and scallops, but not before giving one another knowing looks that said they didn't believe me for a minute.

I took a bite of the salad, still salty from the discarded anchovies, and reminded myself to order a burger next time.

The lunch crowd continued to grow around us, the tables turning over faster than the shrimp rotating on the dancing fish rotisserie, their crescent-shaped bodies speared through the center by spikes that made the cooking apparatus look less like an open pit grill and more like an S and M carnival ride.

"Here, sign this," Sarah whispered in my ear before discreetly passing a card under the table until it rested on my lap. There was no writing instrument included with her covert instructions. I reached into my purse, just as I had almost one year ago to the hour, and pulled out a stainless steel Montblanc pen.

"The salesperson wanted us to get a classic black one, but we thought this was better suited to the task," Maggie had explained to me when I opened their gift the night before Alex and I were meeting at our lawyer's office to sign the papers. We couldn't share a home, a life together, or a future, but Alex had suggested we share an attorney. Despite Claudia's insistence that I needed my own representation, in the end working with one lawyer just seemed easier, seemed more civil than getting an attorney to oppose his own. Maggie couldn't believe I was being so nice, but that was really the point, wasn't it? To prove I wasn't the bitch he wanted to move out on, to demonstrate I was still the woman he'd wanted to marry. To show, once and for all, that I was still the girl he fell in love with. Besides, not going along with Alex's suggestion would have been like admitting that I wanted to drag it out, that I wanted to prolong what was quickly becoming the inevitable. And I didn't want Alex to know that I wasn't ready to give up, that I wasn't ready to give *him* up. So I said yes, and the attorney's retainer fee came out of our joint checking account.

I'd taken the gift box from Maggie and slipped the heavy metal pen from the blue velvet. "It's gorgeous," I told them, noticing my reflection in the polished stainless steel barrel.

"It's the Montblanc version of steel balls," Claudia added. "Not that you need any help, but it can't hurt."

And it didn't. The next day when the attorney handed me a black Bic pen, its logo worn away from all the couples who came before us, I took out my stainless steel Montblanc and held it up to the light. I was packing my own heat. I had my very own silver bullet. If this was the last time Alex and I would face off, if we weren't going to share anything from this day forward, not sharing a pen seemed like a good place to start. I placed the eighteen-carat-gold nib on the page and signed on the thin black line.

Now I used the pen to sign a card featuring Snoopy and all his pals declaring HAPPY BIRTHDAY FROM THE GANG! It was chosen from the hundreds of cards marking today's event, and it wasn't lost on me that there wasn't a single card commemorating my own un-anniversary, my own anticelebration. Divorce wasn't exactly a Hallmark holiday.

In the past few years I'd added a few unexpected items to my list of firsts, although in hindsight I should have seen them coming from a mile away. I was the first of my friends to get married, but only because Claudia didn't accept a proposal from an overeager mime who pledged his undying love by falling to both knees on the cobblestones of Faneuil Hall.

I'd experienced my first engagement, my first wedding, and my first marriage. And after that disintegrated, I earned a new title: Alex's first wife. And here I thought I'd be his last.

When I called Claudia and Maggie that now infamous Friday night, they'd sprung into action, almost as if they anticipated something like this might happen, like they were the relationship equivalent of an emergency rescue team just waiting to slide down the pole and rush out to the scene of the crime. They were at my door, a door that until that day I'd considered *our door*, before I could even begin to comprehend the profound rippling effect two little words—*I'm leaving*—could have.

I'm leaving. I'd heard Alex say it before, so it wasn't the words themselves that sent a shock through my body as if my synapses were firing bullets instead of electrical currents. He'd say it every Saturday morning before heading out the door for the dry cleaner, his arms overwhelmed by wrinkled dress shirts, folded pants, and worn suit jackets turned inside out so only the shiny satiny lining was visible. He'd say it in the mornings before walking out the door for work, and in the evenings after he'd changed into his running shorts and a faded Princeton T-shirt that by now was more rusty marigold than Tiger orange.

No, it wasn't the words themselves that made me take notice. It was the way he managed to turn two little words, three little syllables, a contraction and a word that dropped its *e* before adding *ing*, into a declaration. An announcement. It was his emancipation proclamation. He wasn't just leaving. He was leaving me.

My two best friends didn't waste any time circling the wagons, didn't hesitate to close ranks. The enemy had been identified. He was tagged and labeled for future reference. The enemy was my soon-to-be ex-husband. The enemy was Alex.

It was easy to let them make Alex the villain. It was easier than reminding them that he was someone they used to joke around with, someone they'd vacationed with, someone they'd even liked. It was easier than pointing out that the guy who used to make them laugh with his impressions of Claudia's computer science students had simply decided he didn't love me.

"*Pst*, pass it on," I stage-whispered, and quickly passed the Snoopy card clockwise to my left like a hot potato.

While my coworkers attempted to dissect the Federal Reserve Chairman's psyche and determine whether or not our year-end bonuses would be affected by the ongoing investigation into Verity Financial's trading practices, their own voices rising as they attempted to be heard over the increasing volume of the dining room, the conversation coming from the table behind me suddenly dropped an octave. I turned to see what had happened and noticed a table with two women huddled together over the bread basket.

I strained to hear their conversation, and even though I couldn't catch all the details, the gist of the situation was clear. The woman who'd ordered the fried calamari was quietly listening while the woman who'd asked for the crab cakes relayed the details of how she'd just been dumped.

In the past year I've developed a fascination with breakup stories. They can be amiable partings of the ways or knock-down, drag-out events, and it doesn't matter. I still find myself wanting to know the details. What time of day was it, where were they standing, was there any warning before the bomb was dropped and the announcement filled the room like noxious gas?

I discreetly slid my chair away from our table and closer to the duo behind me, making sure the legs didn't scrape too loudly against the hardwood floor and give me away.

As far as my own story, it was nothing dramatic, nothing like you see on TV soap operas or nighttime dramas with cliff-hanger endings.

The wedding china wasn't smashed against the kitchen walls in an effort to illustrate the shattering of our relationship, and neither of us tossed the other's clothes out an open window onto the street (it was January, in Boston, so opening a window wouldn't have been a smart choice). For such a significant event, it was downright uneventful.

About an hour after Alex walked out the front door, I called Claudia.

"Alex left," I told her, using a variation of Alex's own words.

"By *left*, you mean . . ." She let the question trail off, waiting for me to fill in the blank, even though I now know she understood exactly what I meant.

I didn't attempt an explanation, didn't rewind the scene to the point at which Alex walked into the kitchen and just stood there waiting for me to stop emptying the dishwasher. There was no need to describe the lack of expression on his face, or how, after the front door closed behind him, I realized where I'd seen those same empty eyes, the identical flat line formed by the pressing together of two emotionless lips: ESPN's coverage of the World Series of Poker. Apparently my husband wasn't watching out of mere fascination for the game. He was picking up tips on how to play his hand.

Claudia's question filled the silence, almost seeming to stretch down the phone lines from her apartment in Cambridge to my condo in Back Bay, straddling the space between us until I answered.

I meant he left and he wasn't coming back. I meant he left—left me, our home, our marriage, and from what I could tell, drawers full of clothes he felt he didn't need. But telling Claudia that he left implied he could return. People leave all the time. And they come back.

I chose my words carefully. And that's when I said it out loud for the first time. "Alex is gone."

Claudia didn't ask me whether there was a chance we could reconcile or suggest we see a professional to help us work through our issues.

And we had plenty of issues. Unfortunately they weren't the types of issues that could be easily defined. I couldn't flip through our photo albums, point to a picture and declare, *There, that's when I caught him wearing my water bra and thong while singing "Like a Virgin" into the Baccarat bud vase we got for our wedding.* I couldn't gaze at the calendar hanging in our pantry and identify the day our relationship shifted, a morning I woke up and realized we were irrevocably broken. There was no aha moment, unless you counted the fact that I suspected he had stopped loving me, a fact that was confirmed by the time our divorce was officially recorded by the state of Massachusetts.

"Are you listening to this conversation?" Sarah leaned over toward me and tipped her head in the direction of the two women seated behind us.

"I've caught a few well-chosen words—*prick, asshole, fucking prick, fucking asshole.*"

Sarah leaned in even closer, her breasts hovering precariously over my plate of discarded anchovies. No matter how many buttons she fastened, no matter how pinstriped her suit or broad her lapels, Sarah couldn't hide the fact that she had the double-D cups of a pole dancer, even if she had the brain of a Harvard MBA. "Some guy sent the crabcake girl an e-mail saying that he wanted to break up."

"At least he told her. Maggie didn't find out her last boyfriend was breaking up with her until he called the store and ordered a bouquet of pink gerbera daisies for his new girlfriend. Apparently they were the new girlfriend's favorite."

"What a shit." Sarah shook her head in disgust. "Besides, who'd ask for daisies? I told my boyfriend I want nothing but French tulips."

"He told Maggie that even though he didn't want to date her anymore, he still thought she was the most creative florist in the city—like that was supposed to be some sort of consolation."

"Well, the woman eating the crab cakes"—she nodded toward the table behind us—"she said it wasn't the e-mail that really bothered her. It was that he CC'd the new girl he'd already started dating. I guess he wanted a paper trail."

"He's must be a lawyer," I told Sarah. "Nobody else would think of that. It's just beyond shitty. It's downright . . ." I struggled to find the right word.

"Man-ly?" Sarah suggested, summing up my thoughts exactly. "I don't think he's a lawyer, though. I heard something about him being on call. I think he's a doctor."

Sarah removed her breasts from the table and turned to join a conversation with two foreign currency portfolio managers.

I sat quietly sipping my iced tea, my ears listening for more details of the cyber-breakup. I seriously doubted the guy who dumped her was feeling any guilt about the fact that this poor woman was drowning her sorrows in shredded crab and mango salsa. He wasn't dissecting every dinner conversation, every sideways glance they'd exchanged since the day they met, every morning he left for the office without a good-bye kiss. That's the luxury of being the one who breaks it off. You have the answers. You're the one who called it quits, and there's power in that. It doesn't matter if you're a sixth grader or a thirty-year-old woman. It doesn't matter if his best friend comes up to you on the playground and tells you that the boy who once said he'd always share his Butterfingers doesn't like you anymore, or if your husband tells you he's moving out. The person who walks away will always be the one who had control. The person who leaves will always be the one who didn't think it was worth staying. And no matter how it's spun, no matter how much the other person insists she wasn't happy either, she'll always be the one who was left behind.

Because the truth is, it's not like I wasn't unhappily married, too.

That was actually one of the few things Alex and I shared in the end: a mutual dissatisfaction with our relationship. Alex just decided to do something about it. But even though we were officially through, even though we'd stood in front of a judge and declared our intent to part ways, there was a very small part of me where Alex still lingered. Like the far corners of a closet where dust accumulates, stray buttons settle, and eight-legged creatures spin delicate webs, in some dark crevice in my head a tiny piece of him was still lodged.

I'd thought by now that all memory of Alex and our years together would be eradicated, completely washed from my memory like those first few years of childhood. But even a year later, I can't get rid of them. It wasn't as easy as packing away photos in a cardboard box. I couldn't surround the memories in bubble wrap and place them in storage with all the other remnants of our relationship.

In high school chemistry class we learned about the half-life of radioactive elements, how some of the original substance will always remain, finally disappearing only as time approaches infinity. Maybe my expectations were unrealistic. One year apart seems mighty short compared to infinity.

"Hey, Abby, what do you think?" Jason called to me from across the table, basking in the glow of the festivities we were throwing in his honor. The only thing missing from the birthday grin on his face was a birthday crown perched atop his head.

"About what?" I answered, refocusing my attention toward the birthday boy.

"What do you think is the greatest risk these days?" He repeated the question that plagued the table of financial analysts and portfolio managers. Sarah and I were outnumbered six to two. We were drowning in testosterone, and it smelled like hair gel, four-thousand-dollar Zegna suits and last night's Bombay Sapphire martinis.

The greatest risk? God, that was too easy. "Men," I muttered under my breath. Sarah nudged me and laughed into her napkin.

"What was that?" Birthday Boy asked.

"The yen," I repeated, more loudly, even though my first answer stuck in my mind. "I said the yen."

The table was off and running on how they'd hedge against the yen, but I didn't join in. My first answer was way more intriguing.

What if women could hedge their bets when it came to underperforming men? After all, guys weren't that different from stocks and bonds and foreign currency. Without perfect market information, there was no sure thing. It was all about risk management, about making sure you maximized your upside while minimizing the downside. It was what I did all day for a living, analyzing the market, evaluating investments, providing the information necessary to choose when to buy, sell or hold. What if we could provide women with the data they need to make informed decisions about investing their greatest assets—themselves?

It was brilliant. Rank men like we rank stocks. Compile data, analyze factors and evaluate risk. Give women the objective information they need to assess their risk and invest accordingly.

It was fabulous, if a tad bit unrealistic. Still, one could imagine, couldn't one?

The chair behind me moved, and I turned to see the doctor's ex-girlfriend walking toward the restroom. Even if the market for men was inherently risky, and there were no guarantees, there was one thing I was sure of. A doctor who uses e-mail to cover his ass should be avoided, and the woman walking to the ladies' room had information that could help other women steer clear.

I laid my napkin on the table beside my salad and stood up. "Excuse me. I'll be right back."

The sink area of the women's room was empty when I opened the door. Now that I was here, I wasn't sure what to do. I'd just followed a stranger into the women's room. The person I saw in the mirror wasn't a woman in search of answers. She was a woman lurking outside a stall door waiting for a total stranger to flush the toilet.

When the rush of water finally filled the bowl and the stall door opened, I stared at my reflection and pretended to maneuver an imaginary contact lens.

I caught the woman's eyes in the mirror and smiled. She attempted a smile in return.

Here was my chance. I had about thirty seconds before she left me standing alone in a bathroom that smelled like artificial lemons and Lysol. And about five seconds before she thought I was a restroom stalker.

"Looks like you're having a tough day," I said, and reached for the paper-towel dispenser.

"Not one of my best," she admitted.

I handed her a paper towel and waited while she dried her hands. I knew I shouldn't say anything, but I couldn't stay quiet. I was on a mission. I already knew too much to ignore the situation, and now I had an obligation. "Look, I overheard what happened, and I'm sorry."

She froze, the brown paper crumpled in her hands. "Why? Are you her? Are you the girl he CC'd?"

"No," I quickly answered, acutely aware that the sharp metal edges of a tampon dispenser could cause significant bodily harm if needed. "God no."

"Well, thanks, but you shouldn't be sorry." She balled up the now-soggy paper and tossed it in the garbage can. "You didn't do anything."

"True. It's just that we've all been there."

"I guess we have, haven't we. Like they say, that's life." She attempted to sound cavalier, but her voice cracked and I had a feeling tears weren't too far behind.

"I guess," I agreed, not convinced that life had to be like that. "Look, would you mind if I asked you a question?"

She shook her head.

"Can you tell me his name? I mean, just in case any of my friends come across him in the future. So I can warn them."

She instantly understood. The tears seemed to dry up and her voice was steady. In fact, she seemed all too happy to share the information with me. "Martin Beck." She spoke his name slowly and deliberately, as if she wanted me to commit it to memory. "Dr. Martin Beck."

I nodded and made a point of repeating his name a few times so I wouldn't forget it. "Thanks."

"Do you want his address, too?" she offered, seeming less like the fragile woman stabbing a fork at her crab cakes and more like a woman who'd taken back some control.

"No, that's okay," I told her, not even sure what I'd do now that I had his name. "But thanks anyway."

"My pleasure." She grasped the door handle but hesitated before pulling it open. "And if you ever do happen to run into him, make a point of commenting on his ears. He's a plastic surgeon. It drives him crazy." She pushed through the door and left me alone with my new information. My one piece of data. My *first* piece of data.

Although none of my friends had ever received an Internet rejection, we could relate to that woman looking for consolation in a mélange of crab, mango salsa and Chinese sauce. She was every woman. She was us.

Dr. Martin Beck. He wasn't the first guy ever to break a woman's heart. But it would be nice if I could make him the last.

chapter two

aggie's flower "shoppe" was only a ten-dollar cab ride from my office, but still I was late.

The first thing you notice when you walk into the Flower Carte isn't the way it looks. There are the requisite tall slender buckets lining the walls, of course, the dull, hammered-steel pails neatly displaying daffodils, irises and black-eyed Susans. But it isn't the contrast of colors, or the way Maggie manages to make even an unassuming collection of sunflowers seem extraordinary, that makes you pause in the slate-floor entrance even after the door's closed behind you. It's the smell, a combination of sweet and clean. It's exactly the scent I imagine advertising agencies are attempting to conjure up in those detergent commercials, the ones with people galloping in slow motion through fields of wildflowers, their brilliantly white laundry billowing in the breeze on a rope that's casually strung between two oak trees.

"I'm sorry," I apologized before my mom or Maggie even had a chance to say anything. I inhaled the slightly humid air of the shoppe and made my way over to where they were waiting for me, snapshots of flowers spread out on the wrought-iron table in front of them.

At the very least I expected my mom to remind me that I was supposed to meet them a half hour ago, that we'd had this appointment scheduled for weeks, but instead she waved me over to the table without saying a word. Even Maggie looked up and gave me a reassuring smile instead of appearing put out by my delay. And that's when I knew something was up.

When she made the appointment at Maggie's, my mother clearly didn't remember the significance of the date. But I did. I remembered everything about it. I remembered waking up to a weather report that called for partly cloudy skies with a chance of scattered rain, and debating whether I should slip on practical loafers that could withstand puddles or the three-inch heels I'd planned on wearing so Alex and I would stand eye to eye one last time. I could describe in detail the green nylon collar on the Labrador puppy I found squatting outside my condo taking a pee, and the way his owner shrugged at me as if to say, *Hey, what are you gonna do about it?* And I knew the exact time, how the red second hand swept past the numeral seven as I put my Montblanc to paper at precisely 1:24 p.m. But my mom couldn't know that, and I didn't mention it. As far as she was concerned, today was like every other Wednesday. However, from the kind greeting I received, it was obvious that Maggie had clued her in. And although they didn't come right out and say anything, it was obvious the irony wasn't lost on any of us.

"I think we already have it figured out," my mom told me, reaching for my hand as I took a seat next to her. She traced the knuckles at the base of my fingers with the flat, smooth pad of her thumb, almost seeming to make a conscious effort to avoid the bare skin where my wedding band once took up what many women consider to be a prime piece of real estate. Now that very ring was sealed away in a Ziploc bag stuffed in the back of my underwear drawer, and my mother's left hand was weighed down by a perfect one-carat diamond solitaire. "What do you think?"

On the table Maggie had overlaid four flower photographs so that they resembled an actual bouquet.

"It's going to be beautiful. Blueberries—because they're getting married on Martha's Vineyard—tweedia, popcorn hydrangeas and delphiniums," Maggie explained, pointing to each of the photos as she named the flowers. "Your mom was also thinking you could wear peach, but I told her that might clash with the flowers."

My mom nodded. "Maggie thought maybe something more neutral for your dress."

I bowed my head in thanks, gave Maggie a look that said, *I owe you one,* and then gave my mom a look that said, *They're gorgeous.*

"You really like them?" My mom squeezed my hand, looking for reassurance.

"I really do," I told her, meaning every word.

Popcorn. Blueberries. Peach. If the woman sitting next to me was just another one of Maggie's clients, I would have asked whether she was planning to carry a bouquet or a light snack. I would have said that I liked blueberries as much as the next person, but that they belonged in muffins or on top of a cheesecake, not in the hands of a bride. But the woman on my left wasn't just a client. She was my mom.

In less than three months my mother was going to be a bride for the second time, and I was going to be her maid of honor, an honor that made me actually feel quite matronly. After all, my marital track record was the same as that of a sixty-year-old woman who wanted to carry a berry known for its antioxidant properties. Even though my father took barely eleven months to marry the woman he was seeing when my parents separated, it had taken my mother eighteen years to muster up the courage to say yes to another man. She'd resisted Roger's proposals for six years, and now was finally going to walk down the aisle with a bouquet of blueberries and the hopeful expectation that her second marriage would outlast her first. And I was going to be by her side.

So, even if my mother wanted me to wear a peach dress and carry a bunch of Chiquita bananas, it was her wedding, her day to start over. Who was I to make fun of a preference for fruit? I think my bouquet included poison ivy and something with thorns.

Actually, I carried a bouquet of Orange Unique roses, delphiniums and freesia, the names of which I know only because Maggie had spent so much time going over my selections with me. I'd just pointed to the buds I liked and told her, *The salmony-colored roses, the bluish ones and the little purple things.*

My mother and I sat in these exact two chairs back then, poring over snapshots with Maggie. I remember my mom listening intently as Maggie explained each flower, sketched out options and waited for my reaction. *That one*, I'd wanted to yell every time another slightly different shade of orange rose was put in front of me. *No, that one*, I'd wanted to shriek, practically levitating in my chair like those over-the-top brides they have on reality shows and *Oprah*. But I didn't. Instead I attempted to temper my enthusiasm with restraint, to show the right mix of excitement for Maggie's suggestions and still show my mom that I was a rational, sensible person. Given that I was about seventy-three days away from marrying Alex (at the time, I kept track in my Palm Pilot), it wasn't easy. And now that it was her turn, I thought my mom would be more excited and less tentative. I thought she'd be more like the *Oprah* bride and less like the daughter who was afraid to show her mom how elated she truly was.

Even though my mom never once acted anything less than thrilled with the idea of helping me plan my wedding, I always felt like I was celebrating something that she'd lost, like I was planning to begin what she'd already ended. It wasn't that I felt like I was rubbing it in exactly, but I did make a conscious effort to try not to remind her of what she no longer had.

So, now, when my mom didn't joyfully announce her flower selection, when she didn't gush about how beautiful the blueberries would look next to the popcorn hydrangea, I couldn't help but wonder whether she was doing the same for me.

"So, is that it? Are we all set?" Maggie asked, beginning to gather the loose photos into a pile.

"I think so." My mom let go of my hand and turned to me. "You like them, don't you?"

"They're perfect," I told her.

My mother was sixty years old and didn't really need the consent of her thirty-one-year-old daughter to go through with a wedding, but I got the feeling she wanted it. It was almost as if she was looking for my endorsement, some sort of Good Housekeeping Seal that could be stamped on Roger's forehead, assuring her that he had been thoroughly tested and guaranteed to perform according to expectations. And if there was any way to guarantee her happiness somehow, to warranty that this time around things would be different, I'd do it. But for now, my thumbs-up for her bouquet would have to do.

Maggie slid the assortment of photos into a folder.

"Here, you forgot this one." I picked up a snapshot of pink gerbera daisies just as the small silver bell over the front door tinkled. That tinkle was designed to make people feel like they'd entered a mom-and-pop flower store where the owner, while neither a mom nor a pop, was a sweet flower of a woman herself. *It's all in the tinkle,* Maggie had told me when she hung the silver bell above the door. *When people walk into the Flower Carte, they're buying an illusion.* And it *was* an illusion, tinkle or no tinkle. Maggie was about as romantic as ragweed. Sure, she handpicked her flowers every morning, but it was from wholesalers working out of cavernous warehouses in South Boston. And she wasn't holding wicker baskets in her hand; she was carrying a calculator and negotiating skills as sharply honed as a samurai sword. Maggie may wear peasant blouses and ponytails to appease her clients' sense of romance, but underneath the embroidered Tory Burch tunics beat the heart of a businesswoman—even if her sterling silver anklet screamed *Earth Mother*.

"I hope I didn't miss the good part." Claudia almost knocked over a pail of tulips with her shopping bag as she hurried back to see us. "Am I too late?"

"You're just in time," Maggie told her, and then handed over the four photographs from the makeshift bouquet.

Claudia laid a hand on my mother's shoulder and examined the pictures before bending down and placing a kiss on her cheek. Claudia and Maggie loved my mom. You know those mothers who pack homemade oatmeal cookies into tins illustrated with sweet scenes of country lanes and send them to their children at college? The kind who carefully wrap care packages in brown paper and then draw a big red heart around the return address in the upper left-hand corner? Well, that was not my mom. No homemade cookies arrived in any of the four years I attended college. However, she did win Maggie and Claudia over our freshman year with care packages stuffed full of Chips Ahoy!, Double Stuf Oreos and Pringles, and now Maggie and Claudia were returning the favor. "Celeste, they're gorgeous."

Maybe it was Claudia's unexpected arrival or even the delayed realization that she was picking out the very flowers she'd be carrying down the aisle, but finally my mother seemed to give herself permission to savor the idea of her wedding. "I know," she acknowledged, a smile spreading across her lips. It wasn't the innocent, almost naive smile she wore in the black-and-white wedding photo that reclined on our mantel until my dad left, but my mother's grin was clearly that of a woman ready to be married. "You girls all made your reservations at the bed-and-breakfast, right? It will fill up fast, so you can't wait too long."

Claudia nodded. "Three nights. Queen-size bed. Complimentary continental breakfast."

"Speaking of food"—I turned to my mom—"want to go grab some dinner?"

"I told Roger I'd meet him at home to tell him how it went." She stood up but then paused, as if remembering something. "But I could always call and tell him I'll be home late, if you're hungry."

My mother waited for my answer, but she didn't sit down again. Instead she hovered above the chair seat, halfway between leaving to see Roger and staying with me. Halfway between talking to her future husband about her wedding bouquet and talking to her daughter about any topic except divorce.

I didn't need Claudia's PhD to figure out which would be more enjoyable for my mom. Besides, after a three-hour lunch that included a Greek salad the size of my mom's Vera Bradley purse and a six-layer chocolate cake declaring HAPPY BIRTHDAY JASON, I wasn't just not hungry; I was still stuffed. "That's okay. Another time."

"She seemed happy, didn't she?" I asked once the door closed and my mother waved to us through the plate-glass window. Now it was my turn to look for reassurance, to ask my friends to say out loud what I was silently hoping: that my mom wasn't making a mistake. I knew that after almost ten years with him, my mother was well versed in Roger's assets, but did she truly know all of his liabilities? In the world of finance we performed due diligence before any merger, required full disclosure from both parties. But even if there was no blue book for men, no way to find the value of a used man as easily as we can look up the value of a used car, there had to be a way to avoid the lemons, right? All I wanted was a way for my mom to avoid the lemons. I wanted a way for us *all* to avoid the lemons.

"Of course she seemed happy," Claudia answered, pushing her shopping bag under the table. "In fact, she seemed thrilled."

"Well, she was thrilled to see you. Thanks for stopping by."

"No problem. She did get us a discount on the B and B, after all. And it's Labor Day weekend," Claudia reminded me. "Besides, I was in the neighborhood."

I knew she wasn't in the neighborhood. She was nowhere near the neighborhood. While the excuse may have worked if she lived even remotely near Newbury Street, the fact that Claudia came all the way from Cambridge meant that there was another reason for her visit. It was six o'clock and nobody in her right mind would venture across the river during rush hour.

"It's been a long day," I announced, standing up. "I think I'm going to head home."

"You can't do that," Maggie insisted, sending Claudia a look asking for reinforcements. "I think I still have a bottle of four-dollar red wine my cactus supplier sent me last Christmas. We should try it."

Claudia reached into the brown shopping bag under the table and pulled out a bottle of Grey Goose and a six-pack of tonic. "As tempting as that sounds, I brought my own."

"What are you up to?" I asked, suspiciously.

"Maggie and I thought we could hang out for a little while." Claudia pulled me back down into my chair.

"If you don't want the wine, I think I have a few beers in the walk-in cooler out back." Maggie left us and returned with two Amstel Lights. "I keep them behind the roses in case of emergency."

I sat back and watched as Claudia and Maggie turned my mother's floral appointment into an impromptu happy hour. And I knew that was their intent. To make it happy. To make *me* happy. Because there was only one explanation I could think of for their insistence that we share a four-dollar bottle of sirah from Arizona. They remembered what happened one year ago today, and they knew I would, too.

I wished I could say this was normal, the three of us sitting around Maggie's shoppe like those women you see in magazine articles with titles like "The Top Ten Things You and Your Friends Must Do Before Turning Thirty," or even those ads that have women huddled together sharing a private joke. The only things missing were the Virginia Slims dangling from our fingertips.

But this was not normal. We didn't go out for drinks after work or meet in a coffee shop at the end of the day like the characters in a TV sitcom. We worked. We went home. Then we got up and went to work again. Our professional worlds barely intersected, unless you counted the floral arrangements Maggie provided for Verity's lobby, and the likelihood that the software our bond traders pounded away on was probably developed by one of Claudia's former PhD candidates. Even our personal lives seemed to run in parallel lines while I was married, only sporadically overlapping after multiple phone calls and juggling of calendars. Maggie was occupied with the opening of her new store, Claudia's pursuit of tenure kept her in the MIT computer lab or writing articles for obscure academic journals that sounded like they contained more science fiction than fact, and I was, well, *married*. My job at Verity also kept me busy, but I'd be lying if I said that our friendship suffered from the time I spent researching the U.S. equity market. The truth was, after my wedding, a friendship cultivated during four years of college slowly went on hiatus, almost as if hibernating until it was time to peek its head out of some hole to look for its shadow. And, though I'm not proud of it, that shadow looked nothing like a ground-hog and everything like my divorce.

"So, did you hear from him?" Maggie asked, tucking her bare feet up under her.

I shook my head and reached for the photo of the gerbera daisies. She didn't even have to say his name. I knew exactly whom she was talking about. "That would be a big *no.*"

"They're divorced," Claudia reminded Maggie. "They're not pen pals."

"I have a client who sends a bouquet of two dozen roses to his ex-wife every year on the day their divorce was finalized." Maggie didn't seem to think this was odd. She was probably hoping more ex-husbands would send floral arrangements to express their appreciation for another strife-free year of singledom.

Claudia frowned at Maggie. "Black roses?"

"Actually, South American Leonidas."

"Forgiving guy."

"Considering what she could have gotten in the settlement, he says he's getting off cheap."

"Speaking of cheap..." Maggie and Claudia proceeded to go through their routine. They were like a stand-up act, each practiced in her role and when to come in with the punch line. *Who would walk out on his wife after only two years?* Maggie would ask, as if the short duration of our marriage made the act even more reprehensible. *A prick, that's who,* Claudia would respond, giving Maggie her cue to continue. They were my allies, my number one fans, my cheerleaders, who, if it wasn't for the fact that I'm about four inches taller than Maggie and three inches shorter than Claudia, would probably offer to hoist me up to the top of their human pyramid for a triumphant display of girl power. We were a team, and I'd taken one on the chin for all of us.

But that was more than a year ago, and now my friends' customary team cheer had become less locker room rally cry and more sideline pep talk, less like the fans' eruption after a touchdown and more like a midgame wave. Their ability to rally around me had helped at the time, but I'd signed the divorce papers twelve months ago today, and I didn't need it anymore. And they knew that. They just didn't know how to break the habit.

Claudia reached for the sweaty beer bottle sitting on the table in front of me and slid it toward her. "I hate when you do that," she told me, tapping her fingers against the hardened glue strips running down the side of the now label-less bottle. "Anyway, Abby's over it, so who cares if he didn't call; who cares what he's doing. He was a shit, right?"

I took back my Amstel Light and held it up for a toast. "To moving on."

Maggie met my bottle with her glass of wine. "To Abby."

Claudia's squat tumbler of vodka and tonic clanked against the delicate wineglass. "To Abby."

"Hey, speaking of moving on, what ever happened to your ex-boyfriend, Duncan? Did he end up marrying the gerbera daisy girl?" I asked, methodically attempting to fold the damp gold Amstel label into a tight paper triangle like the makeshift footballs the boys used to flick with their fingers in eighth-grade English class.

"God no. But he has become one of my regular customers. The woman he dated last month preferred aloe plants to flowers." Maggie shrugged. "I guess she was some earthy-crunchy type or something."

"Or maybe she was traumatized from a childhood of really bad sunburns," Claudia offered.

"At least this month's girl has good taste. Nothing but white French tulips. She works for Verity, actually," Maggie told me. "I had a bunch delivered there this morning."

My finger stopped midkickoff, leaving the paper football poised on the table waiting to be hiked. There couldn't be that many women at Verity who knew what French tulips were, no less had a preference for them. "You wouldn't happen to remember her name, would you?"

Maggie considered my question but didn't answer right away.

"What? Is there some sort of florist code of ethics that prohibits you from revealing her name?" Claudia asked. "Some sort of florist-customer confidentiality we don't know about?"

"No, it's just that I don't remember; we had over a dozen deliveries this morning. Susan, maybe. Or Sharon?"

"Sarah?" I offered, thinking I already knew the answer.

"Yeah, I think that's it. Sarah." Maggie shook her head and sipped her wine. "Poor thing, has no idea what she's in store for. It'll be over in a month, but he'll still be calling her for years asking for hot stock tips and help with his portfolio."

"You've met Sarah, Maggie," I pointed out before violently flicking the paper football with my finger and sending it sailing toward a bucket of lilies. "She's the fund manager we ran into on the Cape last summer." Even with my explanation, Maggie had no idea whom I was talking about. "The woman with the . . ." I cupped my hands in front of my chest.

"*That's* Sarah?" Maggie gasped. "*She's* Duncan's new girlfriend?"

"Um, yeah!" I practically shouted.

"Why are you so surprised?" Claudia wanted to know. "Boston's a small town, which is why you have to be careful who you screw—or screw over."

"I can't believe she's dating Duncan," Maggie mused, staring down at her own B cups. "I should have sensed something was off about him when I found out the woman before me worked at the Godiva store in Copley Place."

"So, that's why he always sent you those truffles?" It was unbelievable. Incredibly tasty and fattening at the time, but unbelievable nonetheless. "I am so telling Sarah about him first thing tomorrow morning."

Maggie shook her head at me. "What are you going to tell her? That he uses his ex-girlfriend for his florist? While it may be tactless, it's not a crime."

Granted, it wasn't like he left his wife and daughter for another woman. But still.

"How can you not say anything to these women?" I asked. "How can you call to confirm an address and not just happen to mention that her new relationship has a thirty-day expiration date?"

"This isn't like the Crime Stoppers tip line," Maggie told me. "I'm not here to disseminate information. I'm here to deliver flowers."

"At least you'd be giving them a heads-up of what to expect from him," I went on. "At least these women would be making conscious decisions to be with a guy who could end their relationship but still require their professional services for years to come."

"Look, you can't say anything," Maggie warned. "Really."

"Why not?"

"I don't know; it's just creepy. You of all people should understand. It'd be like sharing insider information or something. Besides, what if Sarah's really the one for him?"

"Come on, you can't believe that. The guy just paid taxes last month; he's probably looking for some good shelter advice before moving on to the next girl. It's the beginning of summer; the next one will probably be a real estate agent who has a line on some properties on the Cape."

"What is it people in your business always say?" Maggie asked. "Past performance does not guarantee future results?"

"It might not guarantee future results, but it sure as hell gives you a good idea of what to expect. Besides, we *have* to include the disclaimer. It's the law."

Maggie still didn't agree. "It's just wrong, Abby."

Dr. Martin Beck's ex-girlfriend didn't think it was wrong. And neither did I.

"Want to know what's wrong?" I told them about the woman at lunch and how I'd followed her to the ladies' room.

"You followed her to the bathroom?" Claudia repeated.

"That's not the point. The point is, I wanted to know who the guy was, and she was more than willing to give me his name."

"And what are you planning to do with this name?"

"I don't know that I'm going to do anything with it, but, like you said, Boston's a small town, and someday one of us might run into this guy."

"That's true," Claudia admitted, even though in the last year, no matter how prepared I was, no matter how many times I checked my makeup before leaving the house or purposely wore a pair of jeans he'd once said made my ass look hot, I'd never run into Alex.

"Anyway," I went on. "Wouldn't you be thankful to find out about a guy's shortcomings beforehand? Forewarned is forearmed, that sort of thing?"

"Okay," Claudia reached under the table for the Grey Goose bottle. "You've made your point. What's this guy's name?"

"Martin Beck. *Dr.* Martin Beck," I repeated. "Ever heard of him before?"

Claudia shook her head.

"Me neither," Maggie added.

"Okay, but if he asked you out, wouldn't you like to know that he broke up with his old girlfriend and CC'd his new one?"

"Rejection in the age of technology." Claudia frowned. "Any guy who'd CC his new girlfriend to prove he broke up with his old one should be relegated to using rotary phones the rest of his life."

"Better yet, Dixie cups and string," I added.

"Okay! You win," Maggie finally gave in. "Dr. Martin Beck is a shit. He's the lowest of the low. I mean, at least I get three orders a month out of Duncan, so I'm making money off the guy. But Martin Beck should come with a warning label—CAUTION: MAY BE HAZARDOUS TO YOUR MENTAL HEALTH."

I liked Maggie's idea. It should be like those labels you contemplate removing from the seam of your Sealy but never do, fearing a surprise visit from the mattress police. And in Dr. Beck's case the label shouldn't be removed until he's proven he's no longer a schmuck.

"You're the economist; you tell us." Claudia handed me the last bottle of beer. "Is demand and supply so off in this city that we're destined to get stuck with someone else's sloppy seconds?"

I shrugged. "I don't know that supply and demand is to blame, even if some men are the human equivalent of junk bonds."

"Relationships seem to be the least efficient market going," Claudia concluded. "Too bad there's not much we can do about it."

"The thing is, I was thinking maybe there *was* something we could do about it. Like create someplace where we could collect this kind of information." I glanced over at Claudia.

"Like a database?" she ventured, seeing where I was going with this.

"Yeah, only I don't know how to make something like that."

Claudia laughed. "But I do, right?"

"You or your students. Isn't there an underachieving sophomore who's looking to earn some extra credit this summer?"

"What would this database entail?" she asked, humoring me.

After lunch I'd toyed with the idea, playing with the thought of

ing to accept a date with some guy who offers her a bite of his Subway sandwich."

"Hey, that's not fair." Maggie choked on her wine. "I just thought it was a sweet gesture. It's not like I was going to eat it—Subway's tuna has way too much mayo."

"Look, it's a nice idea, this whole market intelligence theory," Claudia conceded. "But I think relationships are the one risk you can't mitigate."

"It's fun to think about, I'll give you that," Maggie agreed. "But it would never work."

How could they not see the huge potential? How could they so easily dismiss what was obviously a service women desperately needed?

As someone used to determining inputs and outputs, someone who developed systems and models capable of solving even the most complex problems, I needed to convince Claudia my idea was going to work. And, in order to make sure the data wasn't tainted, I'd have to carefully screen the women who provided the information—and the ones who received it. Although there wouldn't be secret handshakes, we'd have to skate under the radar if this service was going to become a woman's best-kept secret. And if anybody could spread the word, it was Maggie. Women were always in her shoppe buying flowers or stopping in to browse while they shopped on Newbury Street. She was discreet and discriminating. And so were her customers.

"You're right. It's crazy," I gave in, letting the topic drop. For now.

I had to get Maggie and Claudia to buy into my plan. Not that I had a plan, really. Or, I didn't before I started explaining it to them. But now that's exactly what I had. It was an idea that promised to take my knack for risk management to a whole new level. I was going to do for men what Morningstar did for mutual funds.

It was better than insider trading. It was insider dating.

chapter three

It's still hard to believe that there are people who don't know I was married, people I've met in the past year who can't tell the difference between what was me and what is an altered post-Alex version. My new assistant, Elizabeth, had no idea an Abby Madden ever existed. Of course, my former assistant, Lena, would tell you that Abby Madden never *did* exist inside the tastefully appointed burgundy walls of Verity Financial. If Lena hadn't transferred to HR and wasn't now required to demonstrate her heightened sense of political correctness and cultural sensitivity, she would no doubt relish the opportunity to repeat how, three years ago, she'd asked whether I needed her to order a plaque with my new name. My new *married* name. Abby Madden. Or Abby Dunn Madden; I still hadn't decided which it would be. But I had decided one thing for sure.

"I'm going to remain Abby Dunn at work," I'd told Lena, explaining that it would be less confusing.

"Less confusing to who?" she'd asked. "Won't it be even more confusing having two different names—one at the office and one everywhere else?"

I should have given Lena the benefit of the doubt because she was no more than twenty and totally didn't get it. And here I'd thought high schools had replaced home economics with women's studies.

Instead of providing Lena with a recommended reading list and a subscription to *Ms.* magazine, I explained that colleagues and industry acquaintances already knew me as Abby Dunn and I didn't want to have to start over with a new e-mail address and all that. *All that* being who knows what—new business cards? New memo pads with my name and title?

"Women do it all the time," she'd pointed out.

"Men don't," I'd replied, thinking I'd put an end to the conversation.

"They don't have to. Besides, who'd want to marry a guy who'd change his name?"

"I guess a woman who doesn't want to change hers."

"Is Alex one of those men?" Lena asked.

"No," I conceded, leaving out the final *touché* even though she'd earned it.

The truth was, I'd been at Verity all of two years at that point, if you didn't count the summer I'd interned as a research assistant, and I didn't. It wasn't as if changing my name was going to create chaos within the organization or anything. A billion-dollar financial services firm wasn't going to come to standstill because Abby Dunn's e-mail messages were being bounced back to their senders. Verity wouldn't fall to its knees because the receptionist couldn't find my name on the list of employees. And the printer wouldn't exactly contribute to global warming by depleting yet another rain forest for five hundred business cards with the Verity logo and my new last name.

So, there I was attempting to defend my name choice to a twenty-year-old assistant who probably thought changing your name was one of the benefits of getting married, second only to early-morning spooning and having someone capable of opening stubborn pickle jars.

To make a long story short, my original nameplate stayed. Lena transferred to human resources about a month after Alex left. And I remained Abby Dunn.

After five years at Verity, the same brass nameplate still hangs outside my office, just as it did on my first day at work. It still shines, still reflects my distorted image between the engraved letters. Now Elizabeth sits about six feet from the plaque every single day, and yet she has no idea that her predecessor made the three-by-seven brass plate outside my office into either a badge of my feminist principles or a symbol of my total inability to commit to my husband's last name.

I've never mentioned the great nameplate debate of 2003 to Elizabeth, and she's never mentioned hearing anything about it. To her, the Abby she sees every day is assumed to be the Abby I've always been. Even Sarah, who is arguably the only person at work who knew anything was going on during the five months Alex and I had the law office of Steinberg, Gold & Barnes on retainer, seemed to have forgotten my husband ever existed. Alex had become no more than a watermark, visible only when viewing me in a certain way in a certain light. Only I was sure that once you found the right angle, you couldn't imagine how you had missed it the first time around.

Elizabeth looked up from her desk and smiled. "Hey, Abby. Your nine o'clock is in the East conference room."

I thanked her and went into my office to drop off my briefcase like I had done every workday for the past five years.

The senior research team meets with the portfolio managers each quarter. Our meetings were one part fraternity party, one part inquisition, one part ultimate fighting match. There were slaps on the back one minute and plotting where the knife would go the next. We all used to be a part of the same business unit, the portfolio managers and the research analysts, but then there was the whole scandal and then the Chinese wall thing where never the twain shall meet. Except, of course, for birthday lunches and quarterly gatherings in the East conference room.

We were at two ends of the spectrum, the portfolio managers and the research analysts—the ones who examine, investigate and inquire and the ones who put their money where their mouths are. And they were some pretty big mouths. You don't become a portfolio manager without the nerve to make split-second decisions with millions of dollars on the line and the ability to believe your dick swings lower than most. But even if the PMs and the researchers were separated by ego and a Chinese wall, we all had one thing in common: an addiction to the markets.

My addiction started the moment I walked through the lobby of One Exchange Place, soared thirty-two floors above downtown Boston like Willie Wonka preparing to crash through the glass ceiling and pushed open the thick frosted doors that separated Verity Financial from the rest of the world. Only, unlike an addict who wakes up with a blood-crusted needle dangling from a vein, I showed no obvious signs of my obsession. No puncture marks pocking my forearms, no lost days. What was there, the dark circles and bloodshot eyes, was nothing a little concealer and a good blowout couldn't hide.

Sarah waved me over when she spotted me walking into the conference room.

"Want one?" She pointed to the tray of bagels on the credenza.

I shook my head and took a seat at the conference table. A few new faces appeared where former portfolio managers once sat. I didn't envy them, the PMs, even though I knew I was supposed to. As far as I was concerned, portfolio management turned out to be a lot like marriage. Failure didn't impart any sort of real personal growth or an opportunity to learn from your mistakes. It was simply a chance to hear the executive director tell you that *perhaps your skills would be better utilized elsewhere, the nice security man by the door will escort you out, and, oh, by the way, I'd like to introduce you to your replacement.*

I've never met my replacement. I only fear she exists.

Coffee? Sarah mimed to me from across the room, and I shook my head *No, but thanks.*

I joined Verity a year after Sarah, but we'd met the summer I interned in the research department. Everyone in the room had joined the company within a few years of one another. Jason and I even went to business school together, although he was a year ahead of me. Most of the people standing around downing Danishes and bagels went to Harvard and Wharton, Stanford and the University of Chicago, but we were from places as varied as Albuquerque and Albany. It didn't matter. There's a great leveler among men and women, young and old, the privileged few and a girl born 1,216 miles away in a small town outside Chicago—and that's the market's opening bell.

Sarah used to be one of us, an analyst, but she'd made the jump to PM six months ago. She'd gone up against four other analysts for the job, but I wasn't one of them and I had no plans to be. Still, that didn't mean I had no plans to enter another sort of asset management field. In fact, I had about five minutes to do a little prep work before the meeting started.

"So how's the guy with the French tulips?" I asked Sarah as she set her plate and coffee mug on the table.

"Duncan." She pulled out the seat next to me and then crossed her fingers for good luck. I resisted telling her she'd need it. "So far, so good."

"I've got a question: If you were going to put the tulip guy, Duncan, into a fund, which one would it be?" I asked.

"Well, first I'd have to know his financial goals," she started, but I cut her off. She wasn't getting it.

"I meant, if Duncan *were* an investment, if you had to classify him, where would he fall?"

Sarah licked a gob of cream cheese off her lip and thought about it. "Maybe mid-cap growth? I think he might have some above-average potential, but it's not like he stands out in any particular way on paper."

"What about Jason?" I asked as the blessed one walked into the room, leading with his penis. I swear he did. Jason strode forward like his penis was taking him for a walk. I couldn't imagine it was unintentional.

"I heard that," he said, coming over to us. "What about me?"

"If you were going to categorize yourself by fund type, which would you be?" I said.

"Is there any question?" He laughed. "Blue chip, without a doubt."

Blue chip, my ass.

Sarah shook her head and bit into her bagel, probably to keep from laughing out loud as Jason winked at us and went to find a seat.

"Blue chip?" she repeated, her mouth still full. "Is he kidding me?"

"He's kidding himself," I told her. "Jason's a junk bond all the way."

Sarah started to laugh but only ended up choking on her bagel.

"Hey, don't forget about tonight," Sarah coughed, washing down the bagel with coffee. "It's your turn."

"For what?"

"The Analysts' and Traders' Association event."

Shit. I was hoping to stop by and see Claudia about the database. "Is that tonight?"

Sarah nodded. "It is. Boston Harbor Hotel. Six o'clock. Be there or be square."

"Any idea what the topic is?" I asked.

" 'Unwarranted Intrusions in Financial Markets: A Historical Perspective on Regulation.' "

Thrilling. "Sure you don't want to switch?" Sarah and I had rotated our attendance each month when we worked together. Even though she'd moved over to portfolio management, we'd kept the arrangement.

"Are you kidding me?" Sarah lowered her voice as the meeting was called to order. "Last month I sat through forty minutes on 'Competition in a Consolidating Environment'—I think I've earned my thirty-day reprieve."

Competition in a consolidating environment. Sarah had a point. And it looked like my database would have to wait another day.

I don't come from a family of criers. My mom didn't cry when she watched me try on my wedding dress, my dad didn't cry when he walked down the aisle and handed me over to Alex and I didn't cry when Alex walked out of our marriage. We don't cry. At least not for any good reason. I have been known to well up watching the gay pride parade. I couldn't tell you why a transvestite in full-on Gloria Gaynor drag singing "I Will Survive" would move me to tears. I can only assume it's genetic, because how else do I explain that by the time Gloria's gloriously spandex-clad ass passes by, I'm left watching the Moving Violations Motorcycle Club roar by in a watery vision.

It has to run in my family, the inability to cry during appropriate moments and a complete lack of control in others. I caught my mom crying only once after my dad left. Not the night they told me he was leaving or the day I told my mom he was marrying Susan. She sobbed when they canceled *Evening Shade*.

I am my mother's daughter, so when my father left, I didn't cry either. I lied.

I was thirteen and it seemed better than the alternative, telling the truth. "He's in Alaska on a pipeline thing," I'd tell people, or "Business trip in Papua New Guinea" always sounded good. I knew none of my friends would admit they had no idea where the hell Papua New

Guinea was anyway. So what if my dad was really only one town over, living in a duplex he'd furnished with rental furniture and the TV he'd taken from our family room. We were no longer a family, so the room was more of a euphemism at that point than anything. We could have renamed it "the TV room," but my dad had taken care of that, too. So thereafter it became the rec room, the recreation being a game of Trivial Pursuit and a one-thousand-piece puzzle titled "Bonnets of Amish Country."

I saw my father for dinner on Monday and Thursday nights and every other weekend. He'd call every night, ask about my tennis lessons and remember when I had algebra tests, but otherwise all traces of him had been removed from our house in one swift effort resembling a crime-scene sweep. There was one car in the driveway instead of two, empty spaces on the shoe tree in the hall closet, and a dusty rectangular outline on the garage floor where the Craftsman toolbox once sat. I couldn't do much about the car, but I did hang my Keds on the open spots in the closet, and our first Christmas without him, I bought my mother one of those pink toolboxes designed especially for women, the kind that contained small-handled screwdrivers with cushioned grips, and a two-toned hammer, and came complete with a mirror inside the lid. I doubt any of my friends noticed the changes in our house, and they definitely didn't detect the toolbox switch, but I did my best to fill in the holes left by my dad. We didn't have a tremendous need for a ratchet driver, but it was more of a preventative measure than anything else. There was no way I'd let my mom be caught unprepared in the event of a needle-nosed plier emergency. And my mother could always ensure her lipstick wasn't smudged before wielding her new powder pink Allen wrench.

Of course it wasn't one of my friends who outed me. It was a smart-ass in history class who finally got the bright idea to turn around and look up at the huge rectangular map straddling the back wall. And that's when he came out with, "What's he doing in Papua New Guinea? I thought your dad was a paper salesman."

So I lied, at least until I was caught. And my mother bought lottery tickets. Mostly scratch cards, and only the dollar variety. In our house, a celebration for the birth of the baby Jesus wasn't nearly as anticipated as the arrival of the Mistledough Doubler, Winner Wonderland, and Bah Humbucks. Sometimes she even won. About every six weeks my mom would score a winning ticket and we'd both go down to the Star Market and collect the five- or ten- or, even once, fifty-dollar payoff. And mostly she'd end up spending her winnings on me before we even left the store, and instead of walking out with cash we'd walk out holding donuts with rainbow sprinkles from the bakery section.

I don't lie about my dad anymore, but my mom still buys lottery tickets. I bring this up because shortly after Scott Fenton figured out that Papua New Guinea was near Australia, my dad started taking me to the Boston Harbor Hotel for Sunday brunch. And that beat fictitious trips to Papua New Guinea any day.

My dad used to drive us into the city for brunch and valet the car. Up until that point I'd thought only rich people used valets. Then I learned that there's an entirely different class of people who take advantage of valet service at eleven o'clock on a Sunday morning with ample street parking available: newly single fathers attempting to win over their daughters.

But I had nobody to impress at the Boston Harbor Hotel, no car to valet and enough time to walk the six blocks to Rowes Wharf as long as I left my office by 5:50.

By the time I got to the hotel it was six o'clock and I was starving. Luckily, these events were known for two things: an open bar and a never-ending buffet. A seafood buffet. Baked clams and crab cakes and scallops wrapped in bacon. And, of course, the old standby. The recipient of the lifetime achievement award in the finger-food hall of fame. Shrimp displayed on crushed ice, their tails precariously testing the waters of a bowl of cocktail sauce.

I bypassed the buffet and spent the first thirty minutes lingering by the bar.

"Hey, kiddo." I felt a hand rest lightly on my waist. "Did I miss much?"

I turned around and held up my drink. "Only my first two vodka and tonics."

"You look lovely, as usual." Elliott leaned in and kissed my cheek. It wasn't a gesture that grazed the skin, careful not to actually count as a kiss. It was full-on lip-to-cheek contact, a soft center surrounded by a prickly salt-and-pepper beard.

How to describe Elliott? I could simply call him my former boss and leave it at that. Or I could declare him a friend. Or, because he's constantly asking me to leave Verity and go to work for him, even a potential employer. But I think the day we went to a meeting together, back when he headed up Verity's research division, sums up Elliott, and our relationship, best.

We'd left a meeting downtown and were headed back to the office, me towering over Elliott in heels and a skirt, and Elliott in his charcoal gray pinstriped suit.

A car passed by while we waited for the walk light to turn green, and a guy shouted out the window, "How much you paying?"

It was impossible to ignore the comment, or the implication that the thirty-year age difference between a man and a woman could mean only one thing.

"Asshole," I muttered, and nudged Elliott apologetically as we made our way into the crosswalk. "What's he know?"

Elliott, a short, balding Jewish man, had just been accused of paying to be escorted by an attractive younger woman, and yet he was totally unfazed.

"I have no problem with that," he'd told me.

"You don't?"

"Nope." Elliott shook his head.

"You're not offended?"

"Me?" Elliott stopped walking and laughed. "You're the one who should be offended. I may be old, but you're a hooker."

Maggie and Claudia used to question why Elliott and I were friends. They also questioned whether a single woman in her late twenties and a single man in his late fifties could be *just* friends. They were convinced that our *friendship* was all part of Elliott's grand plan, a ruse to lull me into a false sense of security so he could get me into bed.

"So, you're telling me there's no way Elliott would want to spend time with me unless there was the possibility of sex?" I'd asked Maggie.

Yep, she'd nodded.

"And he'd offer me a job, put his business, his livelihood and millions of dollars of his clients' money in jeopardy simply to get me into the sack?"

This time Claudia nodded. "Yep."

"So, he invites me to dinner, we hang out at his house on Saturday nights, he asks me to go to work for him, all because he wants to see me naked?"

They unanimously agreed, and I didn't know whether I should be insulted by the insinuation that the only thing Elliott could find interesting in me was the opportunity to get laid or flattered by their estimation of my desirability.

Of course, I decided to go with the latter.

Now Elliott looked around the room and sized up the crowd briefly before turning back to me. "Do you see anyone I absolutely must talk to?"

Elliott's presence at these events was a formality more than anything. After leaving Verity to head up his own hedge fund, my former boss had left the safety of mutual funds behind to take his chances on high-risk, high-return investments. Whereas mutual funds were the Long Island iced teas of investments, where a single ingredient wouldn't make or break you, hedge funds were the equivalent of a shot of whiskey straight up. You needed a strong stomach and a high tolerance for pain.

"Probably not."

"Come on, let's get out of here," Elliott suggested.

"I can't leave," I told him, although it wouldn't take much to convince me otherwise. "Unlike you, I have to do the whole meet-and-greet thing."

"Kissing asses and sucking up doesn't suit you."

"Neither does losing my job."

"Please." Elliott grabbed my hand and led me away from the bar. I didn't put up a fight.

"Why do you even come to these things?"

We walked past the buffet table, where Elliott reached for a toothpick, speared one of the chilling shrimp and waved it in front of me. "I like to watch you suffer."

He popped the shrimp in his mouth and led the way to the lobby bar.

"So, what have you been up to?"

I shrugged. "Same old same old. You?"

"You know, same old same old," he answered, teasing me. "Went to New York last weekend."

"Did you see a show?"

"*The American Girls Revue.*"

I laughed and Elliott smiled. "Caroline's been begging me to take her. Let me tell you, I was pretty impressed. Who could have known that watching a group of eight-year-olds singing about a quilt could be so entertaining. Or that a ninety-dollar doll in a straw hat could become so uninteresting after Caroline discovered a Pez dispenser in the backseat of my car."

"I used to love Pez."

"Apparently so does Caroline. I just wished I'd known that before I purchased Felicity—the patron doll of guilt-ridden part-time fathers everywhere."

"I'm sure she loved Felicity. The problem is, you can't eat a doll. And toys always lose out to candy."

"Wish I'd known that. Also wish I'd known that Kristie had planned to get Caroline a Felicity doll for Christmas."

Kristie was Elliott's ex-wife, Caroline's mother, and a constant source of entertainment for me, if not Elliott.

"So she gets her a different doll; what's the big deal?"

Elliott shook his head at me and made a *tsk, tsk* sound with his tongue. "Oh, ye of infinite wisdom beyond her years. You'd think it would be that simple. Unfortunately, I learned that I was told this important piece of information sometime in the last six months but chose to ignore it in an attempt to piss Kristie off and turn Caroline against her. I'm a guy. And you know us . . ."

"No, Elliott, you're different."

"I have two ex-wives who might disagree with you."

"Seriously. You're completely different."

"Sweetheart, we're all different. Until you discover we're all the same. Then we become like poor, discarded Felicity. Not all that interesting anymore."

"That's not true," I protested, and then added, "You're way more interesting than a Pez dispenser—of course, it might depend on which kind."

"Simba from *The Lion King*."

"In that case, I don't know," I joked. "Simba's pretty hard to beat."

"I can't believe you even know who Simba is—I can't believe *I* even know who Simba is."

"You know what?" I leaned over and stage-whispered in Elliott's ear. "I wouldn't know Simba if I ran her over with my car."

Elliott crooked his finger, telling me to lean in. "Simba's a boy," he whispered right back.

No matter what Elliott said, I knew he was different. And yet he had a point. In many ways he was the same, as if there was no escaping the XY chromosome thing. When I told him Alex had left me, Elliott didn't act surprised or offer sympathy. He simply asked, "Was he sleeping on the couch?"

"Of course not."

Elliott had seemed truly perplexed. "It's a man thing, the couch."

"We had a guest room. He could have slept there if he didn't want to be with me."

Elliott shook his head as if pitying me my delusions. "It's a symbol, not a sleeping arrangement, Abby. I don't care if you have four guest rooms, a man will choose to sleep on the couch. Preferably with the thinnest, ugliest blanket available. And he'll sleep in his clothes. Maybe even his shoes."

"That's insane. If I didn't want to spend the night in the same bed as Alex, I'd move to the guest room."

"Of course you would. You're not a man."

Well, Elliott was a man, but I still believed he was different. And that's why I wanted to share my idea. If anyone would understand, Elliott would.

"If you could have known more about Kristie before you married her, do you think it would have made a difference?"

"What was there to know? That she couldn't sleep if there was a load of laundry still in the dryer? That she spoke fluent French and yet couldn't pronounce *nuclear* correctly?"

"That she really just wanted a baby?" I said the words softly. We'd talked around the topic before, Elliott's contentment with just living together and Kristie's insistence they get married. His insistence that he loved Kristie and Kristie's insistence that loving her meant he should want to have a baby.

"Well, there's that," he admitted, looking down at the ice melting in his glass before continuing. "But, come on, she was thirty-four years old and I was fifty-eight. Kristie knew I didn't want any children and I knew she did. It was a case of mutual denial. Complicit delusion. We both thought the other one would change their mind."

"And you did," I pointed out.

"Not really. It was simply a battle of wills and Kristie won."

Elliott adored Caroline, so I knew that he wasn't implying that he'd lost. Just that he'd lost the will to fight, the will to persevere at any cost. Kristie had worn him down, whether it was because she wanted a child more than he didn't or because the standstill they'd come to would end only if one of them surrendered.

I used to want to win. There was no such thing as fighting fair, there was only fighting until I'd worn Alex down, ground him into the floor until there was nothing left for him to say, nothing left for him to do but look at up me and cry uncle. He was immature, selfish, cold or whatever it was he had to be for me to prevail. I was a better fighter, and for some reason that made me feel like the winner. Maybe that's why Alex seemed to give up fighting and instead conducted his battles in a less forthright manner. He was the elite force to my atomic bomb, the skilled covert operator who could snap me with a single flick of his wrist while I was still wondering how he snuck by my stable of artillery.

The thing is, even though I was competitive with Alex, there was one thing I never wanted to be better at, one thing I didn't want to want more. And that was *us*.

"So, if you'd been able to talk to her ex-husband or ex-boyfriends and find out what she was really like, would you have done anything differently?"

We sat there silently and watched as the bartender replaced our pale, watery drinks with fresh cocktails.

Elliott stirred his gin and tonic with his finger before continuing. "The real question is, if Kristie had known more about me, would it have made a difference?"

There was no need for me to say anything. We both knew the answer to Elliott's question. It was, without a doubt, a resounding *yes*.

chapter four

In the end, I didn't tell Elliott about the database. While the analyst in Elliott would surely appreciate the methodical approach to gathering and disseminating information, the fund manager in him would want to know the details. He'd want specifics—how I'd maintain the information, ensure secure access and charge for subscriptions. There were still some big holes in my big idea, mainly that I needed someone to program the database to begin with. And while I'd worked out some of the basics, like how I'd allocate member ID numbers and create standardized fields where members would eventually input data, I had to do first things first. I had to talk to Claudia.

It was after eight by the time I left Elliott. He had plans to meet a client for dinner, so I walked home alone. He offered to have me join them, but we both knew I'd decline, much like he mostly declined my invitations to join Maggie, Claudia and me for drinks. Our friendship was like a very bad karaoke duet—something we shared that we were sure nobody else would appreciate. In many ways, Elliott and I were like two sides of a coin: only one of us seemed to be able to land right-side up at any one time. Elliott divorced Kristie and we spent hours on the phone. Alex divorced me and we spent hours at Elliott's house listening to CDs on his Bang & Olufsen stereo—Carly Simon and Van Morrison and Eric Clapton.

Some of my favorite music comes from Elliott. During the first few months after Alex left, I acquired the musical appreciation of someone who'd grown up in the sixties and Elliott learned how to download his entire CD collection onto an iPod, even if he still couldn't figure out how it operated. We'd listen to music in silence—me trying to figure out obscure lyrics that I was sure, somehow, described my situation perfectly, and Elliott describing in detail why Germans made the best sports cars and beer, which explained not only the Warsteiner bottle in Elliott's hand but the Porsche parked in one of his four garages.

"What is it with your generation's fascination with microbrew beer? It's like you think it makes you more special because there's less of it," he'd told me.

"It's finely crafted," I ventured, even though I'm a Miller Lite girl myself and I wasn't sure it was my duty to defend a bunch of nameless, faceless people Elliott insisted on calling "my generation."

"Craft, my ass. Germans know how to make beer—and none of this strawberry periwinkle autumn fest crap. It's just plain old beer." Elliott lifted his bottle and took a long gulp that left drops of Warsteiner clinging to the whiskers around his mouth. "And we both know they're a bunch of Nazis, so that means something coming from me."

Actually, most everything Elliott said meant something to me.

"Don't you ever worry that people will think you're a cranky, eccentric old man suffering a late midlife crisis?" I'd asked, pointing to the Sharper Image gadgets scattered around the living room, most of them still in their original boxes.

"Every day," he'd told me. "Don't you worry people will think you're a crazy thirty-something divorced woman suffering a midlife crisis prematurely?"

"Every day," I'd answered. "But at least you get a Porsche out of it."

After almost forty years of therapy, no topic was off-limits for Elliott. He could always one-up me, so I felt almost normal—I stayed in bed all day washing down a bag of Double Stuf Oreos with warm Amaretto; he spent all day Saturday in bed eating what he thought were pomegranates and what turned out to be bad plums. I had one ex-husband; he had two ex-wives—and he had to send them monthly checks. Elliott had been in therapy since he was twenty-six. Mother issues. And even though he never made me say it out loud, we both knew the labels that belonged to me: Father issues. Husband issues. Ex-husband issues. Pretty much, if it had a penis and liked to watch Monday night football, it was my issue. Luckily, Elliott didn't like sports.

How Elliott felt about being a father was how I felt about being a wife. At times ambivalent, guilty about my ambivalence and yet scared to death of losing what I had. Scared to death of having it disappear because, deep down, the fear that I actually had what I wanted, and could lose it, became more debilitating than having what I wasn't quite sure I wanted and keeping it.

Still, somehow Elliott made me feel like I had my shit together. Better than that, he actually believed I had my shit together. And that didn't just make me like Elliott a whole hell of a lot; it made me love him, too. Just one of the reasons I decided to forgo my short-lived visits to Dr. Sylvia Bartlett, therapist, and spend my twenty-dollar co-pay on drinks with Elliott instead.

"What are you doing here?" I asked, discovering Maggie seated on the steps outside my building. A wicker basket sat beside her feet, making her look like an urban Little Red Riding Hood. Maggie's orders were delivered via wicker basket, yet another facet of the Flower Carte illusion.

"We had a last-minute delivery on your block, so I decided to come by and say hello." She stood up and moved aside so I could slide my key into the lock.

"Don't you know that loitering on my doorstep might attract big bad wolves?"

" 'My, what big feet you have, Grandma.' " She nodded toward my briefcase. "Working late?"

"You think my feet are big?" I pushed opened the door and turned to Maggie. "Started out as work, ended up as drinking with Elliott."

"How's he doing?"

"Elliott spent last weekend in New York watching *The American Girls Revue.*"

Maggie simply nodded, no comment necessary, and followed me upstairs to the second floor, where she waited for me to unlock yet another door.

"Jesus, Abby, do you burst into flames and leave behind a charred corpse if you're exposed to sunlight?" Maggie pushed open my living room curtains and ran a finger along my windowsill. "Ever hear of a Swiffer?"

"Is that why you're here, to disparage my homemaking?"

"No, I'm here because a group of women came in today during lunch and I decided to fly your idea by them." Maggie pulled a pair of pruning shears out of her purse and started clipping the brown leaves off my ailing Spathiphyllum, as Maggie referred to it when she gave it to me, or the green and yellow pointy-leaved thing wilting in the corner of my living room, as I referred to it two months later.

"My idea?"

"You know, the whole stock-market-for-men thing."

"It's not a stock market," I corrected her, yet again. "It's an information clearinghouse."

Maggie waved the shears in the air and a crispy brown leaf flew in my direction. "Whatever."

"So, what did they say?"

People trust Maggie. For some reason, they seemed to think that a woman who spent her days around flowers must be some sort of sage, some zen-like intuit who knows the answers to life's mysteries. Unfortunately, when you inevitably spill your guts and ask Maggie what she thinks, Maggie doesn't interpret this as a polite request to agree with you so much as an opportunity to actually tell you what she thinks. She had the whole confidant thing wrong.

"They asked where they sign up."

"Really?" I didn't even attempt to hide my surprise. "They want to sign up?"

Maggie finished snipping and moved on to the next plant in need of resuscitation. "Really. They loved the idea. Here." Maggie put down the shears and handed me a stack of Post-it notes she'd pulled from her pants pocket.

"What's this?"

"The names of nine guys to put in your database. And, if you're serious about doing this, the women's business cards are there, too. They want to be your first subscribers."

I flipped through the pale yellow squares of paper. Nine names. Nine additions to my nonexistent database.

Maggie moved over to a severely dehydrated amaryllis that had died and come back in its afterlife as a dust magnet.

There isn't a single plant in my apartment that wasn't given to me by Maggie. If it was up to me, I'd have planters filled with silk spider plants, maybe even a few plastic cactuses that never faded to a yellowy brown in an attempt to draw attention to my complete failure in the nurturing department. I guess, really, if it was up to me, I wouldn't have anything in my flowerpots but Oreos and Miller Lite bottle caps. In fact, I probably wouldn't have any flowerpots, period.

In any case, Maggie doesn't believe in artificial flowers—plastic, silk, paper or otherwise. They were bad for business. And as her friend, I was obligated to do my part to keep her livelihood going. And, in return, Maggie was obligated to come by and make sure I hadn't killed off, or at the very least dehydrated to the point of fossilization, the fruits of her labor.

You'd think that someone who spent twelve hours a day around objects designed to smell pretty for a few fleeting moments and then die would have a calling. That as a child Maggie was interlocking the stems of dandelions into makeshift wreaths. But Maggie didn't have a calling or even a grand plan. In fact, in college the only thing Maggie ever did at the Lyman Conservatory was get caught having sex in the student greenhouse during Winter Weekend. On the propagation bench with an automatic mist system that apparently was scheduled to water the orchids at exactly ten o'clock every night. So when the watering system failed to go off, campus security was dispatched to check out the problem. Only it wasn't a problem with the irrigation system so much as two naked people who'd inadvertently kicked the switch while landing spread-eagled on the propagation bench. Maggie could have been arrested or, who knows, even expelled for breaking into the plant house. Only it wasn't the breaking and entering that had her worried; it was the black party dressed hiked up to her shoulders and the pants pooling around her date's ankles.

Luckily, the security guard had only a flashlight and Maggie had an excuse for breaking and entering—something about trying to determine which botany course to take in the spring and deciding to take a stroll in the greenhouse to figure it out. It wasn't sordid sex in a house of glass; it was the contemplation of one's future. But the guard wasn't completely convinced and made a comment about checking out her story.

After the mandatory jokes (references to deflowering, garden hoses and the like), Claudia and I decided there was only one thing Maggie could do. So on Monday she was the first student in line to register for spring-semester classes in an attempt to cover her decidedly white midwinter ass, something she should have been more concerned about on Saturday night.

You'd think the woman who went on to create the most sought-after flower shoppe in Boston (Maggie insisted on the English spelling, the extra *e*, thinking herself something of a modern-day Eliza Doolittle, hence the name of her store) would be in her glory studying stamens and pistils and cross-pollination. But you'd be wrong. Maggie ended up in Horticulture 204 and its accompanying requisite, Horticulture Lab 205, for which she earned the only Ds on her transcript. For the next three years, every time she spotted that security guard, Maggie wondered whether he'd checked up on her. Or whether he knew she'd almost flunked out that semester, and that was why he always gave her a sort of sad grin that she interpreted as meaning, *You should have just told me you wanted to have sex with your boyfriend and saved yourself the trouble.*

While Maggie continued to prune and trim and shape my meager foliage, I read each of the names in my hand. "So, now what am I supposed to do with these?" I asked.

"All three women said to let them know when you're up and running. They want to refer their friends."

"Were they serious?"

"Are you kidding me?" she asked. "They couldn't write down names fast enough. I think the real question is, are *you* serious?"

"I think so." I shrugged. "Why not, right?"

"I thought we went over this yesterday," she reminded me. "How about because it's creepy?"

I glanced down at the business cards. They were all from professional women with seemingly respectable jobs. "Come on, these women seem perfectly normal. How could someone with the title 'Senior Editor—Classics and Ancient History' want to do something creepy?"

"Ever see *Fatal Attraction*? Glenn Close played an editor."

I wasn't going to argue; I had no idea what job Glenn Close's character held. I remembered only one thing about the whole movie: Her name was Alex.

"In any case, if you decide to go ahead and do this, you have your first clients."

"Why'd you even give me the names if you don't think I should do this?"

"I don't believe in superstitions, either, but you won't find me walking under any ladders or breaking mirrors. It's your choice, but remember: What goes around comes around." She sat down on the couch next to the basket and pulled her knees up to her chin. "So, is this your chance to give the women of Boston happy endings? Will I be inundated with orders for wedding bouquets and four-foot-tall table toppers?"

Maggie had zero tolerance for BS but an immense propensity for forgiveness, especially when it came to me and Claudia. This was a woman who never once asked why I didn't return her calls for the three weeks leading up to Alex's departure. Instead she showed up at my place carrying chocolate chip cookie dough and a bottle of Jose Cuervo about sixteen minutes after I choked the words into the receiver.

"Actually, if I went ahead and created some sort of service—which I'm not saying I'm going to do—I wouldn't care if any of the women got married or trotted off into the sunset with their prince or lived happily ever after. That's not the point."

"So, you're not talking about creating some sort of dating service?"

"God no. I'd just like to give women an advantage, an edge. I'd just be enabling the free flow of information. As long as it's helpful, I don't care what they do with the information."

"Well, I do. Weddings make up sixty percent of my business. As a matter of fact, if nobody ever got divorced and remarried, I'd be doing a lot less. So, come to think of it, if this little service of yours works out and people don't make relationship mistakes, you'll be costing me money."

It wouldn't be the first time. Maggie offered her services for my wedding free of charge. I thought she meant in lieu of a present, but when the time came to open all the boxes that arrived at our apartment day in and day out for weeks, there was a distinctive blue box and a card with her name on it. Inside I found a simple crystal bud vase from Tiffany. And on the card was written, "Sometimes one is enough."

I remember thinking she'd meant one flower, a single stem. And that's what I'd filled it with—for about a week, until the first and only flower I'd ever slipped inside the fluted glass, a yellow calla lily I'd taken out of the arrangement in Verity's lobby, died.

After the wedding, where she'd served as a bridesmaid, but before the divorce, where she served as my savior, I wasn't quite sure about the meaning behind Maggie's card. Was one flower enough, or one husband, or merely one—a person by herself, alone?

The thing is, I've never asked Maggie what she meant—at first because I didn't want to seem obtuse, but later because I didn't want to hear her answer. I'd stopped sharing everything with Maggie and Claudia because it felt like a betrayal to Alex. And then, when the idea of betrayal had taken on a whole new meaning, it was too late to go back and fill them in. At that point, there was no way to go back to the way things were.

Still, that didn't stop me from calling them the night Alex left. They were the ones I needed to talk to, of that I never had a single moment's hesitation.

Maggie and Claudia were better friends in the twenty-four hours following that phone call then I'd been in twenty-four months. It wasn't intentional, my inadequate attention to our friendship. It was an outcome of saying *I do.* I wasn't the clichéd new wife who can't stifle her love of all things matrimonial. I was more like the fucked-up new wife waiting for the charade to end. I wasn't an inadequate friend because I fell down the rabbit hole of matrimony and realized the importance of Tupperware and candles and scrapbooking parties. I just wasn't honest. I never admitted more than I had to. And, because Maggie and Claudia passed Friendship 101 with flying colors, they never pressed me to tell them more than I could handle.

"You don't need to be embarrassed," Claudia had responded to the news of the unraveling of my barely two-year-old marriage. "People get divorced; it happens."

"Two years!" I'd reminded them. "We were married *two years.*"

"And that makes a difference?" Maggie asked.

"Or course it does. If you make it ten years, twelve years, at least that's respectable. You proved you could do it. I only proved I could drive a man away in less time than it takes to enter the exciting field of legal transcription."

"You've been watching too much late-night cable again." Maggie shook her head at me. "Please don't tell me there's a Pocket Fisherman in your bedroom next to the Fitness Quest Abdominizer."

They attempted to help with various versions of "the glass is half full" and other clichés from the *Book of Things to Say to Your Friend When Her Husband Leaves Her*.

"Maybe it was just something you needed to get out of your system," Claudia suggested, only I wasn't sure what the *it* was that I had to get out of my system. The designer gown? Alex? The idea that two people could actually be happy together? The idea that those two people were us? "Maybe you're meant to use this experience to be by yourself. Maybe it's Abby time."

I assumed that was similar to Hammer time but without the parachute pants.

"At least it didn't happen when you were forty and had two kids. It's probably better this way," Maggie offered, even though in the first hour alone in our condo, I couldn't imagine anything worse. They reminded me that my new single status meant I could do anything I wanted, like finally taking the sailing lessons I brought up every time we spotted those white little triangles billowing out across the Charles River.

I'd nodded and muttered something along the lines of "Sailing sucks," and instead pictured myself wading into the Charles until my head was submerged, like some tragic character from an Edith Wharton novel.

Only instead of drowning myself I took baths. I took so many goddamned baths you'd think I'd grow fins, or at the very least, mildew. But I smelled good thanks to an ever-increasing stash of bath gels and oils and salts that filled my new apartment and the hallway outside my front door with so many scents, the neighbors across the hall must have thought I was a Bath & Body Works employee on crack.

I'd lie in the tub covered in bubbles smelling like French vanilla or Japanese cherry or coconut lime verbena, and, between wondering what the difference was between a regular cherry and a Japanese cherry, or what the hell a verbena was, I'd watch my breasts floating in the water and wonder whether they were the problem. My breasts. Did Alex want someone with pert breasts? Someone whose breasts peeked through the Japanese cherry-scented suds instead of falling into her armpits when not buoyed by water?

As the foamy white meringue caps faded and my body appeared— a toe here, a quarter of an elbow there—I'd examine the sun spots (spring break in Puerto Vallarta without SPF had seemed like a fabulous idea at the time), the razor stubble on my knees, the single strand of blond hair that had decided to sprout from my right nipple, and wonder what it was that sent Alex packing. And then I'd scoop up the foam and pat it down here, hide an inch of thigh there, and create the perfect Abby, the Abby I was sure he'd have wanted to stay with.

I may have been drowning my sorrows in bubble bath instead of gin, but my pores looked better than ever. People were stopping me in the halls at work to comment on how great I looked, and someone from Verity's IT department actually asked if I'd taken up baking. (How else could I smell like apple cinnamon in July?) I smelled fabulous, my face glowed and there wasn't a patch of dead skin to be found anywhere on me. Did it make everything dandy? Not exactly. Did it make me feel moderately better when I caught a guy in compliance sniffing my hair in the elevator? I'd be lying if I said it didn't.

"Did these women happen to mention how they'd like this service to work?" I asked Maggie.

"I don't think they'd thought that far, but they seemed to like the idea of creating a secret society of women. But maybe they've been reading too much Harry Potter."

Maggie stood up and collected her basket. "I better get going. Big shipment of roses coming in tomorrow for the weekend weddings."

"Any names you'd like to contribute to the cause?" I asked Maggie as I walked her to the door.

"I think I'll pass," she laughed. "I don't want to contribute to the delinquency of a minor, or in this case, a minor lunatic. In any case, let me know what happens next."

What happened next was that I crawled into bed with a legal pad and my Montblanc pen and started making plans. I had nine names, ten if you counted Dr. Martin Beck. Add in a few guys I dated before Alex, some of Sarah's former boyfriends if I could remember their names, and I bet I'd have at least fifteen men by the end of the day tomorrow. Claudia wouldn't be much help in the input department— Claudia didn't date; she worked toward tenure—but that was fine. I didn't need names from Claudia. I needed her to develop the database and some type of security program to keep it all protected. Because *if* I was going to do this (okay, let's be honest, I was *definitely* going to do this), there was no way anyone could know I was the person behind it. I had to be anonymous, the nameless person behind the curtain, the wizard pulling the levers and making the puffs of smoke appear.

By the time I flipped the light switch and called it a night, I had ten pages of notes on everything from database fields that would need to be populated, to an idea of how I'd make sure the service remained a secret available only to those women who needed it.

At two a.m. I finally slipped the cap onto the Montblanc and turned over to go to sleep. Tomorrow I was going to set my new business plan in motion. I was going to make it happen.

One guy is a fluke. Two guys, a coincidence. But *nine* guys? Nine guys is a mission statement.

chapter five

When my mother bought lottery tickets, I calculated the odds. The probability of winning. The likelihood of losing. The slogans would have you believe that "All it takes is a dollar and a dream," "For every dream there's a jackpot" and "You can't win if you don't play." I figured out that what it really takes is 1 in 1,008,000. And even if you play, your chances of winning are pretty damn slim, so rarely are there jackpots at the end of every rainbow-embossed scratch card. I became quite good at it, the determining of probabilities, the looking at odds a million different ways—was it better to play fifty dollars one week or one dollar for fifty weeks? (The answer is, you'd be better off playing fifty dollars in one week, but chances are you're still going to lose.)

Eventually I grew bored and graduated from scratch tickets to Megabucks, and then Mega Millions. We didn't have Powerball in Massachusetts, so I never had the opportunity to examine the grand-daddy of them all. Not that it would have mattered to my mother. She stuck to scratch cards and I honed my skills until there were three obvious professions awaiting me after graduation from college: counselor for Gamblers Anonymous, Vegas odds maker or financial analyst.

Our first night at college, the freshmen in my dorm collected in the living room for a welcome speech from our head resident and the requisite get-to-know-you games. Thirty girls sat in a circle while the head resident, a sociology major named Karen who was way too into the whole bonding experience, told us to reveal one interesting fact about ourselves.

Karen started by declaring that she'd set the record for the most Thin Mints ever sold by a Girl Scout—a whopping 1,863 boxes.

I can't say I was surprised.

As we made our way around the circle, the revelations weren't exactly earth-shattering, and they were far from interesting. Summers spent in Outbound Bound. A Brad Pitt spotting in a Starbucks outside St. Louis.

Finally the group turned to watch the brunette sitting cross-legged to my right. Maggie. "My pinky toe had to be sewn back onto my foot after it was almost severed by a Weedwacker."

She kicked off her sneaker and held up a bare foot as proof. "Right here," she told us, pointing to a raised white scar circling the base of her pinky toe like a noose.

Partially mutilated body parts. Smelly feet. And no fear. I loved her.

I also quickly realized that there was no way I could top a pinky toe that now resembled a cashew thanks to a piece of garden equipment.

So I didn't try to go toe to toe with Maggie. Instead I announced my own undetectable abnormality. "I can tell you the odds of winning any lottery game."

"Mega Millions?" the Brad Pitt girl wanted to know.

"How much do you want to win?" I asked.

"The whole thing, of course."

"Your chances of winning the jackpot are one in more than 175 million."

"Megabucks," another girl called out.

"A little better, just one in 5.1 million."

I looked to my left, where the girl sitting next me nodded her approval and then stood up. None of us had stood up; we'd just sat on our heels or leaned back on our elbows.

As we craned our necks to look up at Claudia, she said, "I have freckles." And then she sat down again.

Freckles. Not so unique, right? Find an Irish girl with blue eyes and red hair and you're bound to find more than a few freckles. Only Claudia wasn't Irish. She was an almost-six-foot-tall black woman. With freckles.

We were a nearly-nine-toed wonder, a girl who could drop out of college tomorrow and land a job as a bookie, and a freckle-faced black girl who went to great lengths to avoid nappy hair (Claudia had to teach me what nappy hair was before I could fully appreciate her success in this endeavor). And from that point on, we were inseparable.

Although Claudia spent most of her time in the computer lab, Maggie was wherever her major-of-the-week took her and I was attending economics lectures, we'd always meet on the lawn in front of Seelye Hall before heading back to our dorm for lunch.

I always imagined we looked a little like Charlie's Angels, the way we came together from the east and west and met in the middle, our hair bouncing in slow motion as we strode to lunch. The only thing missing was the voice-over of a man declaring, "They work for me, and my name is Charlie."

I was the only blond one, but that didn't make me Farrah Fawcett or Cheryl Ladd or any of the other Farrah replacements. About the only thing Farrah and I had in common was the hair color and the once-hyphenated last name. And the fact that she also did away with hers after divorcing the Six Million Dollar Man—a title I never thought much of until the term *divorce settlement* became part of my vocabulary and I wondered whether she got half of that six million.

I once brought up the Charlie's Angels idea to Claudia, whose response was a curt, "You know why there were no black angels? No black woman would take orders from a man over a speakerphone—and she sure as hell wouldn't put up with Bosley."

There was no mistaking Claudia for an Angel now, even if you got the feeling she could crack a safe or take down a rogue nation with a few strokes of her keyboard.

"What are you doing here?" she asked, twisting her head away from the computer screen to look at me standing in her doorway.

"Nothing. I just wanted to say hi, maybe go out for lunch." I probably should have stepped into her office. Instead I lingered outside in the hall like a reluctant student about to discover she flunked Computer Science 101, if even such a course existed at MIT. If it did, it would probably have a much more complicated name—Introduction to Structure and Interpretation of Computer Programs, Circuits and Microelectronic Devices.

But everything about Claudia's office intimidated me—not the least of which was Claudia herself. Granted, I've only ever actually visited Claudia in her office about four times in the past four years, not simply because I figured all the protons and electrons zapping around the Stata Center were surely mutating my genes even as I stood there, but because she seemed like an entirely different person behind her desk. I didn't see the girl with freckles; I saw Professor Claudia Johnson, PhD. The only thing missing was a number two pencil stuck through her makeshift bun.

Claudia's had boyfriends, dated men, but she's never lost her head over anyone, and she's most certainly never given away her heart. Except once, briefly, to a fellow PhD student. But that was more than five years ago, and since then it's been all about her job. While most women our age are counting down their dwindling supply of eggs, Claudia counts down the days until she makes tenure.

"Want to grab some lunch?" I offered, but Claudia wasn't falling for it.

"Maggie already called me." Claudia pushed her chair away from the desk and swung around to face me. "I know why you're here."

"So, what do you think?" I moved a stack of papers off the chair in the corner and pulled it over toward Claudia. "Can we do it?"

"We? What's this *we* stuff?"

"You know I can't do this without you. It's going to take more than a spreadsheet with a few pivot tables."

"I don't know that I have the time to help you, Abby. Like you said, this isn't a simple spreadsheet."

"It doesn't have to be you; it could be one of your students. An independent study project or something. Extra credit, maybe?"

"Extra credit?" Claudia laughed at me. "How exactly would I explain this extra credit to my department head—my friend wanted a dating database so I had my students create it for her?"

"Okay, first of all, it's not a dating database. Second of all, I don't know how you'd explain it; I just know that I need your help."

Claudia leaned back and tipped her head to the side, contemplating my request as if she was deciding whether or not she was going to give me a passing grade. "How sophisticated do you want this?" she finally asked, and I knew I had her.

I laid my briefcase on my lap and took out the legal pad with my notes. "I want to be able to create different fields based on categories women would find important—like family, career, views on relationships, that sort of thing. Then, for each of those we get down to the details, the nitty-gritty reality of who he is. Can he handle a woman who's more successful than he is? How does he deal with conflict? All the things women would find important."

"Does he make you sleep next to the phone because he refuses to answer it?" Claudia offered her own personal pet peeve. "Does he call out his mother's name when you're in bed together?"

"His mom's name was Claudia," I reminded her.

"Still, way too weird." Claudia winced. "Moving on, what sort of outputs do you want? Are you looking for probabilities?"

"Like that he has a 78.6 percent chance of being an asshole?" I asked, thinking that didn't sound so bad. "Could we really do that?"

"You could." She nodded.

"I don't think we need that level of complexity right away. Maybe once we have enough members."

"Members?"

"Yeah. I was thinking we could make this a members-only service," I started to explain, but Claudia cut me off before I could continue.

"Again with the we?"

"Like I was saying, the service will only be available to members, and members will be accepted on a referral-only basis."

"I'm not sure I understand what this is," Claudia said. "A secret club?"

"More like an underground society."

Claudia reached for the legal pad and I handed it over.

"So, what is it you need from me?" she asked, going through my notes. "Do you want real-time statistics, a way to map trends for the men in the database, compare historical performance to current performance?"

"Like is he improving with each woman or getting worse?"

Claudia nodded.

"Absolutely. The more ways to slice and dice the data, the better. In this case, you can't be too analytical."

Claudia continued reading and she didn't look up again until she'd finished the last page. "I know you think you can apply economic principles to everyday life, but doesn't it worry you that every time the *Wall Street Journal* does that dartboard thing, the monkey usually wins?" she asked.

"They don't use a monkey," I told her. "Just a person throwing darts."

I didn't have to ask what Claudia was talking about. Anybody in the financial field knows about the dartboard. Every six months or so the *Wall Street Journal* runs a contest to determine who's better at choosing a portfolio of stocks: professional investment managers, *Journal* readers, or darts flung randomly at stock symbols on a dartboard. Most of my colleagues at Verity have tried this at one point or another—not out in the open, of course. My dartboard was discreetly tucked behind three-ring binders on the bookshelf in my office and hung on the back of my door only when I was sure nobody would be visiting. Not because I was afraid of spearing an unsuspecting cornea, but because I was supposed to know better. I was supposed to believe that research and analytics beat a dart tossed with a random flick of the wrist.

"Besides, I'm not offering advice or recommendations. I'm offering the information women need to make educated investment decisions."

She flipped back to the first page of the pad and bit her lip. "Well, it certainly looks like you've thought this all out."

"I have. There's only one thing. It will all have to be done through a Web site and over the phone; nothing in person." I took a breath and continued. "I want everything password protected and encrypted and firewalled and whatever else it is we have to do to keep nonmembers out. In other words, keep everyone out. Nobody can know I'm the person behind this."

"So, how do you see this working? Throwaway cell phones with untraceable numbers? Morse code? Secret handshakes?"

"An unlisted number and a Web site with a log-in screen—plain black, of course."

"That's it?"

"Yep. A simple black log-in screen with a box to input a user name and password."

"I realize you can't create a secret society without some level of secrecy, but what's the deal? Why are you setting yourself up as the Jimmy Hoffa of relationships?"

There were several reasons, actually. One Claudia would understand, and the other would be a bombshell I wasn't willing to explode. I decided to put it in terms Claudia could grasp.

"If you were a portfolio manager, would you want to discover that the person you rely on to help you make million-dollar decisions is dabbling in a little gender-based database on the side?"

"In other words, you don't want to lose your job."

I knew Claudia would get it. "Bingo."

"So, were you serious about lunch?" she asked.

I glanced up at the clock above the door. "I was serious about lunch forty minutes ago."

"Fine, let me starve." Claudia waved me away and spun around to face her computer. "Go back to work and I'll let you know what I figure out."

By the time I made it back to my office, the red light on my phone was blinking and there was a voice mail from Claudia.

"The eagle has landed. All systems are go. The raven flies at noon," she whispered, and then let out a small laugh before returning to her normal voice. "Consider yourself in business."

I deleted the message with a smile on my face. The eagle hadn't landed. It was just about to take off.

chapter six

Every year Elliott hosts a little shindig at his house for clients and friends—and by *little shindig* I mean huge, elaborate party complete with white linens on tables, servers passing hors d'oeuvres from silver platters and a quartet playing in the garden. Elliott's house is an engineering marvel constructed of varying-sized glass cubes. It always reminded me of a dismembered Rubik's Cube held together by an erector set. Only this Rubik's Cube sits on five acres in Weston and comes complete with small pond, lily pads and four thousand square feet of glass and steel modernity. Wife number one had favored early American colonial, and wife number two was more of a French country kind of gal, so after Kristie moved out Elliott spent the next two years gutting the house to eradicate the six-tiered moldings, chintz wallpaper and faux murals of vineyards and chateaus (he didn't have to worry about the overstuffed love seats and copper pots—Kristie had cleaned him out). I thought it was a pretty expensive *fuck you*, but Elliott loved every minute of it. The expansive glass walls framed in steel that he shares with no one but Caroline on every other weekend and Wednesday nights has all of two bedrooms—one for a grown man who'd rather sleep alone, and one for a five-year-old little girl who sleeps with stuffed animals.

Elliott's parties always took place around the pool, a pool designed to look less like a pool and more like a mirage that just happened to appear in his backyard next to the clay tennis court. And the man doesn't swim. Or play tennis.

But I do—play tennis, that is—thanks to a father who insisted it was more important for a girl to learn a wicked backhand than to master a graceful arabesque. There are very few times I'll ever admit to my father being right about anything, but this time he was. I haven't been called upon to perform a plié with friends on the weekend or asked to join clients for a pas de deux, but the entire portfolio management team knows better than to face me on the court. Even in the end, even after it was all said and done with Alex, I still thought: At least I always kicked his ass in tennis.

Why would an ex-husband I haven't seen in a year jump to mind anytime I see a tennis court—especially an ex-husband who never went to the net (which drove me crazy)? It was vicious. It was uncontrollable. It was a game I called connect the dots.

It starts with something simple, a ride on the T. I'll notice a little girl chewing gum or eating a Hershey bar and remember how my mother always used to make me brush my teeth for exactly ninety seconds on the days she'd let me have candy. She even kept an egg timer on my bathroom counter so I couldn't skate by on a tooth-decaying eighty-nine seconds. An egg timer. We owned one, yet we rarely had eggs for breakfast, and when we did they were scrambled and she'd put a slice of Kraft American cheese in mine, the orange rubbery kind wrapped in clear slips of plastic. Kraft. The summer between my first and second years of business school I had three offers for summer internships—a corporate finance position with Kraft and banking positions with Verity and Morgan Stanley. Stanley. I knew a Stanley; he'd even gone to my wedding. Stanley Madden, Alex's grandfather. And the game of connect the dots is complete.

I almost had a day, one day, five months ago, when I went sixteen hours without playing connect the dots. But at eleven o'clock I was lying in bed watching the news and a story came on about stalled negotiations between the state and the Snow and Ice Contractors Association. Not exactly a story you'd expect to set the game in motion. It took only four dots to get to Alex. Not because he loved to ski or because he'd shoveled the walk outside our condo every winter. But because salt melts snow. And Alex's aunt had high blood pressure. Sixteen hours. I'd made it almost a full day.

"Abby!" Elliott waved me through the glass-enclosed atrium that led to the back patio, where he was surrounded by a group of guests.

I held up a finger and mouthed, *One minute*, before hanging a left down the hallway toward Caroline's room. Elliott's house may have landed on the pages of *Architectural Digest*, but Caroline's room was my favorite, and not just because I'd helped with the decorating. The ballerina pink walls, lavender powder-puff pillows and sheer curtains were Elliott's concession to girliness, and the pink ladybug-shaped rug covering the hardwood floors a concession to me.

The rug had been my idea, my contribution to an afternoon Elliott and I had spent shopping in Pottery Barn Kids. He'd wanted a basic rectangular rug, but I'd insisted on the ladybug. Caroline was only three at the time, so it wasn't as if she was especially fond of the insects. But I was. Well, not the bugs themselves, so much as the cars. My dad and I played the Love Bug game religiously, shouting out every time we spotted a VW bug. The game tapered off once I started carpooling to activities, and by the time my dad moved out, there wasn't a VW bug left on the road. When we'd drive into the city for our Sunday brunches, the only VWs we'd spot on the road were Golfs and Rabbits and Jettas. And there was no more game to play.

My fingers ran along the pink quilted bedspread before resting on the leg of Caroline's American Girl doll. I didn't blame Caroline for choosing Pez over Felicity. She wasn't exactly made for snuggling. Who wanted to play with a doll wearing a yellow gown with scalloped lace and ribbon rosettes, not to mention the satin slippers. Felicity was an ornament, not a toy. She was a doll that looked pretty on a shelf, a decorative touch that reclined against bed pillows until it was time for bed and time to move her aside in favor of more comforting companions.

Before I met Alex, the children's rooms I thought about were always my own. The mint green walls in the house we shared with my dad until he left. The square room with the pale yellow walls in the house I lived in with my mother. After I met Alex, after I started believing that he could be more than a summer fling between my first and second years of business school, I started thinking about children's rooms in an entirely different way. I'd think that the next children's room I'd have a hand in decorating would be for our first child. And then I'd start thinking that my first child was, in an abstract way, Alex's second.

Because Alex got his high school girlfriend pregnant. I've often wondered whether she's happily married, with a kid, maybe two. For some reason I always imagined a boy and a girl, two years apart. The little girl would wear braids and the little boy would always have a ring of dirt around his mouth from playing in a sandbox. When people ask their mother if she has children, she always answers *Yes, two,* but what she's really thinking is, *Yes, almost three.* I wonder whether she thinks about the child she could have had with Alex but didn't. It's impossible not to.

I'd never know this person, the girl who had to tell Alex she was pregnant, so I could assign all sorts of attributes to her. She was the girl all the other girls loved and the guys wanted. She was beautiful, tall and willowy or short and petite, almost fragile. She was a virgin who'd saved herself until she met the guy she thought she'd love forever. My husband.

My freshman year of college I slept with a virgin. I knew this beforehand, his virgin status, and there are only two ways to take this information in when a guy tells you that he wants to sleep with you. You can either think, *Oh, how nice, I am the chosen one, the woman he wants to remember as the first, the only woman special enough to shepherd in his manhood.* Or you can think, *Why am I the only person willing to sleep with this guy?* But that's not my point. My point is, Alex lost his virginity to a girl named Michelle his junior year of high school. The third time they had sex Michelle got pregnant. Six weeks after she missed her period, Alex took her to a clinic in Connecticut and she ceased to be pregnant. The thing was, she got pregnant after having sex in Alex's car (actually, his dad's car). The entire thing fascinated me—the idea that it happened in a car, like something out of *American Graffiti.*

Alex told me about this when we first started going out, not because it was a pivotal point in his life, getting his sixteen-year-old girlfriend pregnant, but because I asked. *Have you ever gotten someone pregnant?* I really thought the answer would be no. I always thought something like that would weigh on a person. When I received an answer I wasn't expecting, it certainly weighed on me.

After we were married, I realized that Alex had the capacity to do that, to just move on. It wasn't as if he'd ruined Michelle's life or scarred her for eternity. She went on to college and was probably living a productive life. Maybe she was a room mom, one of those women who sews her children's Halloween costumes by hand and writes little notes on the napkins she packs in their lunch boxes—*Have a good day! Love, Mom.* Or maybe she was a corporate vice president who sat in first class tapping on her BlackBerry long after the flight attendant announces it's time to turn off all electronics, too busy racking up frequent flier miles to stop and think about what happened when she was sixteen.

I just never understood how Alex could never think about it. There were no moments when he calculated that his son would be in Little League or when his daughter would be expecting her first period. He was the man who never looked back. I truly believed that Michelle never took up any real estate in his heart or his head. And that can be very reassuring when your boyfriend tells you about the girl he got pregnant in high school, and you don't have to worry that one day he'll wake up and decide he must right his wrong by Googling his first love. But it can play with your head when you consider the inevitability of facing a crisis yourself one day, and whether or not, when it's over and done with, it will have mattered to him at all.

Alex was kind enough to help Michelle through the ordeal, responsible enough to handle the situation. He hung in there and did what was right. At first I thought, *This man made a mistake and he didn't walk away. This man is perfect.* Later on I thought, *This man is careless.*

I moved Felicity aside and took the Hello Kitty Pez dispenser I brought for Caroline out of my purse and placed it on her pillow. Then I went to find Elliott.

Elliott was over by the string quartet talking to some people I recognized from last year's party. And the year before that. And if the conversations we'd shared in the past were any indication, this year's conversation could wait until I hit the buffet and filled my grumbling stomach. As always, Elliott's buffet was highlighted with an elegant seafood spread in the center, where another guest was already enjoying mounds of diced tuna tartare on toast points.

Needless to say, I started at the far end of the buffet.

"Not a fan of tuna?" he asked, reaching for a second helping.

"Raw or otherwise," I answered, and selected a serving of the carpaccio of beef instead.

"Not even a good old tuna sandwich?" he asked.

"I was more of a peanut butter and jelly kind of kid."

"Peanut butter and Fluff was my weakness." He held out his hand and waited for me to take it. "Mitch Reeves."

"Any relation to the original Superman?" I asked, wiping my hands on a cocktail napkin before reciprocating.

"Grandfather." He nodded and made a point of looking embarrassed. "Kind of gives a guy a complex, living up to the Man of Steel and all, as I'm sure you can imagine."

I stopped chewing. "Really?"

He laughed. "No, not really. The only grandfather I have to live up to was a milkman in Vermont."

Mitch's hand was still extended in my direction. I took it.

"Abby Dunn."

"Abby? You wouldn't by any chance be the reason I had to figure out how to keep red clay from ruining Elliott's grass?"

"I don't know, am I?"

"When we were designing the backyard, all Elliott could say was that his friend Abby had to have a red clay court. I tried to get him to go for a grass court, or at the least a green clay surface so we wouldn't have red tracked all over the grass, not to mention the drainage issue, but he insisted that you preferred the red clay."

I raised my hand. "Guilty as charged. I'm a baseline player and clay plays slower. You know me, so how come I don't know you?"

"I guess Elliott prefers to talk about his tennis-playing female friends rather than his landscape architect."

"So, you're the one responsible for all this?" I swept a hand toward the white tent pitched on the far lawn.

"I had some help."

"My stepmother could use someone like you. I swear, if I was Home Depot, I'd have her photo taped up in the employee kitchenette—DO NOT SELL LIVING THINGS TO THIS WOMAN."

Mitch laughed. "Don't blame her; it could be the soil. Sometimes you're damned before you even begin."

"I'll pass that along."

"You used to work for Elliott at Verity, right?"

"Did Elliott not leave me with any secrets?"

"He obviously thinks very highly of you. Kept saying he was hoping to lure you away with a clay court."

"I'm not that easy."

"Holding out for the all-season bubble, huh?"

I laughed and Mitch smiled, creating crinkles around the corners of his eyes. Only instead of making him look old, they reminded me of the fishermen we used to see on the Cape, the ones who'd bring the lobsters onto the docks and hold them up for the kids to see before packing them into their trucks and taking them to the local restaurants where they'd become dinner. Even his brown hair had the tousled look of someone who spent most of his day competing against Mother Nature.

"So, what do you do for Verity?"

I shrugged and reached for a second helping of beef. "Nothing very interesting."

"Oh, I get it. You could tell me but then you'd have to kill me."

"No, I wouldn't. If I told you, I'd bore you to death and save myself the trouble."

"I seriously doubt that," he told me, even though I seriously doubted that he seriously doubted it.

"Okay, you want the sordid details, here they are. I'm in equity research. Stocks."

"And what stocks do you focus on?"

The man was a glutton for punishment. We each had our sector, the area we specialized in. Our expertise. Before she moved over to portfolio management, Sarah's was pharmaceuticals. And mine is—drumroll please . . .

"Financial services." Yes, while Sarah was putting on white jumpsuits and touring hermetically sealed factories where they fill IV bags with potential cures for cancer, I was out talking to people just like me. Exactly like me, only not exactly. The companies I visited attempted to impress me with dog-and-pony shows that demonstrated their value to shareholders, and I attempted to see past the show to the shit the dogs and ponies left behind.

"Ah, I'm sure that's fun." Even a guy attempting to flirt with me couldn't do much with that. So instead he pointed to the tennis court. "Do you still play?"

"Not as much as I'd like."

"Yeah, I suck, but more from lack of professional instruction than lack of playing time."

"My dad used to play with me every weekend growing up."

Mitch nodded. "We were more of a badminton family. Less running, but no less competitive, I assure you. We used to have an annual tournament and the winner got one of those little Snoopy trophies.

Our Snoopy was holding a tennis racquet, ironically enough. Guess Snoopy wasn't much of a badminton guy."

"Guess not," I agreed.

"So, isn't this when you offer to give me a lesson, teach me the finer points of the game?"

I couldn't help smiling. "Like I said, I haven't played in a while."

"So, this is when you could start. I know a great red clay court where we could play for free."

"Listen, Mitch." I exaggerated his name, which made it sound like I was reading a name tag. "It's sweet of you and all, but I'm not really interested."

"In tennis?" he asked, although it was obvious he knew exactly what I meant and just wanted to torture me by making me say it aloud.

"In anyone," I answered, although I could have said *In you.* "It's nice of you, but I think I'll pass."

"That's too bad. It's not often you have access to your very own court, and surrounded by such fantastic landscaping, no less." Mitch reached for one last tuna tartare and turned to leave. "Good meeting you, Abby Dunn."

I watched Mitch walk away toward a group of guests gathered under the tent. At least I thought that's where he was headed. Only I was wrong, because before he reached the cluster of laughter accepting flutes of champagne off a silver platter, Mitch stopped, bent over and proceeded to pluck three weeds mingling among the tulips in Elliott's garden.

Would Mitch the weed-picker end up in the database? I wondered. And if he did, what would be wrong with him? Would one woman write in that he had a particularly nasty porn habit, that he cheated at Monopoly or couldn't remember that she was allergic to peanuts? I had to admit, right then and there, standing in Elliott's backyard next to the buffet, I couldn't identify any glaring defect. But it had to be there, somewhere deep down. Somewhere hidden from plain view. Because from my current vantage point, all I could tell from watching Mitch Reeves walk away from the buffet table was that he looked damn good in a pair of khakis.

chapter seven

I try to have dinner with my dad and Susan at least once a month, although during the summer that rarely ever happens. Susan taught middle school English, so she was free from June through August, and that meant visiting friends up and down the East Coast. Most of the time my dad joined her if he could, which meant our dinners had a sort of summer break themselves.

My dad and Susan lived in Belmont, right outside the city. Close enough to visit when needed, but far enough away from my mom that there was no risk of either of them stopping at a traffic light and looking over to see their former spouse gazing back.

When I pulled into the driveway of the ranch house they've lived in ever since my dad moved out of the duplex, Susan was outside in the front garden planting geraniums. My dad once suggested they plant ivy and get it over with, but Susan insisted on trying her hand, or thumb, at a garden every year.

"Your dad is stuck in traffic; he's driving back from Connecticut," Susan told me, sitting back on her heels and wiping her forehead with the back of her gloved hand. "I don't know that he'll make it in time for dinner, but we can still eat together."

I bent down and rubbed away the smear of mud she'd spread across her brow. "That sounds fine."

Susan smiled. "Good. Here, have a seat. I could use some company." She took the padded foam rubber cushion from under her knees and handed it to me.

"Having better luck with the garden this year?" I asked, although the fact that it was June and she was already digging up brown geraniums was a clue the answer was no.

"We'll see. I think once we get some rain these new ones will do better."

"I met someone who mentioned that oftentimes the problem isn't the flowers; it's the soil the flowers are growing in."

Susan looked up from her trowel. "And how do I fix that?"

"I don't know," I admitted. "I didn't ask."

"Well, I'm willing to try anything at this point, so if you find out, let me know." Susan asked, turning her attention back to the geraniums, "How are the wedding plans coming along?"

Questions like this used to bother me, as if talking about my mother, sharing information about her life, made me the divorced child's version of a double agent.

Not that Susan grilled me about my mom on a regular basis. If anything, when I first met Susan, she hung back and waited for me to give her a sign, some indication that I was willing to carry on a conversation instead of avoiding her gaze and looking past her when she spoke.

I think the first words she ever said to me were, *Hi, I'm Susan, your dad's friend. Friend*, I'd thought, *who's she kidding?* Even I knew that wasn't the word for what she was. There were all sorts of nouns I could have suggested—mistress, home wrecker, just to name a few—and *friend* wasn't one of them. My father hadn't left my mother because he needed another friend. My dad wasn't looking for a pal. And there was no way I was going to let Susan pretend that's what they were, although, in hindsight, I can see that Susan's choice of words was exactly how she saw herself. Looking back at the times she'd linger in the kitchen while my dad and I watched TV together on the family room couch, or how she'd offer to stay home when my dad took me to Friendly's for dinner, I realized Susan tried to be a friend to my dad when all he seemed to have was a daughter who sat in the front seat of his car with her legs crossed and eyes fixed on the oncoming traffic.

After a while I realized that Susan's questions weren't an attempt to make me divulge my mother's deepest, darkest secrets; she wasn't probing for my mother's weaknesses. I realized that Susan really wanted to know, to truly hear, that my mom was doing well. That my mother was happy and living her life and some woman with a brown thumb, brown bob and Subaru Outback hadn't ruined her life forever.

"So far, so good," I told her. "Maggie helped us pick out the flowers and we're going to look at dresses on Saturday."

"That sounds like fun," Susan replied, and I believed she meant it, even though her own wedding had been sorely lacking in the flower-and-pretty-dress department.

My dad and Susan were married by a justice of the peace four months after my parents' divorce was finalized. I was there in the courthouse to witness it. Susan's parents and I. It was Susan's first marriage, but instead of a white gown and veil she wore an ivory suit and carried a single red rose that looked like something a forgetful husband would pick up at 7-Eleven on the way home from work. She was being penalized for forgoing the fairy tale prince and instead picking a real-life man saddled with an ex-wife, a kid and child-support payments. And even though I was watching my father marry someone besides my mother—someone who, at the time, I'd thought was the reason my family fell apart—it still didn't seem fair.

I'd stood to the right of my dad, looking directly at Susan as she listened intently to the generic words spoken by a man who, when it came right down to it, was nothing more than a government bureaucrat. I tried to figure out what Susan, basically a decent person, saw in a man who'd leave his wife and daughter. Why she'd choose him to love over all the other *normal* men out there.

There wasn't even a photographer at the ceremony, only Susan's mother with a Nikon designed to eliminate red-eye by flashing a blinking light four times before snapping a picture. Only, with the flashing light, it was difficult to tell when the camera would actually take the picture. So instead of a decent wedding portrait, the best photo my dad and Susan ended up with had him looking to his right while Susan reached over and straightened his tie. Although I'm not in that picture, I remember exactly where I was standing when Susan's mom took it: to my father's right, where he was looking when the shutter snapped closed. The picture didn't compare to the perfectly posed and expertly lit wedding portrait I'd grown up with on our fireplace mantel, but Susan kept it in a frame on her night table, right next to a box of Kleenex and the alarm clock. And I got the feeling she thought it was perfect.

It wasn't until about three months after my father moved out of our home and into the townhouse that I met the woman who would become my stepmother. I'd known Susan existed, but she was a mystery, leaving clues that had me wondering why my father chose a woman who kept bobby pins in a ceramic bowl on the bathroom counter and fuzzy slippers in the hallway closet. Susan didn't fit the mold, the made-for-TV version of *the other woman*. Susan wasn't tall and thin, her graying brown hair was bobbed rather than bleached, teased and sprayed and the only makeup she wore was Chap Stick and Maybelline Great Lash.

Still, she'd stuck by my father, although God knows why. She should have been out of there at the first warning sign. At first I thought she had to be crazy, or at the very least stupid. Sometimes, when I was older, the way Susan loved my father scared me. Not because she was so blindly enamored, but because she saw it all so clearly and yet decided to love him anyway. I don't believe in unconditional love, but what Susan had for my dad was the closest I'd come to witnessing this illusory state in person.

I'm not saying that I embraced Susan. There were the requisite silent treatments befitting a fourteen-year-old forced to spend Saturday nights at her father's townhouse without cable TV. I just didn't understand her. And then, one day I did.

"I love your dad." Susan had spoken the words as if they were a statement of fact. An indisputable pronouncement akin to "The world is round," "Gravity exists" or "Richie Beck has the sweetest ass in the tenth grade."

What was a fourteen-year-old girl supposed to say when her father's girlfriend declares her love while cleaning out the refrigerator's vegetable crisper?

Having never been faced with the dilemma before, I decided that, rather than respond, I'd concentrate on my homework and pretend I didn't even hear her.

While I continued working out the surface area of a box whose length was eight, width was four, and height was four (the answer is 160), Susan turned her attention to the brown bib lettuce and dehydrated baby carrots wedged into the corners of the neglected vegetable drawer.

"This isn't the way I expected it to be either," she'd said, and I wasn't sure whether she was talking about the glamorous life she'd envisioned as the girlfriend of a paper salesman, the step-girlfriend to a fourteen-year-old girl, or merely the state of my father's vegetable bin.

Susan stopped scrubbing, wiped her forehead with the gritty side of the sponge and sat back on her heels. "You can hate me, Abby, but don't hate your dad. I love him too much to watch that."

Once you've been given permission to hate something or someone, it kind of defeats the whole purpose, doesn't it? There's no thrill to sneaking out at night if your parents are watching you crawl out the window, encouraging you to be as quiet as possible, perhaps even suggesting alternate ways to make your escape more daring. At that point, you may as well use the front door. And then it's not sneaking out, is it? Then it's called *going out*, and that doesn't sound nearly as exciting.

After the vegetable-bin declaration, it was harder to picture Susan as the enemy. And my mother kept telling me she wasn't. *A happy person doesn't cheat*, my mother told me more than once, only instead of being convinced that my father wasn't happy, I came away believing that my mother *was* happy. Because she didn't need to find someone else to love. And I remember thinking, *A person doesn't cheat if she wants to be happy.*

I wanted to hate Susan. But she'd taken all the fun out of it. Much like my mom had taken all the fun out of hating my dad. And sometimes it's just so much easier to hate someone than to try to understand them. Because attempting to understand someone, *really* understand someone, takes effort. It takes putting your own opinions aside and trying to see something from someone else's point of view. And once you do that, the person becomes more than simply a symbol, more than a reminder of how your parents' marriage went wrong. The person becomes someone with feelings and thoughts just as complex as you'd like to think your own are. And then it's damn hard to hate her. Even if you want to.

I'd wanted to hate Alex, and it wasn't as if I had any difficulty doing so. But it wasn't just that I'd wanted to hate him. I *needed* to hate Alex, to dissect every inch of him in order to not see the whole person. I needed to hate Alex in 316 pieces—from the tips of his hairy toes and cracked heels to the top of his thick head of hair. (Couldn't the man go bald like normal guys?) Because the truth was, in the end, finding so much to hate was easier than remembering what I loved.

One weekend, when my dad picked me up to take me to the town-house, I remember finding an article he'd ripped out of a magazine—a parenting magazine. It was tucked inside the pocket on the passenger-side car door, and the edges of the pages were torn but even, as if they'd been carefully pulled away from the spine in an effort to not lose any of the copy. It was the first time I actually believed my dad thought about what he'd done to our family. To me. And it probably should have made me feel better, or at least made me feel less bad.

Only, after that, I couldn't help wondering how much of what we did together, what we said to each other, was a result of some article he'd read in a parenting magazine he discovered in the waiting area of a doctor's office or next to the Mr. Coffee machine at Jiffy Lube while waiting to get his oil changed. Or if the questions he asked me when we weren't playing the Love Bug game were in a sidebar next to an article on communicating with your teenage daughter.

Because my father didn't ask normal questions, the standard *How was school?* and *How did you do on your English test?* Our rides to Sunday brunch didn't revolve around discussions of the weather or upcoming exams. Instead my dad asked things like, *If today was a color, which one would it be?* And *If you could change one thing that happened this week, what would you change?*

It took me a while before I finally realized that the man who ripped out articles from parenting magazines was the person Susan married, the man she saw when she looked at my dad—someone who made up games to play with his daughter to get her to talk, or, if he didn't, at least a man who walked out of the convenience store carrying a half gallon of orange juice, a *Boston Globe*, and a glossy monthly magazine he hoped might give him a roadmap to his daughter's heart. She saw the man who did the best he could, and that was enough for her to love him.

And that's when, instead of thinking she was, at best, naive or, at worst, stupid, I thought, *I want a Susan, too.*

"So, what's for dinner?" I asked Susan, helping her collect the gardening tools.

"Chicken and rice. Or, if you'd prefer, we could always go out."

We piled the tools into a small plastic wheelbarrow and headed toward the garage. "No, chicken and rice is fine."

"I'd be really interested to hear more about this soil theory," she reminded me.

"I'll see what I can find out," I promised, just as my BlackBerry vibrated in my pocket. I excused myself and picked up the call with the familiar number.

"What's up?"

"I found two programmers," Claudia told me.

"Who are they?"

"Some students who are staying on campus this summer. I told them it would be worth their while."

"Extra credit?"

"Extra money. I said you'd pay them more than they were making bartending."

"You're going to have to be the go-between, you know."

"Abby, I don't need a second job. I spend enough time making sure I keep my first one."

"I promise I'll make this as painless as possible." Susan waved to me from the garage and pointed toward the side door. I nodded and waved her inside, letting Susan know I'd be there in a minute. "Can you come over tomorrow night so we can go over what we need to do?"

"No can do. I'm busy the rest of the week, but I'm free tonight." I'd have to leave right after dinner.

"That's fine. Nine o'clock. And bring Maggie; we could always use a skeptic's point of view to make sure this works."

"So what do you want to do? Should I tell them it's a go?"

I hesitated and turned toward Susan's ailing geraniums, already slumped over in defeat, their red pom-pom heads bowing to the soil below as if to say, *it's all your fault*. Maybe there was something to Mitch's theory. "Are they good?"

"Abby, they're my students. What do you think?"

"I'll see you at nine o'clock." I started walking toward the house and the smell of chicken wafting out the kitchen door. "Tell them it's a go."

chapter eight

"So, who is this Mitch guy?" Maggie wanted to know.

I stopped tapping my pen, unintentionally taking the bait. "What?"

"Elliott called to thank me for the party's floral arrangements, and he mentioned that you were chatty with a Mitch."

"He's Elliott's landscape architect."

Claudia flipped through the first stack of index cards laid out on my coffee table. "And?"

"And, nothing. He likes tuna tartare. And peanut butter and Fluff."

"Quite the gourmand." Claudia took out an index card and waved it in the air. "Is there a field in the database for food preferences? Are your members going to be able to find out he's had a hotdog phobia ever since a childhood accident with pigs in a blanket?"

"I hadn't thought of that," I told her, and grabbed the index card from Claudia's clutches.

"So, how would you categorize this landscape architect? Earthy-crunchy environmentalist, radical tree-hugging activist or serene poet communing with nature?"

I thought about our brief conversation at the buffet table, how

Mitch made me laugh without trying too hard. How he didn't get pissy when I turned him down or gross me out by smiling with bits of raw tuna caked between his teeth.

"The answer is *D*, none of the above. He seemed perfectly normal."

"Did you get his number?" Maggie asked. "Ask him over to till your soil?"

Claudia covered her mouth with a handful of index cards, but I knew she was laughing at me.

"He asked me for a date," I told them.

"Dinner? Drinks? Wheelbarrow races in the yard?" Maggie winked at Claudia.

"He asked if I wanted to play tennis and give him some tips."

Maggie pursed her lips at me. "That sounds like an hour of instruction, not a date."

I looked to Claudia, but she only nodded. "I have to agree here. Did he suggest anything afterward? A meal, coffee?"

"I don't drink coffee," I reminded her.

"Correct me if I'm wrong here, but he didn't know that when the offer was made, did he?"

He didn't. He knew only that I didn't like tuna sandwiches, which, now that I thought about it, shouldn't have prohibited Mitch from asking me out for coffee.

"What's wrong with him? Why'd you say no?"

"How'd you know I said no?"

Claudia frowned a silent *please*. "So, what's wrong with him?"

"I don't know yet," I admitted. "But there has to be something, right?"

Maggie didn't answer and instead held up a card with a fluorescent pink Post-it stuck to the top. "You've obviously come up with some sort of color-coded system, so, what's pink mean?"

"Pink is a level-one field," I explained. "The basic data all members must fill in—the guy's name, employer, height, that sort of thing."

"And the green?" Maggie asked.

"Level two. More detail about specific areas of importance—communication, social skills, personal grooming, etcetera."

"And blue?"

"My personal favorite, level three. The down and dirty. The real deal. The things you don't usually discover until it's too late."

"Oh, yeah?" Claudia pulled off the blue Post-it and read the card detailing how I wanted the field to work. "And what would you have wanted to know about Alex before you started dating him? What would have been important to find out?"

Too easy. I wish I'd known that one day he'd leave me. That one day he'd *want* to leave me.

Instead I said, "He farted in closets."

Claudia looked up from the card, her mouth the shape of a perfect uppercase *O*.

"That is not what I was expecting," Maggie laughed.

"But it's true." I crossed an imaginary *X* over my heart. "I swear."

Yes, a twenty-seven-year-old man was farting in closets because he didn't want to gross me out (obviously it didn't occur to him that all of my clothes were hanging in that closet and perhaps that idea would gross me out even more). We'd said *I love you* before this revelation, walking back to my apartment after dinner one night. But this level of intimacy was different. I wasn't stuffed full of mushroom risotto and merlot. He didn't have a buzz on from four vodka and tonics and a halo around him from the streetlamps. Instead of a blazer and slacks, Alex was wearing boxer shorts and the faded Princeton T-shirt. He was exposed and vulnerable and looked like I'd caught him shoplifting.

And that's when it happened. I realized that from that day forward

Alex would no longer leave the room and fart in my closet. And someday in the future I'd stop making sure my left arm pressed against my left breast so it seemed to be the same size as my right when we were lying naked together on the bed. Instantly, it became so real, this man and me. This person who, from that day on, would expect to peel me like an onion until he uncovered the raw core of the person underneath. And it scared the shit out of me. And I never stopped being scared. I'd seen Alex the way he didn't want me to see him and yet I still loved him. Probably more. Only I wasn't totally convinced that once he saw me the way I really was, he'd feel the same way.

"He also laughed in his sleep," I added.

Claudia shrugged. "He laughed in his sleep? That doesn't sound so bad."

No, it doesn't. At first it sounds absolutely charming. At first you imagine he's laughing at something you said during the day, some witty comment you made over dinner that was so damn amusing, even his subconscious couldn't forget about it. At least that's what I used to think. Alex was a deep sleeper. I use the past tense because I have no idea what he is now. I didn't know Alex when he left over a year ago, and I sure as hell wouldn't know him now.

Alex slept like a baby. Literally. He'd take all six feet of his body and curl up on his side like a centipede that's been tapped in its center. His fists would be all balled up and tucked under his chin, his elbows squeezed together so that his forearms created two perfectly parallel lines against his chest. In the beginning he faced me, and I'd lie with my head on the pillow we shared listening to his breath escape from his nose and the left corner of his mouth where his lips parted. I'd watch his eyelids twitch and examine the stubble on his chin, looking for blades of gray among the dark brown growth.

The first time he laughed, I was watching David Letterman and I assumed the chuckle was in response to a stupid pet trick. But the next night, when he laughed during a Metamucil commercial, I looked over and noticed he hadn't moved. After that, I didn't turn to face the television screen. I simply watched and waited for the chortle to make its way past the smile on Alex's lips. So cute, right?

Only as time went on and I hadn't said anything especially amusing that day, he still smiled and he still laughed. And that's when I realized it had nothing to do with me. And I started wondering what was making him so happy, if it wasn't me. That made it not so cute anymore.

"I'm not saying it would have made a difference; I just wish I'd known," I told them. "What about you guys? What would you like to know?"

"Remember that guy in college? Robert?" Maggie asked.

"The one who'd get so drunk he'd pee in the corner of the room?"

"That's the one. Would have been nice to have known that before he ruined a perfectly good pair of Nikes."

"I'd like to know if a date is a decent tipper," Claudia said. "I went out with a guy who didn't believe in it. Just outright refused to tip anyone—the valet, the waitress, cab drivers. I kept wondering why, every time we left a restaurant or got out of a cab, we'd get the evil eye. Of course, I didn't know this until one night I offered to pay for dinner. We were walking out of the place and he hands me my fourteen dollars back and says I left too much. It was a deal breaker."

"Why don't women just Google the guy? Isn't that what most people do anyway?"

Maggie was right. Google had become the enabler for every stalker ex-girlfriend out there, and even a few ex-wives, who, while not entering stalker territory, perhaps liked to check up to see whether he'd been promoted or died or something like that.

"Come on, do I really care what he wrote in to his alumni publication? Or what I could find out from some online dating service? Nobody's ever honest in those things because nobody's ever really honest about themselves. If you want to really know about someone, don't ask him. Ask the people who know him."

"Speaking of knowing people, did you ever call that estate jeweler I told you about?" Maggie asked me. "He said he'd make you a great deal on your rings."

I shook my head.

"Why not?"

"They're not antiques," I told her, and then added, "Besides, they're probably worth way more than he'll ever offer me," as if that was the problem: a faulty appraisal.

"Maybe not, but they're definitely relics from the past that have outlasted their use."

"Is that your definition of an antique?"

"It's my definition of an engagement ring sitting in a velvet box next to your Wonderbra."

"It's in a Ziploc bag, not a velvet box." I didn't mention that she'd been right about its location.

"Wherever it is, don't you think it's time to get rid of the thing?"

The *thing*.

"Even if it is an *antique*, who would buy a used engagement ring, anyway?" I asked, choosing the correct term for the emerald-cut diamond and platinum ring.

"Not *used*," Claudia corrected, sounding like a car salesman accustomed to correcting customers while standing in a parking lot next to a six-foot inflatable SALE sign. "Previously owned."

"It's a ring, not a Lexus." Maggie let out an exasperated breath at both of us. "So don't sell it. Throw it in the garbage, toss it into Boston Harbor; that's not the point. The point is, you don't need it anymore."

That was really the point, wasn't it?

"You're right," I agreed, only I didn't. I mean, no, I didn't need the ring; I didn't wear it around the apartment at night pretending that the absence of my husband was obliterated by the presence of an emerald-cut diamond and an eternity band that didn't even come close to lasting an eternity. I could have defended myself, told Maggie and Claudia that I'd had no problem removing the rings once, but it was too late to go back there, to when I'd stopped telling Maggie and Claudia everything about my marriage. I'd gone from sharing everything to hoarding the details. When you begin dating you share everything with friends, how his penis curves to the left, or that he curls his toes before he comes, because hearing your friends' reactions, watching them laugh with you, makes it feel real. Four hours after I learned that Alex got his high school girlfriend pregnant, Claudia and Maggie knew—although I did wait until I got home to call them. But once we were married, what used to be the innocuous sharing of information and comparing of notes started to feel an awful lot like disloyalty. And even though they were my best friends, I started to fear that what I confided was going to come back to haunt me.

Alex wasn't the only topic I skimmed over, the only subject I danced around with all the skill and grace of a ballerina who smiles at the audience while balancing the entire weight of her body on the tips of five tiny toes. I also stopped sharing details that revealed anything about Alex's wife, how she'd crawl into bed at night and quickly close her eyes before lying next to Alex so she wouldn't have to see what he hadn't yet had the courage to say out loud. I didn't tell them that even though Alex had asked his wife to quit smoking, she kept a pack of Marlboro Lights in her raincoat pocket. Or that while Alex went to the gym, she stood outside on the balcony with her back to the sliding glass door, a cigarette cradled between her fingers. Not because she liked the way the smoke filled her lungs or the lightheaded feeling she'd get after each drag, but because she didn't like the idea that she'd have to give anything up for Alex. So they never knew that when Alex walked out one last time, his wife didn't crave a cigarette from that moment on. Not once.

But what I really stopped sharing was the unpleasantness, the desperation that had settled inside me, the uncertainty. I didn't want them defending Alex, but I wanted them agreeing with me even less. Because I knew that a day later, a week after, we'd be on the phone or meeting for dinner and they'd know. They'd know how I was feeling while the man I was supposed to spend the rest of my life with had no idea. The woman who was supposed to be Alex's wife craved something more than cigarettes, only she didn't know how to ask for it, and even if she did, she wasn't sure she could handle it.

And yet, they were my best friends, so maybe they knew all along. Maybe I'd just been going through all that effort and ended up fooling only myself.

"Did you know?" I asked them.

"Did we know what?" Claudia asked.

"Did you *know*?"

Maggie slid her eyes toward Claudia, yet neither volunteered an answer.

"We knew you wanted to marry him," Maggie finally conceded.

"That's a nonanswer if ever I heard one."

"What do you want us to say, that we never thought it would work out and we were right?"

"No, I want you to say just the opposite. That you had no idea it would turn out like this, that you thought we'd live happily ever after with two-point-five kids and a summer house on Nantucket."

Claudia looked confused. "A summer house on Nantucket?"

"Yes. Indulge me."

"You just never struck me as someone who'd have a summer house on Nantucket. You don't even like the ocean."

"I like the ocean; I just don't like going *in* the ocean. I have no problem sitting on a beach and staring at it."

"Besides, you lack the requisite pink and green wardrobe, not to mention the woven basket purse and ribbon belt."

"Anyway, putting my lack of Lilly Pulitzer accessories aside, did you know?"

Maggie pushed a stack of index cards aside and rested her bare feet on the table. "What's it matter now?"

"It doesn't. So answer me."

"We didn't know it would happen, and we didn't know it *wouldn't* happen," Claudia answered. "Who can ever tell?"

"You'd make a great politician."

Claudia flashed me a peace sign and a vote-winning smile. "And you'd make a horrible summer resident of Nantucket."

"Well, it doesn't matter, because I don't foresee an island house in my future anytime soon. But what I do see is a sort of prewedding celebration for my mom. I'm meeting her on Saturday to look for a dress, and I was going to suggest we have a small shower, maybe take her to the Four Seasons for tea or something. What do you think?"

Maggie picked at the polish peeling off her big toe and I noticed that the scar around her pinky toe wasn't as large as I remembered. "I think that's a great idea."

"I'll let you know." I stood up and walked over to the whiteboard I'd propped up against the wall. "Now, back to the database."

Claudia picked up the four-pack of dry-erase markers I'd bought after work and joined me. "So we have, what, thirty fields for level three?"

"Let's add one more for high school jobs," I told her.

"Like that has any bearing on what a guy ends up like ten years after the fact?"

I added the new field in red. "You never know."

chapter nine

Alex was a lifeguard. It didn't matter that, by the time I met him, he hadn't slathered on the zinc oxide in more than ten years, and while I was sure he could still tread water, I seriously doubted he could swim one hundred yards in under two minutes. It didn't matter that, by the time I met him, Alex was working for a large consulting firm and covering up a pale chest in a Brooks Brothers suit. He'd once worn orange trunks, the kind that lace up the front and draw attention to a thin line of sun-bleached hair from his belly button down somewhere inside his swimsuit, a blond arrow identifying every teenage girl's target. And he'd sat up high on a white wooden lifeguard chair staring out at the ocean through a pair of reflective Ray-Bans. He was a lifeguard, a king above mere mortals who relied on him to breathe life into faltering swimmers and return little kids to their parents.

And I'd always wondered what all the fuss was about.

My parents used to rent a house on Cape Cod for a week every summer. The three of us would pack up and head down to a two-bedroom rental, where I'd attempt to sleep on a twin bed that had been slept on by numerous nameless, but hopefully well-bathed, people. And during the day we'd head to the beach with a cooler packed with peanut butter and jelly sandwiches, Ritz crackers and sliced watermelon in a Tupperware container. We lived in a suburb outside Chicago until I was eight, so we were going to do all the things midwesterners think people do at the beach. We collected shells in plastic buckets, built sandcastles and watched them wash away and ate lobster rolls for dinner (I went for the corndogs). Our first day on the beach, my father would pull out his metal detector, and he and I would go to work scouring the beach. There was never a shortage of Budweiser and Miller Lite bottle caps, inevitably some loose change, and even a few broken sunglasses. But no buried treasure, no valuable jewels or treasure chest of rare coins.

By the time I was twelve, I wanted more.

"Why even bother if you know you're never going to find anything worthwhile?" I asked my dad long after I'd given up and he'd continued walking ahead of me, the metal disk skimming along the sand in circular motions.

"How do you know that if you don't keep on trying?" he called to me over his shoulder, and I knew that the next day he'd be out there again looking for treasure.

I was too young to attract any attention from the lifeguards but old enough to know I wanted to. Unfortunately, our beach vacations to the Cape stopped when my dad moved out, and I never had the opportunity to test out a string bikini on the crop of tan teenage boys who looked out onto the horizon.

The thing about lifeguards is that they make you feel safe, but only if you need them, only when you need rescuing. Ninety-nine percent of the time, they're not saving lives; they're gazing out onto the breaking waves thinking about the sandwich they packed for lunch. And once you realize that, you have two choices: You can trust that when you're floundering they'll come to your rescue or you can always be prepared to save yourself.

Was knowing a man's teenage summertime occupations going to provide my members with insight into whether he's the right guy? Probably not. But you never knew.

I caught a glimpse of my mom through the boutique's front window before she even saw me standing outside on the sidewalk. Inside the store, she chatted away with the saleswoman, her hands waving animatedly in the air as she told the woman a story. Under the halogen lights dangling from the ceiling, my mother's engagement ring reflected scattered shards of light against the walls, like a laser show. Not that I've ever actually attended a laser show. The closest I'd come was joining Maggie for a consultation at Sleek MedSpa, where she'd hoped to eliminate the need for bikini waxes but decided that the idea of some technician playing Luke Skywalker around her delicate parts was a tad more frightening than a monthly wax appointment.

"I'm here," I announced, pushing open the door and stepping onto the hardwood floor. "You must be telling one heck of a story."

My mom dropped her hands to her sides and smiled. "I was just telling Nora about something Roger did. Nora, this is my daughter, Abby."

"We'll start in the back, where the gowns are," Nora told me, and then led us past the front racks and toward the more elegant gowns hanging along the wall in a back room.

The boutique didn't specialize in wedding dresses, not like the stores my mom and I had visited when it was my turn to select a gown. We'd hit all the small stores tucked up on the second floor of the gray stones along Newbury Street and spent hours among white crinoline, taffeta and sheer netting.

Instead of a boutique catering to brides, my mother had selected a small dress shop in Brookline. She'd bought her mother-of-the-bride dress in this same store three years ago, and, at the time, had chosen a graphite blue chiffon number. We'd been like two little girls the first time around, spinning in our full skirts until they mushroomed out at our waists as if about ready to take off. Together we must have tried on fifty dresses, with fewer than half of them even remotely resembling what we were looking for. My mother wanted something simple but elegant for her daughter's wedding. I'd wanted to be Princess Diana.

I was five when I started hearing about the princess, how she was marrying her fairy tale prince—although even at five I knew she could do better than a gangly guy who looked like he'd sucked one too many lemon drops. The night before the wedding, I'd begged my mom to set the Cinderella alarm clock I kept on my night table, and the next morning it was still dark out when Cinderella's white-gloved hands gracefully pointed to the twelve and the five. I plopped myself in front of the TV with a bowl of Cheerios and a teacup filled with chocolate milk, my version of an English child's breakfast. My mom's Polaroid camera sat poised on my lap, ready to snap a picture of the princess bride in all her ivory taffeta glory. Only rather than capturing Diana in yards of obscenely ruffled ballooning taffeta, the flash bounced off the glass screen and captured my reflection instead. And even though my yellow cotton nightgown with the Smurfette iron-on across my chest made me feel quite beautiful on several occasions, when my hands were holding the developing photo of a large white burst outlining my ponytailed head, there was no mistaking me for a princess.

"So, what are you thinking?" I now asked my mother, running a finger along a burgundy taffeta waist that looked more appropriate for a Christmas party than a summer wedding.

"Something simple but pretty. None of that beige old-lady stuff, no long sleeves and no high necks."

"Watch out, Nora. This is a woman who knows what she wants."

Nora clapped her hands. "Well then, let's get started!"

Helping your mom choose her wedding dress is a surreal experience, especially after she once helped you pick out your own. There she was, standing barefoot in a slip and strapless bra. The woman I used to watch prepare for a night out with my father, the woman who seemed so glamorous with her hair up in hot rollers and her reflection lit up in the magnifying mirror on the bathroom counter. She'd lean forward, her face bigger than life, her hand poised with the lipstick brush laced through her fingers, and prepare to wield the tool like an artist painting a canvas. My mother wore her yellow robe with the mandarin collar, the zipper pulled all the way to the top. And I'd watch her like that the entire time, watch the Saturday-night routine that seemed so mysterious to me because I always wondered where she was headed that required such care, this woman who walked out the front door looking more like a movie star than the woman who boiled water for my morning Cream of Wheat.

It was one of the rituals I missed the most after my father moved out. Instead of preparing for nights on the town, my mom and I ate popcorn and watched *Mr. Belevedere*. She started dating Roger after I'd gone to college, so I don't know that she ever used that lipstick brush again, or if she forewent the artistry and went straight to the slanted tip in the tube. I hoped she kept the lipstick brush and the ritual that went along with it.

Funny how routines become rituals after you miss them, after they cease to exist. The way my father would come upstairs and take off his suit and tie while my mom and I sat on their bed and recounted our days. How my mother ordered pizza on Sunday nights while all the other families were having roast chickens and mashed potatoes, just so we could all sit in the family room with my dad while he cheered on the

Patriots. The drive to pick up the pizza, and how it was my responsibility to hold the pizza on my lap and keep the hot cheese from sliding off the pie when we turned the corners. The steam rising from the holes on the side of the box, and how I'd always write my initials in the condensation that formed on the passenger-side window, *AD* inside a freeform heart.

There were rituals I missed when Alex left, things that were part of our life together that became so ingrained, so a part of the daily workings of our relationship, I'd stopped noticing them. When fractures began forming between us, the routine filled in the cracks like mortar. The dailiness of life let us ignore the growing distance, the increasing silences, the more frequent frustration. The rhythm of our marriage, the ordinary sounds and background noises—the ice maker humming in the freezer, the second hand sweeping around the living room clock one hatch mark at a time—swelled together to fill in the silences so that we didn't have to. It became deafening, and I always wondered what the neighbors thought of us, the couple next door. Did they hear the silences? Did they notice the absence of noise that seeped under the doors and filled the rooms of the apartment next door? Were they surprised when the moving trucks arrived and our names were removed from the mailbox in the lobby, or did they hear the end long before the boxes were stacked in neat rows lining the hallway?

"What do you think the Kramers make of us?" I'd asked Alex about a week after we moved into the condo. We'd introduced ourselves to the Kramers, a couple in their forties, in the lobby the day before, when we ran into them at the mailbox.

Alex continued reading *Business Week*. "I don't know, they probably think we're a normal couple who gets more junk mail than anything else."

"Do you think they think we're happy?"

This time Alex looked up at me, but he didn't put down the magazine. "I don't think we gave them any reason to think we weren't. Do you?"

I shrugged. "No."

He stood up then, and came over to me on the couch. "Why do you care what the Kramers think, anyway?" Alex laid an arm over my shoulders and I let my head fall against his chest, where I could feel his heart beat out a rhythm.

"I don't care what they think. I was just wondering what they saw when they met us."

Alex rested his chin on the top of my head and I remember wondering whether he'd always ground his teeth while he slept or if it was something that started when he met me.

I closed my eyes thinking about that, Alex's molars slowly grinding away at night. When I opened my eyes the apartment was dark, the only light a green shadow coming from the digital clock on the microwave in the kitchen.

"How long was I sleeping?" I asked Alex, sitting up and running my hand through the right side of my hair, which had been pressed down and probably made me look lopsided.

"Not too long, maybe forty-five minutes."

Forty-five minutes. I glanced over at the *Business Week* still lying open on the chair across the room. All he'd had to do was get up and go back to his reading. Instead he sat on the couch in the dark listening to my sleepy breath.

We'd been married two months at that point, and I remember thinking that Alex had done something only a newlywed would do. In six months, a year, he'd feel me go limp against him, realize he couldn't reach the remote control or a book or a magazine, and he'd stand up, leaving me to sleep alone on the couch, which would probably be more comfortable than the awkward incline I'd been in against his chest, but not nearly as desirable.

And so I began waiting for that moment, counting down to it. The first time he slipped out of bed without kissing me. The first afternoon I was sitting at my desk and he didn't call just to say he loved me. The first Saturday he forgot to ask whether I needed anything at the store on his way back from the gym. The first Friday night he didn't initiate sex, and the second Friday night I followed suit just to see how he'd react, to see whether he'd pass the test. When he didn't react, the failing mark was recorded next to the other things that bothered me. That he didn't know they bothered me, bothered me. Even though the apartment was silent, I could hear the crescendo beginning to build, like at the Emmys—the orchestra had started to play, signaling to me that it was time to wrap it up.

Did the Kramers ever know, in the end, that it was the silences that did us in? That the quiet unraveling of our marriage, our relationship, our friendship, had less to do with the building's well-insulated construction and more to do with my ability to build a wall so impenetrable, there was no way Alex could ever break through?

"Why don't we start with this one?" Nora suggested, handing my mother a pearly gray dress with a full skirt and capped sleeves.

"It's pretty," I told my mom, and she nodded and turned toward the dressing area.

I started to follow her, but Nora stepped between us.

"No, let me help." Nora pulled back the curtain and stepped into the dressing room beside my mom. "This way when she walks out you won't be biased."

Nora swept my mom behind the curtain and I headed back toward the front of the store, where I lingered over the jewelry display.

"My sister says I can't join unless she puts in a good word for me, though," a blond woman said, sifting through the sale rack behind me. "I guess there's some sort of screening system in place."

"Well, if you get in, you'll help me, right?" her friend asked, holding up a sleeveless turtleneck and admiring her reflection in the full-length mirror against the wall.

"Of course. I don't really know much about it, yet. My sister said she'd let me know as soon as it's open for membership."

I moved closer to the duo, taking a sudden interest in a beige tweed skirt priced to sell at fifty percent off.

"Well, I'm in," the blonde's friend told her, now sifting through a row of silk camisoles. "Remember that guy I went home with a few weeks ago? Steven? Before we went to bed he went to brush his teeth, which is fine; I like a guy with minty-fresh breath as well as the next girl. Then he asks if I'd like to brush my teeth as well, only I'm not using this guy's toothbrush."

"So, you're willing to sleep with him, but you're not willing to use his toothbrush?"

"Not the point. I didn't have to use his toothbrush. He offered me a new one, still in the package and all."

The blonde was impressed. "That was nice of him."

"You think? Only the next morning I discovered a box under the sink filled with toothbrushes—Oral B, Reach, Colgate. So there's two options here: one, the man was raised by a hyperactive dental hygienist, or, two, he has way too many overnight guests."

"You think that's bad, I once went out with a guy who had a stuffed animal. Only it wasn't a cute teddy bear—which would be bad enough. He had a squirrel. Named Nuts."

"Sounds like he's nuts."

"Yep," the blonde agreed. "And he's going to be my first contribution to that database."

The database! They were talking about *my* database! Two women in Brookline, two strangers who had no idea who'd thought up the database or how it would work, were talking about becoming members.

The database was going to be filled with men who slept with stuffed roadkill and lived in fear of periodontal disease. It was just too perfect. And if I was going to get the database ready before another woman had to sleep next a squirrel named Nuts, there were going to be some long nights ahead of me.

"It's really going to happen," I mumbled, and then sighed a tad louder than I'd intended.

"Tired?" Nora asked, appearing in the doorway to the dressing room with a pale sage dress draped over her arms.

"Just thinking about all the work I have to do tonight."

"Well, stop thinking about work. Your mom's ready for you."

"Then, let's go see," I agreed, and followed her in the direction of the bride-to-be.

chapter ten

"You look like shit." Maggie walked into my office and placed a vase of bright pink tulips on my desk. Every quarter a bouquet landed on my desk before Maggie met with our purchasing department to go over floral orders for the foyer and meeting rooms.

"Tell me something I don't know." I yawned, then rubbed my eyes so I wasn't viewing Maggie in triplicate.

"The tulip is the national flower of Turkey."

"Really."

"And Iran."

"I had no idea."

"Shall I go on, then?"

"Please don't. I'm shamed by your abundance of botanical knowledge. I might have to retaliate by explaining how the Black-Scholes model provides the arbitrage-free value of a call option."

"In that case, consider my botany lesson for the day over." Maggie parked herself in my visitor chair. "So, what's going on? Why do you look like someone I'd see resisting arrest on an episode of *Cops?*"

A pinstriped suit strode past my open door, and it took every ounce of energy I had to get up from my chair and close my office door. I hadn't told anyone that my diligent six a.m. arrivals and late-evening departures had less to do with my commitment to discovering the next great investment than with the fact that Verity had a T1 line and all I had at home was a dial-up connection. It was something I was remedying this afternoon when my new hyperspeed DSL connection was getting installed.

"The database is finally done." I flopped back into my seat and sunk down until my head was resting against the black leather upholstered pillow. It was about the only thing holding me upright at that point. "I finished it at four o'clock this morning."

"And?" Maggie asked, as if I'd left her hanging, as if she knew there was more to the story.

"And I'm taking it live tomorrow. Claudia's coming over tonight to go through it and fix any bugs."

"Whoa. Step back a minute. Going *live*? So, this is really happening?"

"I just wrote a check to Claudia's students for sixty hours of programming, and I have thirty-seven members and almost two hundred men in the database, so, yeah, it's really happening."

Maggie picked up a legal pad and ripped off the top sheet. "I hope you know what you're doing."

"You've already made it clear that you don't approve of my new venture, but look at it this way: It's no different from what men have been doing for ages on bathroom stalls—sharing information gained through experience. You don't have to believe everything you read, but I'm sure there's been a man or two who's appreciated the heads-up that Rita Sandler gives good head."

Rita Sandler did, indeed, give good head, at least according to the eighth-grade boys lucky enough to be on the receiving end. I might not have known this, even though I suspected it, if I hadn't ventured into the boys' bathroom myself to see if my kissing skills had earned immortality above the urinal. Only, instead of discovering my French kisses were second to none, I learned that Rita Sandler wasn't terribly discriminating, and Ms. Juanita, our Spanish teacher, went commando under her pleated skirts.

"So you're ushering restroom graffiti into cyberspace?" Maggie folded the yellow rectangle in her hands until she had a perfectly crisp paper airplane.

"I'd like to think my Web site will be slightly more sanitary," I told her.

"Well, for the record, I think you're asking for trouble." She positioned the airplane for takeoff and then launched it across my desk and watched as it hit me in the forehead. "Maybe that will knock some sense into you."

"Claudia has no problem with it."

"Claudia has one thing on her mind at all times. If she actually stopped for two minutes to think about what it is she's helping you do, I doubt she'd be so supportive." Maggie reached for another sheet of paper, apparently determining that the situation had become a full-on military initiative that required reinforcements. "Something tells me Claudia wouldn't think sharing oral-sex tips on bathroom walls was something worth bringing into the technology age."

But at this point it didn't matter what Claudia thought. The database was completed. And tomorrow I'd be open for business.

Riding the T on the way home, I watched the women watching the men, wondering what it was they wished they knew about the guy in the blue paisley tie or the redhead with the compass dangling from his backpack's zipper. A yellow legal pad was always on my lap, its blank lined pages covered in notes by the time I reached the Copley Station stop. I had less than twenty-four hours to makes sure the database included all the areas a woman needed in order to make a solid investment of her time, not to mention emotional energy. Did he have a good relationship with his family? And his mother in particular? Was he still convinced he had the makings of a professional _____ (insert answer here: baseball player, sumo wrestler, soapbox derby champion, etc.)? Had he ever been in therapy?

This wouldn't necessarily be a strike against him. In fact I might argue that someone who'd submitted to the couch could be more well adjusted than the average guy. Then again, he could just be completely fucked-up. Again, it wasn't my place to judge, just to put the information out there.

I tried a therapist. A woman. It had to be a woman because I figured only a woman would be on my side. I didn't believe a man, no matter how many degrees hung on his wall or how many capital and small letters and periods came after his name, would be able to truly fully understand me. Because I didn't care how hairy he was, or how old, or if he smelled like Listerine and Ben-Gay, I still imagined him sitting there trying to figure out if Alex left because I was bad in bed. Or because I was ripe with classic woman ailments—the woman who loves too much, the woman who married the man she wanted to fix, the woman who (God forbid) married her father.

But even my female therapist wasn't much help. Therapy is a lot like analytical modeling—garbage in, garbage out. And in my case, the poor woman, Dr. Sylvia Bartlett, PhD, EdD, was dealing with the equivalent of a waste management cavalcade, corrupted data from start to finish.

I don't know what I thought it would be like, having never needed the expertise of someone like that before, but it felt like a job interview. Her probing, open-ended questions designed to delve into my warped psyche were met with answers designed to get me the job of Woman Who Is Really Okay and Doesn't Need to Be Sitting on a Leatherette

Couch Talking About How Fucked-up She Is Since Her Husband Walked Out on Her. Things like "I'm a team player but also work well independently," "Communication also means being a good listener" and "My weaknesses are also my greatest strengths." But never once did I tell her the one piece of information that I knew she was waiting to uncover, the one tidbit that would blow the lid off my case.

Sylvia Bartlett, PhD, EdD, tried hard, I'll give her that. But I couldn't give her what she wanted, which was for me to tell her, a complete stranger, the truth.

Elliott understood, but he thought the problem lay with Sylvia Bartlett's credentials, and not me. I liked his thinking. And I thought there must be something to it. After all, Elliott was on a first-name basis with most of the Harvard Medical School's department of psychiatry and psychopharmacology, not to mention he was probably responsible for more than a few lovely ski homes and had helped put a fair share of their children through Ivy League colleges.

Somebody's always the engine and somebody's always the caboose. That's what Sylvia Bartlett, PhD, EdD, told me after our second meeting. I'm telling her about how my husband left and she's giving me some bullshit about how relationships resemble the workings of an antiquated transportation system. Sylvia Bartlett had a habit of doing this, tossing out metaphors and analogies and parables that were supposed to impart some deeper truth that I, being the one seeking therapy, was obviously missing. I knew she expected me to nod, to have my very own aha moment, see the lightbulb go on, get down on my knees and scream, *Hallelujah.* Instead I pictured a children's cartoon, a runaway train with Alex's face superimposed on a steam engine, his eyes for headlights, a Boston Red Sox cap positioned over his steam pipe, and me at the long end of the train, whipping around corners uncontrollably.

"So I'm the caboose in this scenario?"

"Actually, I see you as the engine," she'd told me.

I canceled my next appointment and never rescheduled. Maybe Dr. Sylvia Bartlett wasn't so clueless after all.

"Are you ready?"

Claudia and Maggie were huddled around the desk in the corner of my living room. The lights were dimmed and the apartment silent. Sure, it was a tad melodramatic, but I'd been up until the wee hours of the morning for the past two weeks and I wasn't letting my moment of triumph pass by without milking it just a little. Besides, I hadn't had more than three hours of sleep a night for the past twelve days. I was entitled to my moment of eccentricity.

"Ta-da!" I lifted the sheet dramatically draped over the flat-screen monitor. "We are officially open for business."

Claudia bent in and squinted at the colorful screen glowing on my desk. "Again with the *we*."

"Are you going to explain all this?" Maggie tapped the monitor. "All I see are graphs and blinking numbers."

"Actually the blinking numbers are just for fun. Claudia's students were showing off, I think. What I've done is create different fund categories that contain men with similar characteristics. When the data is input into the system, an algorithm takes the information, sorts it, and allocates the guy to the most appropriate fund or funds." I looked over at Claudia to see whether I was doing all the database hocus-pocus justice, and she nodded her approval.

"Like this one over here in green," I continued. "This is a balanced fund. The guys are pretty much average in every way, stable, sort of the ones you can take home to Mom."

Maggie nodded.

"Over here, in the purple, that's our long-term growth fund. This is for guys who have some areas in need of improvement but show great potential if you're willing to put in the time and effort. And the orange one, that's the global fund, for women who like a little international flair."

"What's that?" Maggie asked, pointing to the fund highlighted in blue. "A contra fund?"

"A contrarian fund. That one is filled with the guys most women avoid."

"Who'd want a guy from there?"

"Maybe a woman who likes a challenge."

"So they're masochists?"

"I like to think of those members as eternal optimists."

I took Maggie and Claudia through the rest of the funds—the limited-duration fund, for women who don't have the time or inclination to pursue long-term relationships; the special-values fund, for women with particular religious or lifestyle requirements; the socially responsible fund, for Birkenstock-wearing vegans and the like.

"So this is where I'd find that guy in the VW van with the WHAT WOULD JESUS BOMB? bumper sticker?" Maggie asked. "Or the one in the hybrid with NICE HUMMER, SORRY ABOUT YOUR PENIS plastered on the back?"

"Exactly."

"You're talking about half the guys in Cambridge." Claudia laughed.

"What do the stars mean?"

Maggie may not endorse my approach, but her curiosity was certainly piqued. And that's when I knew I had a winner. All the lost sleep, the money spent on Claudia's students, it was all going to be worth it.

"It's a basic system to rank men based on their risk-adjusted performance over various periods—a five-star rating is the best, and one star is the worst." I reached for the mouse and clicked on the toolbar. A menu popped up. "Okay, here's where it gets fun."

I took them through a few of the tools I'd had the programmers develop, charts and functions that enabled even more in-depth analysis.

"This here calculates a man's interest rate—the higher it is, the more positive feedback we've received on him." I double-clicked the menu and brought up a graph. "This is an index so we can chart a man's performance compared to the average—is he outperforming the mean or underperforming? It kind of gives women an idea of where he's tracking. And then this"—I pulled up yet another screen—"is where we list the IPOs, the initial public offerings. These men have just come back on the market after being off for a while, so they're a little risky. They could have learned a lot from their long-term relationship and be an ideal choice, or they could just want to go drinking with their buddies and get laid."

"Are your members going to understand all of this?" Claudia asked. "Don't they just really want to know if he slurps his soup?"

"I'll be there to help them along the way." I picked up the brand-new cordless phone sitting next to the monitor, as well as its accompanying wireless headset. "Support is included in the monthly dues."

Maggie scrutinized the screen, still trying to make sense of the charts and graphs and data fields. "How much are you charging these members?"

"A flat fee every month—thirty bucks. I opened up a PayPal account, so they just do it all online." I nudged Claudia, grinning at the brilliance of the whole idea. "I take back every time I called you a geek. This technology stuff is great."

Maggie was finally out of questions, her skepticism exhausted. She stepped away from the desk and gave me one last defeated shake of her head. "You've thought of everything, haven't you?"

"I'd like to think so." Blame it on my day job, but I was nothing if not thorough.

"Have you thought of what happens when guys start figuring out that their nasty little secrets are being cataloged for the world to see?"

"Not the world, just womenknowbetter.com's discerning members. Besides, it's not all bad; there'll be positive things in the database, too."

"You sure make it sound easy enough."

Yeah, I did. And that wasn't an accident. In fact, it had been anything but easy. The biggest challenge was figuring out how to make the entire site a black box of sorts. I couldn't risk having some fourteen-year-old with a Game Boy and his father's electric razor hacking in. Or some thirty-four-year-old guy getting wind of the service and creating an account for himself. That's why Claudia's students created a referral system that required an introduction by an existing member. Once verified and approved by yours truly, new members would be assigned an ID number that they'd use to log on. Then members could submit new additions to the database and retrieve information at will. Of course, I'd always be there to make sure everything kept running smoothly. The benign moderator who ensures that the free market system doesn't fail its members. The Adam Smith of relationships, only without the powdered wig and Scottish accent.

Claudia hiked a thumb at me, indicating she was giving me the boot. "Get up and let me take this baby for a spin."

I relinquished my chair and let Claudia take the driver's seat. "Now we'll see if we have any problems with the programming and fix any bugs."

An hour later Claudia gave me her seal of approval and Maggie gave me her final word of disapproval.

"What goes around comes around, Abby," she warned, pausing in my doorway. "I may not be superstitious, but I do believe in karma."

Who was this woman all of a sudden, the Dalai Lama?

"Don't worry," I assured her, basking in the blue glow from the flat-screen monitor. "I know exactly what I'm doing."

After Claudia and Maggie left, I collapsed onto the couch. The past two weeks I felt like the only place in my apartment I spent any time was my desk chair. It was a lovely antique white swivel chair that matched the antique white Bedford desk I ordered out of the Pottery Barn catalog. They were the first purchases I made for my new apartment. Alex would never have gone for the antique white. Too feminine. Of course, that was half the point in ordering the pieces in the first place. They didn't say *man*, or *couple*. They said, *This is a woman on her own*. The chair also said, *I have a flat wooden seat and no cushion; therefore, I wasn't meant to be used for long periods of time*. Of course, the catalog left that part out of the description.

In any case, my desk chair was nowhere near as comfortable as the chenille sectional I was currently lounging on, my bare feet propped up on the armrest. I loved my couch, although it used to be *our* couch. Not that *we* picked it out, or *we* paid for it, which is why there was never any doubt who would keep it. Except for the dark walnut desk we'd kept along the wall in the guest room, there was no doubt who would keep most of the furnishings in our home. Not that Alex seemed to mind. He took so little when he left, not even the Christmas ornament his mother gave him one year, a moon carved out of wood with a Santa hat. I've thought about that a lot since he left, that stupid freaking ornament his mother tied to a shirt box with a flimsy red ribbon. *He didn't even miss it.* Like a political refugee, Alex left everything behind and escaped over the wall without looking back. Not because he was afraid he'd change his mind, but because he had to keep moving to survive. And the ornament, like our marriage, was a casualty he left behind.

We spent Thanksgivings with his family. All whopping two of them. Those stories you hear about horrible mothers-in-law, the jokes and parodies of the boozy, chain-smoking Joan Crawford or the repressed June Cleaver? His mom was neither. And she liked me, so I wasn't about to complain. I often wondered whether from now on, when his family gathered around the dining room table, would they remove the chair I used to sit in, the one against the credenza that I'd always bump into and end up apologizing when the gravy spilled on the tablecloth? Will his mom ask Alex whether he's talked to me, whether he knew how I was doing, or will she simply say, *What ever happened to that silly girl who wouldn't even try my oyster stuffing?*

Or maybe my chair was already filled by a new woman, a woman who would ask for seconds of the oyster stuffing. Maybe even thirds. A woman I'd never know but already hated.

Although Claudia and Maggie were led to believe there may have been someone waiting in the wings, who knew what Alex had waiting for him when he walked out of our home for the last time? A breathy woman did call once and ask to speak with Alex, but she could have been trying to sell him a timeshare in Boca Raton for all I knew. What I did know was that it was easier to believe there was another woman. To believe he was leaving me for something else, something he thought was better, or even just different. Because if he was leaving me without that safety net, without warm arms and crazy Cinemax sex, then he was just leaving me to be alone. And that meant that even having nothing at all was better than having me.

I thought about her, Alex's next girlfriend, or next *wife*. Would she be taller than me, blonder, easier to get along with? Would she have tattoos, small ones, like a delicate daisy the size of my pinky nail in the crease of her thigh or just below her belly button? She could be brave and have a big tattoo, a butterfly with its wings spread across her shoulder blades or Yosemite Sam on the small of her back. Maybe she'd have a sense of humor. Or just really poor taste. I was hoping for the poor taste.

Would the next woman Alex chose be like me? That thing in movies where the man leaves the woman and ends up with his ex-wife's twin— right down to the perfume she wears and her favorite color nail polish—that's got to be bullshit, right? Because I can't think of anything worse than waking up next to a man who smelled like Alex, someone whose chest had a small bald patch where his brother once burned him with the tip of a cap gun, a man with the same two hollows carved into the spot where his thighs met his perfectly white ass. Alex had taken up residence in my brain and I hadn't been able to evict him, and so the memories stayed there, cordoned off with that yellow tape police use to mark off a crime scene.

As much as I was ready to take the Web site live the way it was, I knew I'd forgotten something. And as much as I hated the idea of getting up off the couch, I knew there was more work to be done.

I reached my feet as far over the armrest as possible and clapped them around the phone sitting on the end table. After bending over to grab the antenna, I dialed Claudia's voice mail at work. "We need to add some new fields to the database," I told her. "We need a whole section on holidays."

chapter eleven

The next morning I called in sick to work. Not right away, not before I'd picked out a suit and blown my hair dry. Not before I took my T pass out of my purse and slipped it into my jacket pocket. I even went through the motion of packing a vanilla yogurt in my briefcase for a midmorning snack. But it was all a show. A hoax. Because there was no way I was going to leave my apartment, not when a computer screen taunted me with colorful graphs and indexes and blinking numbers that defied me to miss out on the first day of my new endeavor.

Even when I *am* sick, I don't call in sick. I'll sneeze and sniffle, clutch a tissue in my hand and suck on menthol cough drops until I smell like those old ladies wrapped in crocheted scarves and plastic, foldable rain bonnets. But I never give in, never admit that an inability to breathe air through my nasal passages or a pink, crud-crusted eye is enough to break me. Much to my coworkers' dismay, I was sure.

That's why this morning I simply called Elizabeth and said, "I have a headache."

"Well, take it easy and get some sleep," she'd prescribed, not even the slightest bit suspicious. "Sometimes a cool washcloth on your forehead helps, too."

Elizabeth had to believe me. It was just so perfectly normal. If someone were going to make up an excuse to blow off her first day of work in five years, wouldn't she attempt to be more creative—perhaps a case of whooping cough or Legionnaires' disease? And she certainly wouldn't come up with something so common that it could be cured with a hot shower and over-the-counter medication.

Only, instead of taking two Tylenol and lying down in a darkened room, I sat down at my desk and tried on my new headphones. I adjusted the small foam pad against my ear, testing various positions I'd seen the operators-standing-by use on late-night infomercials. By ten o'clock I'd perfected my very own rendition of *one ringy-dingy*. By ten thirty I'd clicked on every single screen, admired the new fields where members could recount their manly holiday horrors (Claudia was nothing if not hyperefficient), and checked my inbox 3,027 times waiting for an e-mail from one of the members, or maybe even a new referral to approve.

By eleven o'clock I really did have a headache. A throbbing, stabbing pain that started in the back of my neck and ended behind my left eye.

Around noon, just as I was about to pack it in and admit that I'd been wrong and Maggie was right, the phone rang.

Only it wasn't the new unlisted phone number. It was my home phone, which meant it definitely wasn't a new member and was most likely a telemarketer.

"Playing hooky?" Elliott teased when I answered. "I called the office and they said you weren't feeling well." The total lack of concern in his voice meant he wasn't quite convinced I was on my deathbed just yet.

"Woke up with a headache."

"Come on, it's me, Abby. I've seen you show up at the office with a Petri dish leaking from your nose. What's up? Are you interviewing somewhere else?"

"I'm not leaving Verity, Elliott. Like I said, I had a headache." At this point there was no reason to tell Elliott about the database. There was no database, just a few women who'd thought the idea was intriguing as long as that's all it was. An idea. Now that I'd spent too many late nights and too much money to actually create the service, nobody was interested. Build it and they will come, my ass.

"As long as you're playing hooky, Caroline and I were wondering if you'd like to come to the aquarium with us this afternoon," he explained. "We're heading over after the market closes."

"Thanks, but I think I'll take a pass."

"You're missing out on a good time," he continued. "Not to mention it would be the perfect opportunity to get over your fear of fish."

"I don't have a fear of fish; I have a dislike for them. There's a difference."

"Is that why you told Mitch to leave you alone? He seemed fishy to you?" Elliott laughed at his own joke.

"I didn't tell him to leave me alone. I told him I didn't want to play tennis."

"So you thought he was a good guy but he wouldn't be able to hold his own on the court?"

"I'm just not looking for a tennis partner right now."

"He asked about you," Elliott persisted, and if my head wasn't about to implode right there in my kitchen, I might have asked him to elaborate. Only I didn't have to, because Elliott wasn't leaving it alone. "Do I have to convince you to take him up on his offer?"

"I don't need convincing. He seemed fine, really," I repeated. "Almost too fine, if you know what I mean."

"Too fine? Sorry, you're going to have to clarify that."

I hung my head in my hands and rubbed my temples in circular motions. Elliott wasn't doing much to help my head. "Remember when you were little, and it was time to go to camp?"

"Abby, I grew up on Long Island with a Jewish mother who had me convinced spiders were the root of all evil. I did not go to camp."

"Well, let me fill you in on what you missed. First your mom would give you a brochure filled with pictures of kids laughing together, sharing toasted marshmallows with campers who would become your best friends for life. Then you'd look at photos of Sailfishes gliding across crystal-clear lakes and archery tournaments and arts-and-crafts classes where you'd make stained-glass creations worthy of installation in St. Patrick's Cathedral. And you'd believe it all, hook, line and sinker. Only do you know what you'd find when you got there?"

"I'm sure you're going to tell me."

"Instead of all-night slumber parties with your best friends, you're sleeping in a log cabin under a canopy of mildew, the Sailfishes belong to the camp on the other side of the lake and the kid in the bunk next to you is a bed wetter who's stealing the bag of Chips Ahoy! your mom packed in your duffel bag."

"So you're saying you're afraid Mitch is going to steal your Chips Ahoy!? Or, worse, be a bed wetter?"

"No, I'm saying if something seems too good to be true, it usually is."

"You know, Abby, there are two kinds of people in this world."

I held my pulsating head in my hands and ventured a guess. "The haves and the have-nots?"

"The ones who stop trying because they're afraid of disappointing someone, and the ones who stop trying because they're afraid of being disappointed."

I knew Elliott expected me to get his point, but the thing was, I didn't know which was supposed to be me.

I'm not the first person to get divorced. I realized that. In the grand scheme of things, the odds were against me from the beginning, even if statisticians would have us believe that our chances are fifty-fifty. Now, if I'd been diagnosed with a brain tumor (odds: 5 out of 100,000) or been struck by lightning (1 in 280,000), perhaps I should have been thrown for a loop by the sheer unlikelihood of such an event happening to me of all people. But divorce? My odds were one in two. I should have known I wouldn't beat them.

I tried bargaining for a while, attempting to reverse what was happening to us. I'd wake up thinking, *Today's the day.* The day I tried harder to be a better person, someone who walks to the staff kitchenette and tosses her water bottle in the recycling bin instead of stuffing it into the wastebasket under her desk. I'd give up aerosol hairspray and volunteer at an animal shelter (our building prohibited animals, so even though I thought adopting a stray might score me some points, it was out of the question). I'd even commit to reducing my greenhouse emissions by ten percent (an arbitrary number, but, considering I wasn't quite sure what greenhouse emissions even were, I figured I could achieve this small step toward betterment). I'd decide that today was the day I'd be a better wife. Because a better wife would make Alex happy, and if Alex was happier, then I'd be happier, too, right?

Only all along I knew he'd leave me. I knew the same way you know, no matter which line you pick at the grocery store, the other one will move faster. That no matter which pasta dish you order, the steaming plate on the other table will taste better. Because I wasn't lucky. My mom played the lottery because she thought she could defy the odds, but I wasn't under the illusion that was possible. I never believed I'd be one in a million.

At twelve thirty I decided that, if nobody was going to use all the valuable data that I'd slaved away on for weeks, then I'd be the first one. I typed in the names of a few coworkers, and two guys in derivatives actually appeared along with some inside scoop: fear of flying, wears white Hanes underwear inside out—on purpose, shaves his chest. Just imagining the stubble gave me chills, and not the good kind. I almost felt obliged to drop by the derivatives department tomorrow and leave a brochure for laser hair removal on the poor guy's desk. Then I looked up a few men Maggie dated, and one was right there, as well as the information that he was afraid of the dark. She'd never mentioned that.

I already knew that Alex wasn't in the database—yet. Although I let Claudia's students program the system, I wasn't about to let them get their hands on the information that made the Web site valuable to begin with. So I'd had to manually input the information for every single man, and even though I went on autopilot after about the fourteenth hour, I would have known if my fingers tapped out the ten familiar letters in Alex Madden's name. His conspicuous absence could mean only one of two things: either he wasn't dating anyone (the preferred answer), or he'd been dating women who thought he was a risk worth taking. Sadly, these were the women who needed womenknowbetter.com the most.

Once I'd exhausted the pool of coworkers and my friends' past boyfriends, I typed in a new name. Someone who seemed too good to be true. Mitch Reeves. But when I pressed ENTER, all I got was a pop-up telling me that no data existed. There were only two hundred men in the database, and while that sounded like a lot to begin with, it didn't even begin to scratch the surface of all the available men in Boston. If I was going to learn more about Mitch, it might take a few weeks until he became another data point in the system. As much as I trusted Elliott's opinion, the mere fact that Mitch could design a retaining wall to complement an infinity-edged pool wasn't exactly the sort of information that provided any sort of useful insight into the guy's psyche.

By two o'clock my unlisted phone number still wasn't ringing. The blinking fields on the database had become more annoying than anything else, and I was beginning to regret telling the programmers to go ahead and add the flashing stars that were now lighting up the corner of my living room like a disco ball gone awry.

I had to get out of my apartment before I reached over and pulled the plug on the whole thing. And fast.

So I threw on my sneakers and went for a walk around the Common.

Statistics show that only twenty percent of murders are committed against total strangers. That means that a significant majority of people are hurt by someone who's seen them in their pj's, watched them down the last piece of birthday cake when they thought no one was looking and sent them annual holiday wishes. The lesson here: It's not the strangers we need to watch out for. It's the people sending us Christmas cards.

I once had the great idea to play a little Halloween joke on Alex. We'd had all of two trick-or-treaters, and the bowl of Snickers and Twix bars had ultimately ended up serving as my dinner as well as my after-dinner snack. Sure it was the middle of the night and after emptying his bladder Alex probably wasn't going to be in the mood for a joke, but that didn't stop me. I had the power of chocolate, caramel and cookie crunch in me.

It had to be three a.m. when I felt the weight on the bed shift and heard Alex walk toward the bathroom. He didn't flip on the light switch, so the only light in the room came from the streetlamps outside our bedroom window. Before he flushed, I slid out from under the sheets and hid behind the bedroom door waiting for him to return. And when he did, I sprang into action, jumping out at him and yelling *Boo*. Needless to say, Alex wasn't exactly expecting to find me behind the door, no less have me jumping out at him. He reacted with a scream and a fist that punched out at the only thing he could see, the brass door handle reflecting the light from the street.

I liked it, seeing him frightened. The confusion, the vulnerability, seeing the fear in his face, his eyes wide. I liked taking him by surprise. And I liked scaring him. Maybe too much. Definitely more than I should have.

I didn't tell Maggie or Claudia how much I'd enjoyed Alex's reaction, how I'd laid in bed smiling to myself as I replayed the sound of his fear. They'd undoubtedly compare me to the psycho woman you read about in men's magazines, the wife who gets turned into a joke and e-mailed to strangers across the country. And even if intentionally scaring your husband in the middle the night is slightly unorthodox, I wasn't feeling like the psycho wife yet. It would take a few more months before that happened, before I started feeling that his *I love you*'s weren't emphatic enough, that his hands weren't holding mine as tightly as I'd like. That I'd become the one saying the *I love you*'s, the one who reached for his hand first and wouldn't let go. And that I needed him more than he needed me became the most frightening thing of all. I started to be scared, and Alex didn't even need to get up in the middle of the night to make it happen.

When I returned home from my walk two hours later, I went right for my desk and picked up the cordless phone. All I wanted to hear was the fast beeping of my voice mail telling me I had a message. And I did. In fact, I had sixteen voice mails and twenty-nine e-mails waiting for me. Not one of them was from a telemarketer.

My hand shook as, one by one, I took down the names and numbers of the women who left messages. And then I started making my way through the e-mails, my fingers lingering on the keyboard as they savored every keystroke. A few of the messages simply included the sender's name and the name of the person who referred her to the service. Most included the names of the men they'd like to add to the database as well as some highly annoying behavior, undesirable traits and bizarre habits. One name I even recognized, although he would have stood out anyway because there wasn't a single bad thing said about the guy. A member named Melanie had given him a glowing recommendation, and out of all the men in the database so far, he'd probably be the only one with a solid five stars.

By the end of tomorrow I'd have forty-five new members and at least seventy new men in the database. And I couldn't help wondering what additional information the members were going to provide for their first entries, especially the name that was fourth on the list. The data point provided by Melanie. Someone who, in a few short sentences, already seemed too good to be true. A guy named Mitch Reeves.

chapter twelve

I grabbed a cab and headed to the aquarium in search of Elliott and Caroline.

By the time I found them in front of the jellyfish exhibit, Caroline was already loaded down with a stuffed penguin and a Myrtle the Turtle mug. Elliott carried a dolphin DVD and a two-foot-long glow-in-the-dark jellyfish wrapped around his neck.

"Nice tentacles," I called out, and then waved at Elliott and Caroline when they turned around.

"You know, if buy souvenirs when you leave, you don't have to carry all that stuff around," I told Elliott when I reached them.

"Yes, but then we would never have made it past the gift shop, now, would we, Caroline?"

"I liked my Pez." She smiled at me through purple chapped lips.

"Ring pop?" I asked, dabbing at her lips with my sleeve.

Caroline shook her head. "Gummy starfish."

"I should have known." I gave up on the wiping and decided that Caroline didn't look so bad with a purple mustache. "It is an aquarium, after all."

"Daddy said you weren't coming."

"I guess Daddy was wrong," I told her, and Elliott rolled his eyes at me.

"Not bad enough I get it from her mother," he whispered. "Now you, too?"

Elliott handed me the jellyfish and I stuffed it under my arm.

"Headache all gone, I see."

"Yep, feeling all better."

"So you'll be getting back to work?"

At first I thought he meant the database, but then I realized he meant Verity. I shrugged. "I guess so."

Elliott hit me in the head with a two-foot-long tentacle and then wrapped it around my arm and pulled me along to the next exhibit. "You sound positively thrilled."

Elliott and I took turns reading the exhibit descriptions to Caroline as we walked past the oversize tanks on our way toward the penguins. We stopped about every ten feet, so Caroline could make faces at each blue, purple, yellow and orange fish that swam by the glass and turned to look at us.

"They're so pretty, aren't they?" Caroline asked, reaching for my hand.

"They are," I agreed.

"Did you ever have a fish?"

"I did. Once. It died."

Elliott watched me with a look of curiosity, his mouth a half grimace, half frown, like an S lying on its side. I couldn't tell whether he was surprised I'd had a fish, or unhappy I'd told Caroline it had died.

Caroline didn't seem fazed by either pronouncement. "Daddy said I can get a fish, right?"

"Right," Elliott answered, and then added, "As long as Mommy wasn't planning to get you a fish first."

"What was your fish's name?" Caroline wanted to know.

"Fish."

She rolled her blue eyes at me. "That's boring. I think I'll call mine Daisy."

"You're right," I agreed. "That sure beats Fish."

I never had a pet growing up, although if I had, it would have been a cat. A calico cat I would have named Marmalade and dressed up in my dolls' dresses. Alex was a dog person who complained cats shed too much. So when he moved out, my first impulse was to get a cat. The hairiest goddamned cat I could find. The white hairy species James Bond's nemesis used to have. The white cat in those Fancy Feast commercials. Then I thought, *a cat*? I'd be a divorced woman with a cat. A cliché. What next, I'd take up crochet? Put a rocking chair in the corner of the living room, where I'd knit long winter scarves while my cat sat on my lap and licked herself? And that's when I went to look in the freezer to see whether Alex had taken Fish.

I bought him the reddish blue Siamese fighting fish, a compromise between the dog he preferred and the cat I still wanted to dress up in doll's clothing. There was a method to my madness. Bettas can't get along with other bettas; if they see one, their fins flare out and they prepare for a standoff. So I knew we'd have only one fish; there'd be no danger of that single betta turning into an entire tank of tropical finned creatures, and maybe, when it died, Alex would let me get a cat.

Fish, as we'd come to call him (that we couldn't agree on a name should have tipped me off to the fact that we weren't exactly playing on the same team), didn't live through his first winter. So when he died we had an idea.

Alex and I stayed up late, so late that we'd end up watching infomercials that otherwise were viewed only by insomniacs and demented Nielsen households. And commercials on cable at one a.m. being what they are, we ended up making a few purchases that required only three easy payments of $29.95, the Seal-o-Matic being one of them. (We managed to resist the Flowbee, which seemed the ideal add-on for the taxi yellow Dyson we purchased after seeing an ad with that clever British man disparaging our American vacuums and their inadequate bags.) In the age of Costco and Sam's Clubs, the Seal-o-Matic seemed to be a no-brainer.

So when Fish died we had an idea. It wasn't as if we thought someday we'd thaw Fish out when the technology to bring him back to life was available. Fish wasn't Walt Disney. We just thought it was time to get some use out of the gadget, considering we didn't vacuum seal one other thing the entire time we owned it. The twenty pounds of chuck roast that was supposed to last for four months went bad before we'd even gotten around to opening the box the Seal-o-Matic came in.

But even if we weren't enjoying chuck roast long after we'd paid off the three easy payments, Fish lasted a year in our freezer thanks to the Seal-o-Matic.

The Seal-o-Matic was designed to defy the expiration date, extend the shelf life. And I totally related to that, because that's what I wanted to do long after I knew it was just a matter of time. Because before we even started, Alex and I had an expiration date, only the numbers were rubbed off so that I couldn't know exactly what it was. And no amount of vacuum packing could save us, even if Fish was still in the freezer for a week after Alex left, when I finally decided to throw him out along with the Seal-o-Matic stuffed in the back of the hall closet.

"You had a fish named Fish?" Elliott asked as we moved toward the next large glass window.

I nodded.

"I wouldn't go around telling people that."

"There's a lot I wouldn't go around telling people," I answered. I hadn't come here to tell anyone anything. I'd come to ask Elliott a question. "Listen, I was hoping you could give me Mitch's number. I wanted to give him a call."

"Really?" Elliott paused, then reached into his pocket and pulled out his BlackBerry. "Decided your Chips Ahoy! weren't in danger after all?"

"It's not for me. It's for Susan. She's having some gardening issues."

"Sure she is." Elliott tapped on the miniature keyboard. "All set. Just e-mailed it to you."

"Thanks."

"Do you want me to give him a heads-up that you'll be calling, so he can be prepared for this pressing gardening issue your stepmother is facing?" Elliott winked at me and nudged Caroline. "I think Abby might have a boyfriend."

Caroline scrunched up her face and nudged Elliott back. "Abby doesn't need a boyfriend."

I patted her on the back. "Thank you, Caroline; my sentiments exactly."

"Did you ever bend the rules?" I asked Elliott as we made our way toward the exit. "Were you ever tempted to tip the scales in your favor?"

Elliott slowed his pace and looked down at the ground before answering. "I don't know that I want to have this conversation, Abby." Elliott's tone was serious, the kind of *serious* he usually reserved for meetings with clients and imitations of CNBC broadcasters. "Have you done something I should know about?"

"No, of course not," I told him, when what I really meant was, *Not really.*

"Then, what's with the question? Are you in some sort of trouble at work, because if you are, you can tell me. You can tell me anything."

"No, not at all." He didn't look convinced. "Look, it was just a question. Really. I just came down here for Mitch's phone number. If I was looking for a confessional, I would have gone to church."

We both knew that wasn't true. I hadn't stepped foot in a church since my mom and dad split up. Alex and I weren't even married in a church, which would make one wonder if we were damned from the get-go, as his great aunt Mary Ellen had suggested after giving us the sign of the cross and a twenty-five-dollar gift card to Target's Club Wed.

Elliott reached for my hand and squeezed it, a bit too melodramatic for my taste. "If you want to talk, I'm here."

What next, an earnest hug and the eight-hundred number for the Good Samaritans?

I shook my hand free and handed him the jellyfish that I'd been carrying under my arm. "Take your jellyfish and stop worrying. Everything's fine."

Geraniums. Who would have known that Susan would provide me with my opening line.

"So, any suggestions?" I asked Mitch, after explaining my stepmother's problems with her wilting annuals.

"Like I said, it could be the soil. Sometimes even the hardiest plants won't flourish if the soil's not right." Mitch paused and then went on. "I could stop by and see if I can help," he offered. "It would have to be next weekend, though, because of the holiday."

I'd never actually thought of the Fourth of July as being a holiday so much as a midsummer break for working people and an excuse for boys to set off bottle rockets.

"I'll talk to Susan and see what she says," I told him, and realized too late that I'd probably just ended our conversation.

Only instead of using this opportunity to get off the phone, Mitch continued talking. "If you don't have plans this weekend, I'm having some people over for the Fourth."

"The whole summer cookout thing?" I asked.

"Complete with hot dogs, hamburgers and s'mores for dessert."

"Sounds like somebody's been watching too much Martha Stewart."

"Actually, I'm lying about the s'mores. I hate marshmallows."

"And yet you love Fluff," I pointed out.

"Just one of life's bitter ironies."

I wrote down Mitch's address and we hung up.

The guy didn't like marshmallows. Who didn't like marshmallows? As long as you didn't actually think about what it took to make sticky white puffs that could withstand a nuclear catastrophe, marshmallows were the perfect anytime snack.

So Mitch wasn't a marshmallow guy. It wasn't a fatal character flaw, but it was a place to start.

God, that sounded nice. Novel. Even foreign. It practically required a certain level of optimism to even think about it. And, as Maggie had pointed out a few months ago, I'd become a glass-is-half-empty kind of gal lately, so having my morale boosted by a campfire snack was a pretty positive thing. It had come to the point where I was convinced that if I went to the doctor for a sore throat, I'd discover I had only days to live. Is it any wonder I never called in sick or went to the doctor? Is it any wonder that when Alex walked out, while I imagined him pressing the DOWN button on the elevator, it didn't even occur to me to go after him, to get him to change his mind? Instead, I thought about the last time I had sex. And how it wasn't with the man who waited in the hallway for the DOWN arrow to light up and signal his descent away from me and the home we'd shared. And how I never imagined infidelity would taste like garlic and baked clams.

chapter thirteen

Alex left seventeen days after the incident. The indiscretion. He never even knew. Nobody did. Except me, and I wasn't exactly announcing the news.

How do you keep something like that to yourself? It isn't easy, the keeping quiet, but it's easier than the alternative: saying it out loud. I knew that if I spoke the words they'd float out into the universe with the finality of a last breath, and everything would change. Once the words were spoken, you became a person who could cheat. A person who made bad choices. A woman who would sleep with a man who wasn't her husband. A bitch.

I did it once, and once was enough. But that single act, the fifty-eight minutes I spent in a hotel room in Manhattan with a man whose name I've blocked from my memory, wasn't the reason we got divorced. My action was merely a reaction, a side effect, a side order—*Would you like some careless extramarital sex to go with that disintegrating marriage?* That's what it was, extramarital sex. Not an affair. To me, an affair always implied some grand event. I pictured women in taffeta ball gowns, suave men in three-piece suits, clandestine meetings in the bar at the Ritz before heading upstairs to Egyptian cotton sheets with gold-foiled mints perched on the pillows.

An affair is something to remember, or so the movie title would like us to believe. And, while that night is committed to memory much like the time I stole a glance at Charlotte Willmette's spelling test and hesitated, my number two pencil pausing while I waited for Mrs. Murphy to catch me, it certainly wasn't memorable.

Nobody knows. Not Claudia or Maggie, not my mom, and certainly not my dad, but least of all Alex. Alex, who, when he moved out, didn't even look at me when he said good-bye.

I almost told Claudia and Maggie a million times, but the words stalled before I could get them out. I knew they'd be surprised, maybe even disappointed, but I also knew they wouldn't judge me. They didn't have to. I did.

I'd relegated the entire occurrence to an outtake, one of many scenes you delete from a relationship because they don't fit with the story you've constructed. Only instead of creating extra bonus footage for the DVD version, I'd burned the film on the screening room floor. It had just been easier to let Claudia and Maggie think I'd married a cheater than offer up the truth: They were friends with one.

So there it is, the nasty little truth. Or the nasty little lie, depending on how you look at it. However you choose to view the situation, this I know: People don't like cheaters. They don't trust them. Hell is filled with them, and so are cheap motels and dimly lit restaurants and bars that reek of stale cigarette smoke, drunken desperation and selfish delusion. So what makes me any different from the rest of them? I can only hope that my culpability is somehow mitigated by the fact that I loved Alex. That even when I was letting another man watch me undress, allowing him run his tongue along the collar bone that I'd once showcased so exquisitely in my lovely ivory Vera Wang gown, I loved him. Somehow, I hope that makes me different.

How do you cheat on someone you love? The answer is, it had nothing to with Alex and everything to do with me. I needed to prepare myself, to feel like we were on equal ground. I needed to level the playing field. By cheating I thought I'd prove I didn't need him. I thought I would prove he didn't have all of me if I gave a part to someone else.

Because the truth is, I knew Alex would leave me. I trained for it, prepared for it, told myself it could happen, that given enough time it *would* happen.

Like a stewardess preparing for a crash, I smiled while we were spiraling into oblivion. I wouldn't react. I couldn't. The seventeen days between the night Alex walked out and the night Alex's wife had another man's dick inside her merely solidified what hadn't yet been spoken. We both knew it was the end, even if it was for different reasons. Even though he didn't know it, Alex had a reason to leave. I played it cool. I gave him the woman I wanted him to see. Somebody who no longer cared enough to put up a fight. I watched as he found his briefcase and carried the Nike duffel bag to the front door, the one we purchased after American Airlines lost our luggage the first three days of our honeymoon. Not the monogrammed suitcase with matching garment bag and carry-on. A fucking black nylon Nike duffel bag. Smile, smile.

We never had sex once I returned from New York, after the invisible *A* on my chest made it difficult to catch my breath without feeling like my lungs were caving in. Or maybe it was my heart. There's a difference between sleeping with your husband and sleeping with a stranger, but it isn't good sex. Because, I'm going to be honest here, you don't have to love someone to have good sex. Mind-blowing sex. The kind of sex that makes you forget you haven't used your tube of Clarins anticellulite cream in ages. The kind of sex that makes you almost believe you're as fabulous as you'd like to be. It has nothing to do with how you look to someone else, and everything to do with how you see yourself. Because it's born out of something that can be even more seductive than love, and that's power. The power to make someone want you. The ability to control someone by mere virtue of your desire to do so. It's the difference between yielding on yellow and running a red light. It's dangerous and stupid and any advantage you gain is fleeting, but you do it. You do it because you want to prove you can.

It wasn't meaningless sex. It was just about the most meaningful sex I've ever had. It meant everything and nothing. It meant that I'd officially declared war with Alex, only I wasn't willing to admit that in doing so I'd become the casualty.

When Alex left, I said it for the first time: *Don't go.* But I didn't say *Stay.* I screamed, yelled at the top of my lungs with what little air was left inside me. *Don't go.* Only I waited until the door was closed and I knew he wouldn't be able to hear me.

I walked over to the couch and sat down when what I'd really wanted to do was stand at the window and watch him leave. To see which way he went, to see his first decision as a free man, assuming that his last decision as a married man was to stop being one. I can't say I was stunned. I wasn't. And I don't want to say I felt slightly vindicated, vaguely self-satisfied. But I was. He'd left. He'd proved me right. Just like I knew he would.

chapter fourteen

"You're late."

"Do I need a note from my mother?"

Sarah shut my office door and watched as I unpacked my briefcase, which took all of three seconds since the only items in it were a vanilla Dannon and my Montblanc pen.

I hadn't taken work home with me in weeks, ever since I started working on the database. There were no annual reports, no 10-Ks, no spreadsheets analyzing competitive pricing and market share. Just a pen and a low-fat snack. And I didn't feel the least bit guilty about it.

"I don't care that you're late," Sarah told me, even though she'd never loitered outside my office before in anticipation of my arrival. "I just want to know what's going on with you."

"Nothing, why?"

"You work sixteen hours a day for weeks straight and then you call in sick and now you show up late." Sarah crossed her arms over her chest, not an easy task. "I know what's going on."

I froze. "You do?"

"I do." Sarah narrowed her eyes at me and moved around to my side of the desk. "You're seeing someone."

"God no!"

"Then, what's with the erratic work schedule?"

"It's my mom," I lied. Poor mothers, always getting the short end of the stick. "You know, I'm helping her with the wedding plans and all, and between the dress and the shower plans, it's taking more time than I anticipated."

"Well, you better not have any plans to go register for china or linens tonight—you have to go to the monthly meeting."

"Oh no, I don't. I went last month," I reminded her.

"Oh yeah, you do, I'm flying out to Denver this afternoon to speak at a conference—Jason had to bail at the last minute and I'm his replacement."

Tonight of all nights. It was barely past nine o'clock and already I couldn't wait to get home and see what I had waiting for me—more members, more referrals and more data points.

"What's tonight's topic?" I asked, as if seriously considering the idea of taking Sarah's place.

"A panel discussing the benefits of an intermarket trade-through rule."

Yeah, that did it. There was no way I was going to make it. I had more important things to do.

"I'll try, but I did promise to help my mom listen to some CDs of wedding bands." I shrugged and attempted to appear truly disappointed. "I'll call my mom, but I can't promise anything."

"Fine, do what you can." Sarah picked up the Dannon cup and started reading the ingredients.

I picked up the Montblanc pen and acted as if I was writing a note to call my mom, when what I really wrote was *Goal: 100 members by July 1.* An aggressive goal, considering I had only two days to add more than fifty new members. Still, I set the bar high. The exponential effect of member referrals was infinite. All I needed was one member to refer a friend, and have that friend refer a friend, and so on and so on (so what if I was riffing on an old commercial).

"So, have you heard about this new advisory service for women?" Sarah asked. "The one where you can get the inside scoop on a guy's dating history?"

I tried not to let my hyperventilating give me away. "How do you know about that?"

"My neighbor just became a member and she won't tell me anything," Sarah complained. "She said if Duncan and I don't work out she'll give me a referral or something but until then I'm not eligible."

Inhale. Exhale. Inhale. Exhale. "What else did she say?"

"Not much, the whole thing is so hush-hush, she acted like she'd be compromising national security if I learned the details." Sarah flipped up her jacket sleeve, glanced at her watch and then settled herself into my visitor chair. "I'm feeling quite left out of this whole membership-only bitchfest. What, just because I found someone to date, I don't need a little inside information?"

"It hardly sounds like a bitchfest," I told Sarah, using a tone that could best be compared to that of a mother who'd just been told her baby is ugly. "I heard it's more like a compilation of independent investment research."

"Whatever it is, my neighbor's convinced it's going to make her life a hell of a lot easier."

"Did she happen to mention who's behind the whole thing?"

Sarah shook her head and checked her watch again. "Nope. Why, do you know?"

She had no idea that I was the Fort Knox of secret keepers, someone so well versed in the art of concealment, I was one of only two people who knew what happened between myself and a man who, although good looking, wasn't even my type. He was blond. The type of blond you imagine went to boarding school and wore rugby shirts and played soccer until his shaggy bangs turned almost brown as they clung to his sweaty forehead.

If my name got out, if *Abby Dunn* was on the lips of every better-informed woman in the greater Boston area, I was afraid, somehow, he'd hear about it. The guy behind the grassy knoll, which, in this case, was a room on the tenth floor of the Carlisle Hotel. The witness who blends into the crowd until he decides to step forward to reveal what he knows. And in this case, what he knew would turn the founder of Boston's best-kept secret into Boston's most public fraud. Because while I was cataloging the flaws of Boston's male population, I had a flaw of my own. And the last thing I needed was a blond soccer-playing witness coming forward to tell everyone that one night, while Abby Dunn's husband was at home in Boston doing the laundry, she'd slept with another man.

I wasn't naive enough to feel bad because I didn't love the guy. A guy whose name I still can't say out loud because, although it was written in bold letters on a name tag announcing, HI, MY NAME IS . . . , I refused to register what it said. Instead I liked to think that maybe he existed for only that moment, that purpose. Because to think that there was a man out there who knew what I was capable of, who knew that what I did was more than simply a demonstration of my lack of impulse control, terrified me. Because what I did was anything but an impulse. It was carefully planned out, right down to the fact that I slipped my wedding rings inside my suit jacket pocket before Blondie even slipped the card key in the hotel room door. Where to put my rings, that was the dilemma. Not whether or not I should let a strange blond man take me to bed. Not *What will it feel like to have a man other than my husband inside me*, but *Where do I put my rings?*

Didn't college exist to rid yourself of the antiquated notion that you have to love someone to have sex with him? I'd had sex with men I didn't love. Shit, I'd had sex with men I didn't know well enough to like. But having sex with a man you didn't love while being in love with someone else? That was new to me, and my body refused to respond at first, leery of the unfamiliar touch, as if it sensed that this was not something it should be doing, no less enjoying. Fortunately, it was nothing five Stoli and tonics couldn't cure.

Once I set my mind to it, there was something exhilarating about the newness and the unexpected feel of someone you haven't traced with your finger a million times before. Only the newness isn't like that new-car smell that lasts for months. The novelty goes away when you close your eyes and realize that the new-car smell is toxic. And maybe that's why I kept thinking about the toiletries. The free single-application-size bottles in the bathroom. The shampoo (even though I wasn't going to wash my hair), the shower gel and the body lotion. What was I going to smell like when this was all over?

I was fully aware that after it was over, after I put my underwear on and hoped my skin didn't smell like latex, everything would be different. I'd be different, or at least I hoped I would. Because all I really wanted was to not care so much when the other shoe dropped.

Sex was never one of our problems. At least Alex and I got one area right. We set the bar high the first time, drunk after downing three scorpion bowls in just over an hour. I'd always heard that waning sex was one of the warning signs, along with wearing granny underwear and forgoing your daily leg shaving. But even when we were winding down, our sex was furious, as if I could somehow fuck him into loving me again.

But that night in New York I'd touched the third rail of relationships, and as much as I'd liked to believe I could hide the burn, it left its mark. I lived to tell about it, only instead of making me feel more in control, I knew I'd lost it, given it away. Alex had won. I'd failed at my marriage and here I'd thought Alex was the one who needed to tested.

"So, do you know who's behind the Web site?" Sarah asked again.

"Sorry, no idea," I answered, and gave Sarah's shoulder a squeeze, a gesture that translated as, *But if I did, you'd be the first to know.* "So, what do you think of the idea?"

She took one last look at her watch, stood up and turned to leave. "I think I want in."

Knowing what I knew about Duncan, I didn't blame her.

Oh. My. God. It was really working.

chapter fifteen

planned to meet Maggie and Claudia between Exeter and Fairfield streets. And that plan would have worked out perfectly if it wasn't for the other forty thousand people who'd planned to meet their friends between Exeter and Fairfield streets. Red Radio Flyer wagons packed full of toddlers and coolers and blankets rolled over my toes as everyone made a mass exodus for the Hatch Shell. The Boston Pops didn't start playing until eight thirty, and you'd think getting there an hour and a half before the first triangle tinkled would be enough. Only the rest of Boston had decided to show up four hours earlier. It wasn't like we were novices at this, so we should have known better.

The Fourth of July Pops concert and fireworks were a tradition for us. As long as something can still be considered a tradition after it went on hiatus for two years (during my marriage to a man who didn't like crowds) and on hold for one (during my postmarriage hibernation).

This was my first Pops concert at the Hatch Shell in three years, and I could almost finally understand why Alex often drew the comparison between the Fourth of July concert and an evening in hell.

The esplanade along the banks of the Charles River was packed—families carrying folding beach chairs (I always wished I'd brought a chair but never enough to lug it through the streets of Back Bay), couples holding wicker picnic baskets (ditto the baskets filled with food), and the die-hard patriots decked out in togas and metallic green body paint in homage to Lady Liberty (never once did I envy these people, especially when it was nearing ninety degrees and humid). While I was sure somewhere along the line my mom must have given me a stars-and-stripes T-shirt or perhaps a cute pair of socks with Uncle Sam parading around my ankles, the best I could do tonight was navy blue capris from the Gap and a white tank top.

If only my divorce could have been finalized a mere month later. July Fourth, Independence Day. How perfect that would have been. The entire city gathered on the esplanade, the Boston Pops playing, crashing cymbals culminating in fireworks. Now, that's how you usher in a new beginning, a new era of freedom. Instead, when the papers were signed and the decree finalized, it felt nothing like freedom and everything like failure.

After waiting an hour on the sidewalk, my toes bore the black remains of Radio Flyer tread marks, my tank top bore some very unattractive sweat stains and my face bore the blotchy red marks of a woman ready to pack it in and head home to her air-conditioned apartment. A year ago, that's exactly what I would have done. But now I had something to prove, and even if the throngs of strangers had no idea I was striking out for divorced women everywhere, I knew that sitting on the lawn watching a concert by myself did not exactly constitute a giant step for womankind (although stabbing an American flag into the ground would certainly have been in keeping with the occasion), but it was a small, baby step in the right direction.

There was no way I'd find a spot on the oval in front of the Hatch Shell, so I set off to find my own piece of public recreation space, finally settling down on a two-by-two spot of vacant grass. I had no picnic blanket, like the family of four on my left, but I also wasn't pumping noxious fumes into the public airways like the teenage couple smoking clove cigarettes to my right. It was just me. Sitting on the hard ground. Tapping my tread-marked toes on the dusty grass. By myself. Celebrating independence. Yippee.

I was about two zip codes from the Hatch Shell, so I couldn't tell the percussion section from the Porta Potties, but at least I could hear the music swelling over the park.

"All alone?" The teenage boy asked me, pointing his cigarette a little too close to my arm for comfort.

I nodded and shifted away from the burning orange tip that threatened to brand my right shoulder.

"Just me," I confirmed, thinking maybe this was where they offered me a drag on the joint I was sure they were about to pull out.

"Then, can you move over a little? We'd like to lie down."

No communal doobie, no sharing of the peace pipe or passing of a portable bong. Instead I'd been asked to give up my prime real estate to an eighteen-year-old and his slutty girlfriend with the clear plastic bra straps hanging out of her tank top.

I edged over the eight inches I could spare, and the couple managed to lie down on the Mexican blanket they'd spread beneath them.

All around me, couples of all shapes, sizes and ages negotiated to land one of the last few remaining spots on the esplanade. Families unpacked coolers and positioned strollers while teenagers paired off holding hands, their fingers tucked into each other's pockets. It was hard not to notice that everyone celebrating independence was conspicuously dependent.

I held my ground for the next half hour, literally. The family to my left kept edging their picnic basket in my direction, and the teenagers were in the throes of some serious heavy petting. I tried to concentrate on the music drifting from the shell, and not the moans and groans coming from the Mexican blanket. Not so easy a task when you haven't had sex in more than a year.

By nine o'clock the sky was finally dark and the teenagers on the blanket next to me were rounding third base. Although leaving meant I'd miss the fireworks I'd been determined to see, I decided to leave before they made it home.

I navigated my way through Back Bay, past the front window of the Flower Carte and the other darkened storefronts on Newbury Street, until I reached Mitch's building on Beacon Hill. I ran a finger down the list of residents until I found M. REEVES written in neat block letters on a label beside a small square buzzer.

"Come on in," he crackled over the intercom, not even bothering to ask who it was before buzzing me in.

I pushed the door open and wondered whether the large brass planters on the steps were Mitch's contribution to neighborhood beautification.

The brick building with black shutters had to have been at least two hundred years old, but the hallway and stairs leading to Mitch's fifth-floor (count 'em, ten flights of stairs) condo had been completely gutted. Which was good. Maybe he'd have central air, which I'd be desperately needing.

The door to his place was cracked open, and I waited for the eruption of laughter and clanking of beer bottles that usually accented a summer party. Only when I pushed the door open the only noise was a stereo playing in the background.

"Hello!" I called out, peeking around the corner, looking for someone, anyone.

And I found them. The someones. Three of them. And Mitch.

"I thought there was a party," I said by way of an apology for breaking up the two cozy couples.

"There was, there is," Mitch told me, coming over and placing his hand on my shoulder as a polite welcoming gesture. "Everyone left a few minutes ago to head over to the Cambridge side to watch the fireworks."

Excellent.

"I don't have to stay," I offered, and Mitch dropped his hand from my shoulder and made his way toward the kitchen.

"Don't be silly; we were just finishing up our beers." A slash of light illuminated the granite breakfast bar, and I suspected he was opening the refrigerator. He confirmed my suspicion by returning with a cold Corona, which he handed to me.

"These are my friends, Travis and Delia, and this is Willie."

Contrary to the expectations her name might produce, Willie wasn't wearing a quilted trucker jacket and baseball hat. And when Willie smiled at me, she had all her teeth.

"Wilhelmina." She reached for my hand and shook it. "Nice to meet you."

Travis and Delia. Mitch and Willie. And me. How cozy.

"They were just leaving." Mitch pointed to the door, where Travis was waiting for the women to join him.

Mitch walked his guests to the door and I excused myself to go to the bathroom, where hopefully I'd find something to wipe away the thin sheen of sweat that I was sure made my face appear capable of being wrung out, its proceeds used to fry a pan of bacon. What I saw in the mirror didn't exactly dispel that thought. Only I changed it to sausage links to reduce the sodium content.

I slid open the medicine cabinet, hoping to discover Mitch was evolved enough to own a bottle of Sea Breeze, or even just a bottle of rubbing alcohol and a few cotton balls. Instead I discovered the man had shoplifted aisle three at CVS. NyQuil, DayQuil, Sudafed, you name it. There were more bottles and capsules and caplets than any one person could possibly consume without heeding warnings about operating automobiles and heavy farm equipment.

"Abby?" Mitch called my name and I slid the mirrored door closed.

"Coming!" Forget the cotton balls and astringent; a quick swipe with some toilet paper would have to do.

"I was going to meet everyone over there in a bit," he explained to me when I joined him in the living room. He walked around the room picking up a bowl of peanuts and some empty Corona bottles. "I just wanted to clean up before I went."

"Are you always so conscientious?" I handed him a half-eaten plate of nachos.

"Only when I have to take off in the morning. I'm heading down to the Cape first thing to see a client's new place." He piled a bowl of salsa onto the plate and headed into the kitchen. "I shouldn't even be going out."

"Well, my friends blew me off, so I'm pretty much on my own." I didn't realize how pathetic I sounded until it was too late. He was probably standing next to the stove wondering why he'd invited a woman he barely knew to his party when her own friends didn't even want to hang out with her.

Mitch peeked over the breakfast bar and rested his elbows on the counter. "You know, we don't have to go to Cambridge. The traffic will suck and we have a great view right here." He dangled a couple of empty beer bottles between his fingers. "We could just take a couple of these and go up to the roof."

"Having just braved the crowds, I can tell you, there's no way I'm heading back toward Cambridge."

"Then we're all set—on one condition." Mitch reached for a dish towel and tossed it to me.

I thought it was a pretty fair trade-off considering the other option: going home alone.

While Mitch carried a box of empties out to the recycling bin in the hall, I wiped down the coffee table. And the end tables. And the floor where one of his friends had spilled a glass of wine. And then I spotted it. Sitting on the fireplace mantel. The trophy. Snoopy holding an oversize tennis racquet, grinning triumphantly over a base with a bronze plaque: WORLD'S GREATEST.

The man cleaned his apartment. He recycled. He kept a Snoopy trophy on his mantel.

I had no idea what to make of him. And it made me want to figure out the puzzle that was Mitch Reeves even more.

"What do you think?" Mitch pointed to a pair of Adirondack chairs on the roof deck and waited for me to sit down.

"Of what?" I asked, taking in the sweeping view of the Charles River. Mitch wasn't kidding when he said we'd be able to see the fireworks. There wasn't much we couldn't see from the rooftop.

"Not what. Who. Willie."

Besides the funny name, I thought. "She seems nice."

"She's a friend's cousin's neighbor, or something like that." Mitch hopped up onto the deck railing and sat there dangling his feet. "She comes highly recommended."

"Is she a potential date or a restaurant?" I half joked, and Mitch laughed.

"I just meant that she's supposed to be a lot of fun. I was thinking of asking her out."

I hoped Mitch wasn't looking for my endorsement, because I wasn't about to provide it. "If you want to ask her out, why are you blowing her off to stay here?" I asked, although I left off the part about staying here *with me.*

"I'm not blowing her off. I wouldn't say that sweating in a crowd on the banks of the Charles River constitutes a great first date. I'd rather be remembered for my scintillating conversation than for my ability to perspire while telling little kids to put their sparklers away before they poke their eyes out." Mitch tsk-tsk'd me. "Blowing her off, what kind of a guy do you think I am, anyway?"

"Apparently not the kind who tries to impress a woman with his poor hygiene and lack of tolerance for sparklers."

"You're so right, although, for the record, I am pro-sparkler." Mitch took a sip of beer while I contemplated my own view on sparklers.

"Me, too, on the sparkler thing," I told him, just in case he'd been waiting for me to weigh in.

Mitch nodded his approval and continued. "Then again, what do I know? I thought discussing childhood food preferences while dazzling you with my accomplishments on the badminton court would do the trick."

"So, when's the last time you played badminton?"

"It has to be seven years ago—at least." Mitch took a sip of his beer. "Why?"

"No reason." A few rogue fireworks popped in the distance. "I noticed the trophy."

"I just keep it up there in case my brothers come over."

"For seven years you've been adorning your mantel with Snoopy so you can rub it in your brothers' noses when they come over?"

Add hypercompetitive to recycling neat freak.

"You don't have any brothers, do you?"

I shook my head. "Only child."

"Well, then you wouldn't understand," he explained. "But believe me, my brothers do."

"They can smell weakness a mile away, right?"

"The only thing they can smell is a free dinner if I'm barbecuing, but you're on the right track."

Now it was my turn to laugh.

"Hey, what are you doing tomorrow?" Mitch asked.

I didn't have to think very hard. "Nothing."

"Want to come to the Cape and keep me company?" he offered. "A client just bought a new beach house that needs some work and he asked me to look at the yard."

"Wouldn't you rather invite the woman who comes so highly recommended?"

"Nah, too much pressure for a first date, all that time alone in the car and then being stuck together all day with no way to get out of it if things aren't going well."

"So it wouldn't be a date?" I clarified.

He didn't need to laugh so hard. "I think you were clear about your level of *interest* at Elliott's house. I can take a hint—especially when it's not exactly subtle."

"Come on, I wasn't that bad, was I?"

Mitch shook his head. "No, not at all. But you know what they say: *reject me once, shame on you, reject me twice, shame on me.*"

"I don't think that's exactly the saying, but I get the point."

"So what do you say? You know how to read a map, right?" he asked.

So I was not being asked out. I was being asked to copilot.

Mitch didn't want to hold my hand; he wanted me to hold his Burger King order when he pulled away from the drive-through.

Mitch noticed I was hesitating. "Come on, the weather is supposed to be great. I'll even buy you lunch for keeping me company."

"You weren't planning on making it a trip through the Burger King drive-through, were you?"

"I wasn't, but if that's what you'd like . . ." He let his voice trail off just as the air whistled and white, blue and red flames burst into the sky. Mitch jumped off the railing and came over to sit in the chair next to me. "Look, the fireworks are starting."

"As long as it's not Burger King," I conceded, my answer punctuated by a flash of purple trailing above the river.

"But I like Burger King," he replied, his soft voice feigning disappointment. "They flame-broil."

Truth was, I liked Burger King, too.

"What time will you pick me up?" I asked.

"Eight thirty."

"It's a date," I told him, and then quickly added, "Or not," just as a canopy of green lit up the sky around us.

chapter sixteen

"Where the hell were you?" Claudia spat into the phone. "We waited for over an hour."

It was a quarter after eight, and Mitch would be pulling up outside my apartment any minute.

"I was there. Me and six hundred thousand other people."

"We called you."

"You're the technology whiz, how many ring tones do you know of that can compete with an entire symphony orchestra?" I asked. "I ended up leaving around nine."

"So you didn't even watch any fireworks?"

"I saw some. What about you?"

"Not exactly the fireworks I expected. Maggie met a guy. She tripped on a soda bottle and twisted her ankle. This doctor just happened to be waiting in line at the Porta Potti and saw the whole thing. He carried her back to our blanket and asked her out."

"Do you know his name?" I asked, getting up and walking over to my computer. I still had a few minutes and the welcome screen was already greeting me from the monitor. At seven o'clock this morning, before I'd brushed my teeth or gone to the bathroom, I'd sat at my desk with a full bladder and read last night's e-mails, all fifteen of them. Must be the holiday rush. Some of the existing members had even added new data points to the system, including information on Mitch Reeves. Apparently Mitch was a great first date who preferred Italian restaurants in the North End to trendy places in Back Bay, had a weakness for chocolate chip cannolis and was color-blind.

"I don't remember his name," Claudia told me.

"Do you know what hospital he's affiliated with? I can look him up by employer."

"What are you doing over there?"

"Checking up on the guy. You don't want Maggie dating a deadbeat, do you?"

"He's a doctor, Abby. I hardly think he's a deadbeat."

"Occupation has nothing to do with it. One member submitted a Harvard classics professor with a spanking fetish."

"How does that work? He recites Homer while swatting your ass?"

"And dresses up as Helen of Troy just to make things interesting."

Claudia laughed. "How perfectly epic of him."

"So, which hospital?"

"Listen, I'm not getting involved. You'll have to ask Maggie. Give her a call."

"Can't right now. I'm heading to the Cape with Mitch."

"You have a date with Mitch?"

"He needs to check out a client's place," I explained. "It's hardly a date."

I met Alex on a date. Only he wasn't the man I was supposed to be dating. The summer I interned at Verity, Claudia set me up with a sales rep who called on her store every other week. He sold packaging. My dad sold paper. If nothing else, we could talk business. Only, when we met at the restaurant, I was out of my league. This guy could talk about long white cardboard boxes for roses, plastic sleeves, tissue paper, even that soggy green foam that makes a mess when you toss the dead arrangement. A guy at the bar was obviously listening to our conversation, because when Packaging Man got up to go the bathroom, Bar Man came over to our table and handed me his business card.

My first reaction? Alex was in the market for some packaging and he'd been won over by my date's pitch. My second reaction? He had some pretty nice packaging himself.

We went out two nights later, and the day after our date Alex sent flowers to me at the office. A single pink rose. In a pizza box. "Hope you like the packaging," the card read.

See, I think about things like that. How a man who figures out how to score a clean, empty pizza box for a single pink rose couldn't figure out how to make his marriage work.

Before Alex, there were two boyfriends of little consequence. Two men I'd slept with in business school, both during my first year. One ended up going to New York after graduation for a position with Goldman Sachs. Adam. The second took a job as a brand manager for Proctor & Gamble, and I took a sort of perverse pleasure in picturing him attempting to come up with new product-line extensions for Tampax. There could be no greater justice for a man who couldn't find his way to a G-spot if he followed the alphabet.

We all knew we'd scatter after graduation, so it wasn't as if any of us expected a sleeping partner to evolve into much more than a footnote from our graduate school experience. We weren't taking out sixty thousand dollars in student loans to follow our hearts. It was about following the job offers, not some person we'd been screwing between Bayesian Econometrics and Supply Chain Strategy. In the grand scheme of things, the men before Alex were statistically insignificant. And the men after Alex, practically nonexistent.

I knew Mitch wasn't going to show up with a rose, no less a pizza box. He wasn't even coming up to my apartment. Instead he said he'd call me when he was outside. So it definitely wasn't a date, even though I was never a stickler for the whole pomp and circumstance of having a man come to your door to pick you up. Ever try to park in Boston? Any man willing to do that either really wanted to get laid, had a relative who worked in the parking clerk's office or had great parking karma. Even in high school I didn't buy into the whole boy-should-pick-up-girl-and-ring-her-doorbell crap, which is why I drove myself to my senior prom, while my date, Alan Frost, followed behind me in his parent's silver Honda Accord. We still had our pictures taken in my living room, he still placed a corsage of pink and white carnations on my wrist, but after the photo op was over I climbed into my mom's car and Alan into his. And we drove separately to the banquet hall, where we met again in the parking lot and walked under the arch of balloons in the lobby holding hands. Alan never complained that our dueling modes of transportation would severely impact his plan to get me naked in the backseat of his car. Not that it would have mattered. A girl who wasn't willing to give up the ability to leave the dance whenever she wanted, or let someone else decide which after-party she attended, certainly wasn't afraid to show up to a dance by herself. And I think Alan knew that. And he knew he had a better shot of getting me into his backseat than his second choice, Amanda Proust.

"It's definitely not a date," I told Claudia. "I'm merely conducting a little *field research.*"

"And what does that consist of?" she wanted to know, and I could tell from the high squeak of her voice that Claudia was stretching in bed.

"Getting to know more about him, so I can figure out what the other women he's dated can't."

Claudia yawned. "Yeah, good luck with that."

✳   ✳   ✳

Mitch called me from downstairs, where he'd parked in front of a fire hydrant.

"Right on time," I told him, climbing into the passenger's seat. It took me a second to realize what he was wearing on his head.

"Here." Mitch handed me a paper bag before pulling out into traffic. "You didn't say anything about breakfast. Hope you like Crois-san'wiches; there's one sausage and one bacon in there."

I took the bag and couldn't help laughing at him.

"One more thing." Mitch leaned over and placed an adjustable cardboard crown on my head. "I may be the Burger King, but you are now officially my queen."

And with that, we drove away from my castle.

Forty minutes later we were on Route 3 headed toward the Cape. It didn't occur to me until we were outside the city that I really didn't know much about Mitch other than his odd eating habits, his successful badminton record and Elliott's backyard. He knew even less about me. So after an abridged version of twenty questions, which included where we grew up (me: Chicago and then a suburb of Boston; Mitch: Massachusetts his whole life), college (me: Smith undergrad and then University of Chicago for graduate school; Mitch: Williams undergrad and then Cornell for graduate school), and favorite thing about living in Boston (me: my two best friends; Mitch: the annual Beanpot Hockey Tournament), we had a better handle on who was sitting in the throne next to us.

"So, are you seeing anyone?" Mitch asked question twenty-one as we waited in a line of traffic to cross the Sagamore Bridge.

Didn't he know he was breaking the rules of the game? It was called twenty questions for a reason, mainly the comfort of the person who had only so many answers she wanted to give.

I was attempting to discover what Mitch was hiding behind the veneer of a good guy, and yet it never occurred to me that he might be trying to figure out what I was hiding.

I shook my head and was ready to leave it at that when I caught sight of myself in the passenger-side mirror. I was the queen. I had nothing to hide.

"I was married until a year ago."

"Yeah, Elliott mentioned something like that."

Elliott mentioned something like that? Mitch said it like it was no big deal, like Elliott had brought it up in passing—*Oh, and Abby just happens to be completely psycho since her husband left; can you pass the potato salad?* There was no way somebody *happened* to mention divorce. It wasn't like *happening* to mention you enjoy a good merlot or that you had season tickets to the Red Sox. It was like bringing up somebody's raging case of herpes.

"He did?"

"We were talking at the party and he mentioned you were married."

I knew he meant *used to be* married, past tense, not that I *was* married, currently. Elliott had told him that I was married, so was Mitch trying to discern why my marriage didn't last? Did he try to picture who I was before it happened, or wonder whether I was ever the same? I almost stole a line from my short-lived therapist and asked Mitch how that made him feel. Instead I changed the subject.

"So, where's the house?" I asked.

"Falmouth; not too far. I run the road race there every August; that's how I met Bruce, my client."

We followed the slow stream of traffic onto the bridge, and I gazed out my window at the Cape Cod Canal, remembering how I used to squeeze my eyes shut and cover them with balled fists as a kid, convinced the bridge would collapse just as my family crossed its center.

I wasn't as paranoid now, although I wished the traffic would move faster, just in case a few bolts were loosening beneath us. Maybe looking at the water below wasn't helping.

I slid my eyes toward Mitch's right hand, where his fingers were curled around the steering wheel, holding it lightly beneath his fingertips. His left arm, already tan, rested along the base of the open window, where the sunlight reflected like glitter off the strands of sun-bleached hair. Even Mitch's hands were tan, creating darkened crinkles around his knuckles like parentheses. I've always liked men's hands. I loved the moment when Alex held out his left hand and let me take it before slipping the gold band onto his fourth finger.

I used to watch Alex leave for work in the morning, waiting for him to walk out the door without the band I'd placed on his finger that day. But even when he left that last time, there it was, a flat band of yellow gold against his skin. I almost thought it meant something, that he hadn't removed the ring I'd given him and laid it on the dresser next to the alarm clock. Only at that point it was no longer significant enough to leave behind to make a statement. To Alex it was simply costume jewelry.

When I finally removed my own rings, the skin underneath was pale and smooth, like the pure, unblemished skin of a baby.

"The house should be down here," Mitch told me, turning left off the main road. A few seconds later a gray-shingled house came into view. "Bruce said it needed some work."

It may have needed work, but the view overlooking Buzzards Bay mirrored the postcards tourists sent to their friends back home. "Wow."

"You can say that again," Mitch answered.

"Wow."

"Not bad for a little beach cottage, right?"

"Who is Bruce and where do I find him?"

"Quite possibly where his second wife found him, getting head from his secretary." Mitch removed a spiral-bound notebook from the backseat. "Do you mind if I walk around and take some notes?"

"Not at all. Mind if I check the place out?"

"Help yourself."

While Mitch surveyed the property and took notes, I headed down to the water to take full advantage of the view. The boats in the distance resembled distorted triangles, their pregnant sails straining against the wind. When my mom and I used to sit on our beach towels, waiting for my dad to return from his treasure hunting, there were two things to do: watch the lifeguards and watch the sailboats. They both seemed equally unattainable, the boats too far away and the lifeguards too preoccupied by the sixteen-year-olds who didn't need padding in their bikini tops. Even when my mom would venture away from our towels to cool off in the water, I stayed behind and watched the sail boats.

"Come on in," she'd always call, dipping her hands into the waves and splashing herself. "We can swim out to the boats, I'll race you."

But I always declined, knowing that even if we attempted to swim out to them, the boats would be out of our reach.

I was never the kid who ran into the surf and dove under the breaking waves. I didn't beg my dad to play Marco Polo with me or complain when the chalkboards resting against the lifeguard stands announced the presence of jellyfish. And yet I managed to convince everyone that I wasn't afraid of the water. It was either too cold or too warm or too rough or too calm, and nobody ever argued otherwise. But the thing is, it wasn't the water I was afraid of. It was the things *in* the water that I wanted to avoid. Give me a choice between running up against a lion or a sea bass, and I'd pick the lion every time. At least I could see it, hear it, be warned it was coming and prepare appropriately. But when you're waist deep in the ocean, there isn't much you can do when coming face to fin with danger. It sneaks up on you and takes you by surprise, and at that point, there isn't much you can do to protect yourself except hold your nose and take one final breath before going under.

I always wanted to learn to sail. What I didn't want to learn was how to capsize, and I figured that in order to not fear one, you had to not fear the other. Only the water crawling up the rocks toward me didn't look nearly as menacing as I remembered. The boats in the distance effortlessly slid along the horizon without so much as a hint that they could turn over at any minute and drown everyone on board. And it was hot. And getting hotter. Walking down to the beach below didn't just sound like a good idea, it seemed like the only logical thing to do.

I turned my back to the bay and searched the lawn for Mitch. After a few minutes I spotted him near what looked to be an overgrown garden strangling a haphazard stone wall running the length of the property.

"So, what do you think?" Mitch called out to me when he caught me staring. "Want to hit the beach before we head home?"

"You know what?" I answered. "I do."

Twenty minutes later we parked the car along the road at Bristol Beach. This wasn't a date, so there was no picnic basket in the trunk, no bottle of wine tucked behind the backseat and no wheel of Brie nestled against a loaf of French bread. I was pretty sure that if Willie had been with him, Mitch would have suggested they do more than stop at a deli and pick up sandwiches. Not that I didn't like a good turkey sandwich, but it wasn't exactly romantic to be biting into a bulky roll while wondering whether you had mustard on your face.

I guessed Mitch saved the table-service meals for the women he thought were worth asking out. And I obviously wasn't one of them.

Which was too bad, because I was really enjoying our day together, even if my field research hadn't yielded more than the knowledge that Mitch prefers mechanical pencils to pens and whole wheat to white.

I pointed off to the west of Nantucket Sound. "My mom is getting married on Martha's Vineyard Labor Day weekend."

Mitch bent down and removed his shoes before stepping onto the beach. "Do you like him? The man she's marrying?"

"Yeah, I do." I kicked off my flip-flops and dangled them from my fingers as we walked.

"How long have your parents been divorced?"

"Long enough. She dated Roger for almost six years. I never even thought they'd get married."

"Is she making you wear a hideous pink dress and sun hat? Maybe carry a parasol?"

"You joke. Peach was the first color of choice, but now I think we've settled on navy blue. Sort of like a nautical theme and all."

"Will the guests be required to wear Topsiders?" he wondered.

"Not if I have anything to do with it, but I'm not averse to a peg leg and eye patch, in case you were wondering."

"Sounds good, but that parrot on your shoulder might get a little messy." Mitch shook his head. "Yeah, definitely don't go with the parrot."

"You might be right," I reluctantly agreed. "But now I'll have to re-think the whole outfit."

I watched as a teardrop of sweat slid down Mitch's cheek and landed on his collar. It was a perfect beach day—a clear blue sky without a single cloud to offer even a brief moment of shade. My dad used to love days like this, while my mom usually stayed under the beach umbrella, reading a book.

"Is Elliott going to your mom's wedding?" Mitch asked. "Are they friends?"

"They've met a few times, but never really became friends. I actually used to think that maybe if Roger didn't work out I'd set them up, but that was before I really knew Elliott."

"Why wouldn't Roger and your mom work out?"

I shrugged and felt my shirt cling to my damp back. "No reason. You just never know."

"After six years I'd think you'd know," he told me. "What's with the pessimism?"

"Not pessimism," I disagreed, fanning my face with my hand. "Pragmatism."

"Was this pragmatism something you learned from your own experience?"

I wiped my damp forehead with the back of my hand, but I didn't answer.

"What was his name?" Mitch asked. "Your ex-husband."

"Alex."

"Alex," Mitch repeated. "And where is Alex today?"

"Still living in Boston, the last I knew. When you get divorced, you tend to lose touch."

"Have you dated much since Alex?"

I shook my head. "Once. It was enough."

Hi, I'm Marcus. That's how it started, my first date in four years.

Thanks for dinner. That's how it ended. And I wasn't even thanking him for paying, because I'd insisted on splitting the bill. It was more of a courtesy catch-all that substituted for *I kept my eyes open during our good-night kiss because I was afraid what I'd see if I closed them.* Only it wasn't *what* I'd see but *who* I'd see that made me fight every reflex I'd learned in the nineteen years since I first kissed Kevin Carpenter in sixth grade.

"Was it weird dating again?"

"You could say that."

"Dating can be weird even if you haven't been married, so you're not alone." Mitch smiled. "So why didn't you jump ship when Elliott left Verity?"

"I wasn't ready. I'd only been there two years at that point. I thought I still had a lot to learn."

"So after five years what have you learned?"

"Do you always ask such difficult questions?"

"Is the question really that hard to answer?"

It was when you couldn't think of a good answer. "Let's just say that at this point, going to work is like being on autopilot."

"So why not leave now?"

"Because working with Elliott would be like becoming a kamikaze pilot," I told him. "And I'm not quite ready to go down in flames just yet."

"Probably a good idea. I hear those peg legs are highly flammable, too." Mitch rolled up his sleeves and I waited to see if he'd go so far as to take off his shirt. "It's really hot out, isn't it?" He didn't.

A man passed us on the beach, his metal detector beeping sporadically as he swept the round base along the sand.

"My dad used to bring one of those to the beach with us every summer."

"Did your dad wear black socks and a camera around his neck, too?" Mitch asked, smiling at me, or maybe at my memory of my dad.

"It was really cool," I insisted, even though by the time I was twelve it was anything but cool. I'd turn down my dad's invitations to go treasure hunting with him, and instead lie on my towel waiting for the lifeguards to notice I'd just started shaving my legs. "Really, it was."

Mitch stopped walking and laid his hand solemnly on his chest, as if he was about to recite the Pledge of Allegiance. "And I believe you. Really."

The detector beeped rapidly and the man kneeled down to uncover what he'd discovered.

Mitch watched him, waiting to see what buried treasure he'd pull from beneath the sand. "Ever find anything worth keeping?"

"No, but we had fun looking."

Mitch made his way to a rock and sat down. "Do your parents still come to the Cape for the summers?"

I shook my head and sat down next to him. "My dad and his wife do. My mom and Roger started going to Martha's Vineyard."

"Hence the pirate-themed wedding," he concluded.

"Exactly." I watched the man pick up the metal detector and move on after realizing he'd dug up a Sprite can. "Guess he has my luck," I told Mitch, and then asked, "Were you ever a lifeguard?"

"Me? No. I was the kid cutting your lawn at seven a.m."

"Man, I hated you."

"You weren't the only one. People used to run outside in their boxer shorts and yell obscenities at us. I always thought it was way too early to be screaming at some teenage kid to turn off his fucking mower."

"If it's too early to be shouting obscenities in your slippers, it's too early to be mowing a lawn, don't you think?"

"You may have a point. But it was ten bucks an hour and I was sixteen. As long as they weren't throwing things at me, I was going to keep on mowing."

I pictured Mitch pushing a mower with his shirt off and traced a mental finger along the outline of his chest. I used to love Alex's chest. I'd rest my head on it and listen to every double heartbeat and think that was one less he had in him. And then I'd wonder how many he had left. If his heart would last another fifty years or if maybe we should switch to garden burgers and soy milk. I'd listen to the unidentifiable noises making their way through his body and think about all the things going on inside him that I didn't understand, and yet how still he remained unchanged on the outside. It almost seemed prophetic now.

"We better get going." Mitch stood up. "I have to be back in the city by five."

"Hot date?" I joked, only Mitch didn't laugh.

"Yeah, we're meeting at seven and I still have to shower and shave."

I didn't really want to know, but I asked anyway. "Willie?"

"No, Tracey."

Who the hell was Tracey?

Mitch pointed toward the road, where a policeman was inspecting windshields for parking permits. He was making his way toward Mitch's car, a pad of parking tickets in one hand and a pen in the other. "In fact, we better go now."

Mitch grabbed my hand and pulled me off the rock. "Come on, before the car gets booted."

"It's probably only a ten-dollar ticket."

Mitch let go of my hand as he started running toward the car. "Yeah, but when you're already on the Boston Police Department's list of most-wanted parking offenders, you can't take the chance."

So finally Mitch gives me something to work with. He was a parking scofflaw. It wasn't exactly the smoking gun I thought I'd find, but it was something a little more significant than marshmallows.

"Run, Mitch, run!" I called out after him as a huge grin spread across my lips. There was something so enjoyable about watching Mitch sprint toward the car in an attempt to beat a cop on a bicycle.

I jogged after him but didn't exactly break a sweat trying to keep up. It was only three o'clock and I wasn't ready to leave. Not because it was too early, but because it was too soon.

By the time I reached the street, Mitch was already in the car with the motor running. "Get in," he yelled through the open passenger window.

We pulled away just in time to see the policeman waving to us in the rearview mirror.

"That was a close one."

"Aren't you overreacting a bit?" I asked.

Mitch reached over, pushed the button on the glove compartment and let it fall open. A pile of fluorescent orange envelopes with the familiar Boston Police Department logo fell onto my lap.

"We better get the hell out of here, Clyde," I told him, thumbing through at least a year's worth of unpaid parking tickets.

Mitch smiled. "Whatever you say, Bonnie."

chapter seventeen

Mitch sneezes when he's horny. At least according to Member 137, a woman named Patrice who logged on last night at 9:12 p.m.

Maggie needed clarification. "You mean, he actually sneezes?"

"More than once, apparently. And the more he sneezes . . ."

"I get the picture."

"It's totally normal," Claudia explained.

Maggie and I turned to Claudia. We knew there was some sort of scientific explanation forthcoming.

"Okay, it's not exactly *normal*, but it's not abnormal either." Claudia took a deep breath and prepared to recite her seminar on the sneezing and erectile habits of North American males. "Erectile tissue has arteries that can carry blood into it, and in humans you can find erectile tissue in the penis and in the nose."

"So instead of saying *bless you* and handing him a tissue, I should ask if he needs a condom?" I asked.

Claudia didn't crack a smile. "Look, if you really want to understand, I can pull up some articles on your computer and you can read all about it."

She stood up, but I grabbed her hand and pulled her back down onto the couch.

"No, really, if you don't believe me, I'll show you." Claudia attempted to stand up again, but I tossed my leg over her lap and trapped her.

"Honestly, that won't be necessary. We believe you, right, Maggie?"

Maggie bit her lip and shook her head. "I don't know; sounds sort of like you made that up to me."

It was always great fun to get Claudia all wound up. It never ceased to give me a good laugh if for no other reason than she fell for it every time.

"That's it." Claudia pushed my leg off and jumped up. "I'll show you both. Is your computer on?"

"Are you kidding me? It's always on—I've been averaging twenty-three new-member referrals a day and about fifty new data points."

Maggie wrinkled her nose at me. "Data points?"

"Men that members input into the system."

"Of course."

Claudia took a seat at my desk, and Maggie and I moved on to Mitch topic number two.

"So, why would a man be stockpiling decongestants and cold medicine?" I asked. "Mitch must have had three bottles of NyQuil, a case of Sudafed and more Benadryl, Dimetapp and Sominex than CVS."

"You were snooping in his bathroom cabinets?"

"I was looking for cotton balls. And you should have seen how many unpaid parking tickets I found in his car," I went on. "At least fifty."

You know what bothered me? Not the idea that Mitch was hoarding unpaid parking tickets in his glove box, or even that he wasn't paying them—not that he was paying them late, or just not paying them, period. No, what I kept wondering was, *Why so many tickets?* He wouldn't even leave his car to come up to my apartment Saturday morning, but he was double-parking for all the other women he asked out? I'd had three—count 'em, three—requests for data on Mitch in the past week. How was it possible that women were bitching about no good men being left, and Mitch was spreading himself around like Philadelphia cream cheese?

"I've got something," Claudia chimed from the corner. "An abstract from a urologist at Albert Einstein College of Medicine: 'Pharmacological Studies of Human Erectile Tissue: Characteristics of Spontaneous Contractions and Alterations in Alpha-Adrenoceptor Responsiveness with Age and Disease in Isolated Tissues.'"

The poor girl sounded so proud of herself. "Want me to print it out?"

Maggie and I ignored her. "So, what do you think? About the stockpile of cold medicine? Do you think he's one of those people who drinks cough syrup and stuff for a cheap high?"

"I thought only teenagers did that when they weren't off doing whippets with cans of Reddi-wip."

"Are you suggesting I should have checked his fridge for cans of dessert topping?"

"I don't know. I'm not telling you anything. Maybe all that stuff keeps him from sneezing when he has erections?" Maggie suggested, her voice raised over the printer spitting out paper on my desk.

"I think you're underestimating the number of products in that cabinet—we're talking at least six brands and thirty bottles and boxes."

Claudia rejoined us, placing two perfectly printed copies of the abstract on the coffee table. A little bedtime reading. "Perhaps you're underestimating the number of erections this man obtains."

Leave it to Claudia to make even an erection sound perfectly uninteresting. "You don't *obtain* an erection, Claudia. You have one."

"Actually"—Claudia sat down before she corrected me—"I don't."

"So what's up with this doctor you met at the esplanade?" I asked Maggie.

"Actually, he's a paramedic." Maggie cleared her throat and waited for Claudia and me to give her the attention she obviously required. "The other day we met up at Parish Café for lunch and then he asked if I wanted to walk over to the Common."

"The verdict?" I asked.

"Good guy. Sort of a Renaissance man."

"Renaissance man?" I repeated. "Like he jousts and drinks mead? Did he call you *m'lady?*"

Claudia laughed. "So, does your Renaissance man have a name?"

"He does."

"And are you going to tell us what it is, or are you going to play charades and make us guess?" I wiggled my ear and held up two fingers—*Sounds like, two syllables . . .*

"I'd rather not tell you his name."

"How can we look him up if you won't tell us his name?"

"I don't want you to look him up." Maggie sighed. "I don't want to know what your database says. Thanks for the offer, but no thanks."

"More than two hundred of Boston's finest women are paying good money to find out what's in that database, and here I am offering it to you for free, and you say thanks, but no thanks?"

"Yep."

"Funny, you never struck me as a romantic."

"Not wanting to find out a guy I'm dating doesn't wash his hands after going to the urinal qualifies me as romantic?" Maggie said. "I'm not the romantic here, Abby. You are."

"Me? I'm a realist, not a romantic, Maggie. I'm just trying to add some much-needed clarity to the process. Full disclosure. Enabling the free flow of information."

"Is that what you call snooping through a guy's medicine cabinet to find out his secret addictions?"

"That was not what I was doing."

Maggie shrugged, her shoulders telling me, *Prove it*.

Here I was busting my ass on the database and she dismissed it as some silly extracurricular activity. This from a woman whose job required tying bows with brightly colored ribbons.

"I've spent a lot of time on that database, Maggie, and I don't know what your problem is with it. I'm just trying to help."

"You see, that's what I just don't get. You really believe you're helping people."

"Women," I clarified. "I'm helping women."

"And how are your computerized undercover investigations helping these women?" she challenged. "Do you think it would make me feel better to hear what my date's ex-girlfriend has to say about him?"

"It's not about making you feel better. It's about making you smarter."

"Because you're so smart?" Maggie responded, and I knew, just by the way she raised her eyebrows at me, that she was thinking about Elliott's fund-raiser, and how she'd run after me when I took off in a cab without even saying good-bye.

"Ladies, return to your corners, please," Claudia ordered, finally deciding it was time to step in. "We're supposed to be planning Celeste's shower, or tea, or whatever it is we're having."

"Tea." I didn't look at Maggie when I spoke. "At the Park Plaza."

Claudia asked Maggie about the floral arrangements, and it was all shower talk from there. But even though I'd begun writing names for the guest list, I hadn't stopped thinking of the night I'd slumped down in the backseat of a cab so I couldn't hear Maggie calling my name.

We were at one of Elliott's charity events, the ones someone was always asking him to host or chair or donate money to. Because he has trouble saying no, as evidenced by the Felicity doll on Caroline's bed, Elliott purchased a table and invited us. Actually, he invited me and I invited Maggie and Claudia to fill up two of the four empty seats that would be surrounding me and Elliott at a table for six. Because, while he was always willing to open his wallet, Elliott wasn't always willing to admit that he had plenty of contacts in his Rolodex but few friends in his address book.

After Kristie left, I was responsible for filling the seats at his tables. Maggie called me his charitable beard, but since she was providing the flowers for most of the events anyway, she didn't mind the invitation to make use of the front entrance and the complimentary cocktails.

Because I once worked for Elliott, everyone at the events made sure they knew me. And because Elliott was bad with names, I made sure I remembered them.

"Bernie?" Elliott would ask, waving to a bald man across the room.

"Barney," I'd tell him, and he'd nod as if he'd known all along.

That night, though, Elliott was by the podium preparing his welcome speech with Karlyn Sneed, the organizer of the event. And I was standing outside the ladies' room waiting for Maggie, making small talk with whatever Betsy, Bitsy or Buffy stopped to envelop me in a cloud of Chanel No. Five and insincere embraces.

"Abby!" Sherry Longly cried out when she saw me loitering by the door. "How are you?" Kiss, kiss, cheek, cheek. All air. "I just saw Alex in the lobby. I was wondering where you were."

That's the thing about people you see every other year or so, the people who have only a cursory knowledge of what's going on in your life. They simply assume that your life today is similar to the one they knew the last time they saw you.

Sherry continued to babble on about innocuous topics, and I stood there with my eyes fixed on the hallway leading to the lobby. It was going to happen eventually, me and Alex coming face to face without a lawyer present. I just never imagined I'd look so good when it did. That I'd be perfectly made-up, my cocktail dress hugging my flat midcycle stomach, my feet in shoes that podiatrists relied on to send their kids to private school.

"What's wrong?" Maggie asked, coming out of the ladies' room to discover me immobile and mute. Sherry had come and gone, guests were swirling around us, but I stood there without blinking.

"He's here. Alex is here."

"What's Alex doing at a fund-raiser? The closest he's ever come to philanthropy was tucking a quarter into some little kid's cardboard Unicef box at Halloween time." Even in a strapless cocktail dress Maggie could remember her solo routine. "Are you sure it's him?"

"He's here," I repeated.

I always believed I'd *know*. That I'd feel a shift in the air or the conversation in the room would dim, like someone turning down the radio. But Alex was one room away from me and I'd had no idea.

"I have to leave," I gasped, and started running down the hallway toward the lobby. Well, maybe running was an exaggeration given the shoes.

"Wait!" Maggie ordered, but I didn't listen. I darted through the revolving doors and demanded the doorman hail me a cab.

"You're in quite a rush," he noted, blowing a long, thin silver whistle that instantly resulted in a taxi appearing before me like the pumpkin coach in "Cinderella."

"Abby!" I heard Maggie call out the door and down the steps.

"Where to?" the doorman asked, opening the taxi door for me.

I ignored the question and instead stuffed a dollar bill in his hand before slamming the door closed. He watched me through the tinted backseat window as I slumped down into the lumpy leather seat.

"Where to?" the cab driver asked.

I gave him my address and, after we'd pulled away, I turned to find the doorman. He was still standing there, his gloved hand holding the dollar bill, trying to figure out why the woman in the black dress just made a fast getaway.

He didn't know that I was rushing away from a man, a man who used to be my husband, a man who still had the ability to make me run. The doorman knew only the license plate of the cab I drove away in. And that the cheap woman in the expensive heels and cocktail dress had tipped him only a single dollar bill.

chapter eighteen

Two weeks later, my field research continued. I'd managed to wrangle three "dates" with Mitch—an invite to lunch to talk about Susan's Japanese beetle problem (she didn't have one as far as I knew, but I'd pressed Maggie for a good garden parasite and the Japanese beetle had come highly recommended), Saturday afternoon coffee to discuss Susan's nonexistent slug problem (again, thanks to Maggie) and a drink after work to talk about Elliott's tennis court (my father really could be interested in a tennis court someday, so I didn't feel like that was a total stretch of the truth).

The problem with these encounters: Mitch didn't expose his seedy underbelly as I'd hoped. Instead he exhibited a thorough knowledge of garden ailments and a polite upbringing, which is why he offered to take our off-site meetings to the source of all the problems: my father's yard.

And then there was the other problem: the dates. Not ours, his. And the fact that he had them at all. Because, let's face it, I'd asked Mitch out on three nondate dates, and yet he was still asking out other women. Only they weren't just women; they were also womenknowbetter.com members. And all their feedback ended up on my computer monitor the morning following dinner or a movie or drinks. And the comments populating the fields for Mitch Reeves were just as glowing, just as benign, as the first data provided by Melanie. Either he really was exactly as he seemed, or Mitch was doing one hell of a snow job on these women. And me. Because you'd think that at least I could ferret out the real man behind the shiny veneer. So what was I missing?

All of his feedback from members was just too pleasant, too normal (allergies, gets up too early, can only sleep on the side of the bed closest to the bathroom). Where were the annoying habits, the bizarre behavior, the little things that gnawed at his dates until they just want to pull their hair out? Mitch was skewing the data. He was an outlier that threatened to ruin the model if I couldn't figure out his flaws.

"Is that your dad?" Mitch asked as we pulled into the driveway.

"The one and only," I answered, and waved to the man sitting on the front stoop.

I heard my dad call for Susan, and she came out of the front door a moment later. My father took her hand and they met us in the driveway.

After the kisses and hugs, Mitch came around to my side of the car and I made the introductions. "This is my friend Mitch," I laid a hand on his shoulder. "And this is my dad, Stewart, and Susan, who can't wait to get you into her garden."

"Stewart and Susan." Mitch shook my dad's hand and then returned Susan's hug.

"Stew and Sue?" he whispered to me as we followed them around to the back of the house.

"Stew and Sue," I repeated, glad he noticed.

Scientists once conducted a study that asked people which couples they thought were better matched, only they didn't give participants anything but couples' first names: Bob and Stephanie, Lisa and William, Jennifer and John, Vicki and Frank. Sixty-five percent of the respondents chose Jennifer and John for no other reason than they liked the way it sounded. They sounded good together.

We sounded good together. Alex and Abby. Abby and Alex. When the justice of the peace pronounced us husband and wife, I remember thinking that. *Damn, we sound great together.* Maybe that's why I didn't read the name tag that night in New York. I knew whatever his name was, we wouldn't sound good together. We weren't supposed to.

It was just an overnight trip, down to New York one morning, back the next, and I relished the idea of one last battle, savored the opportunity to finally see whether we'd survive. To see whether, when it was over, he'd still love me—or whether he ever did. I was going put Alex to the final test—how could he not be able to tell his wife had sex with someone else?

Only, flying into Boston, over the harbor, instead of smiling triumphantly, I covered my mouth with my hands and prayed I wouldn't get sick. Sick, like throwing up right then and there, on our descent. I checked my seat-back pocket to see whether the airline still gave away free airsickness bags or they went the way of free peanuts and those gold plastic wings pilots used to give out to little kids. Alex was down there on the ground, maybe walking to work or even still at home reading the morning paper. And there I was, hovering above him wondering how he'd feel if my Boeing 757 plunged to the ground. Wondering whether he'd be able to see it out his office window, and whether it would occur to him that it could be me in that plummeting body of steel. Or whether he'd feel even the tiniest twinge of relief.

Mitch didn't waste any time getting to work. By the time Susan had given him a tour of her flower beds and the meager growth she hoped would one day produce tomatoes, Mitch was ready to go.

"Let me figure out what we have going on here, and then I'll call you out and we can go over it," he told Susan, who looked as if she'd been given the gospel by Mr. Greenjeans himself.

I turned to follow Susan into the house, but Mitch stopped me. "You're not going anywhere. I need an assistant."

"To do what?" I asked.

"First order of business, how about something to drink?"

"It's a Saturday, so I hope you know I'm getting time and a half for this," I told him.

"Then make it a really big drink," he answered, "as long as it's costing me."

I brought two tall lemonades out to the backyard and found Mitch kneeling beside what should have been a flowering hibiscus. Susan and my dad watched us from the porch as if they were spectators at a sporting event. Mitch waved to them and they waved back.

"How long have they been married?"

"A long time, almost seventeen years." I kneeled down and pushed aside some dead leaves so Mitch could see what he was doing.

"Why'd they get divorced, your parents?"

I never knew why my dad finally left. I never asked, maybe because I was afraid of the answer. Me. My mom. Us. Or maybe the reason— no reason at all. He just wanted to. He'd just changed his mind. At any time, someone could change his mind.

"Why's anyone get divorced?" I nonanswered, and I could almost see Mitch asking himself, *Why? Why? Why?* "I mean, I'm sure there were a bunch of reasons."

"You know, relationships are a lot like this right here." Mitch shook the flower he cradled in his hand. "They come in all shapes and sizes, some look beautiful and some not so great, but they pretty much all need the same things."

I waited for the punch line, but Mitch wasn't giving it to me. "And what is that?" I finally asked.

"This." Mitch picked up a handful of dirt with one hand and his lemonade with the other. "And this."

"I don't know about your relationships, but I think you're being a little simplistic."

"Maybe. But whatever the reason, Stew and Sue seem pretty happy now." Mitch bent a branch over toward me. "Is this purple or bright pink?" he asked, and then explained, "I'm color-blind."

"I know."

Mitch looked up at me. "You do?"

"I meant I know what you mean," I quickly recovered. Claudia wasn't color-blind, but I figured she could go along with it for the purpose of this exercise. "My friend Claudia is color-blind. And that's purple."

"Did you know you can change the color of a hydrangea just by changing the pH of the soil?" Mitch pointed to a bush wilting in the shade of a much larger tree. "And that one over there needs more sun. It looks like it's in mourning."

The hydrangea wasn't any color, which probably didn't bode well for the pH level or the aluminum content or whatever it was that Mitch was trying to explain to me while I started to feel really, really sad for the poor bush with its wilting flowers that were just brown tinged and dusty looking. "All it needs is a black veil."

"And relatives showing up with lasagnas," Mitch added, and then laughed. "We could probably dig it out and relocate it before the rain starts."

I looked up at the sky, which had grown gray and overcast but certainly didn't look that menacing. "What are you, a meteorologist, too?"

"Nah." Mitch stood up and started to walk over to the ailing bush. "Trick knee, it always starts to hurt when it's going to rain."

"Can your knee do any other tricks? Roll over, sit up and beg?" I sat down on the grass and watched him examine the plant. "Pull a rabbit out of a hat, maybe?"

"We're working on it, but the rabbit keeps getting it wrong."

"Sure, blame the rabbit; it's always the rabbit's fault."

For the next two hours I watched as Mitch tagged plants that shouldn't be in the sun and then tagged other plants that should. He showed Susan how overgrown shrubs should be pruned and pointed out dead leaves that should be cut away. He even showed Susan how her rosebuds were choking, even though I didn't hear any gasping coming from their direction.

"There's a lot more to do, but we should probably get going." Mitch's hands were covered in dirt and the grass had stained his knees green. "The rain will be good for everything, and that's a start."

"You could stay for dinner," Susan offered, and my father joined in. "You're more than welcome to stay."

I waited for Mitch to answer before I said anything. Dinner actually sounded good, since at this point I'd been made to feel woefully inadequate in the yard and my night would most likely consist of watching HGTV marathons in hopes of honing my landscaping vocabulary.

Mitch took the damp towel Susan offered him but declined dinner. "That's nice of you, but I can't."

"Me neither," I added. "But thanks. We should get on our way before it starts to pour."

"Big plans tonight?" My dad asked us. Us, as if the reason we couldn't stay was that we'd planned to do something together.

Mitch wiped his hands on the towel, leaving brown smudges on the terry cloth. "Not so big, but yeah."

"I've got some work I have to finish up before Monday," I explained, leaving out the part about HGTV.

We said good-bye and Susan insisted she was going to talk to my dad about hiring Mitch to transform the yard into something worthy of Martha Stewart.

"Date tonight?" I asked Mitch, climbing into the passenger seat.

"Nothing big, just meeting someone for drinks, maybe dinner if that goes well." He slipped the key in the ignition and turned on the car. "What about you?"

"What about me?"

"Why aren't you dating?" He laid his arm across the top of my seat and turned to look out the rear window as he pulled out of the driveway.

"Nobody's asking."

Mitch didn't act shocked by the revelation that there wasn't a line of men circling my block waiting for a chance to ask me out. Instead he gave me a look that said, *I'm not surprised.*

"Not that I'm rubbing it in or anything, since at this point I think we're beyond that, but I asked," he reminded me, putting the car into drive. "You said no."

"Yeah, I guess I did," I agreed.

"So while I'm enjoying drinks, you'll be home crunching numbers on a spreadsheet?"

I leaned my head back against the headrest where, a few minutes ago, Mitch's arm had rested against my shoulder. "No spreadsheet, a database. I have some new information that needs to be added."

"Sounds terribly interesting."

"It might be," I told Mitch. "You ever watch HGTV?"

"No, never." He shook his head. "Why?"

"No reason. I was just wondering."

chapter nineteen

On Saturday night Mitch's date canceled. I should have been surprised, but I wasn't.

"They stopped all the flights out of New York, so she's stuck there until tomorrow."

"Did she reschedule?" I was curious.

"No, she said she'd call me next week."

I seriously doubted that.

"That's too bad," I said, silently thanking the meteorologists for incorrectly predicting that the massive rain and thunderstorms we'd been having would be gone by the weekend. If I ever had any doubt, I didn't any longer. Mother Nature was definitely a woman.

"Everyone seems to have plans tonight or is out of town or something," Mitch went on. "So I was thinking maybe you could come over and we could grab dinner."

It wasn't exactly the invitation I'd been waiting for. "After *everyone* was unavailable you thought of me?"

"That's not what I meant," he backpedaled. "What I should have said is that it's pouring out and there isn't anyone else I know who isn't afraid of a little rain."

An hour later I was at his door, flip-flops in hand. Moisturizing my feet sounded like a good idea before I left, but Vaseline Intensive Care, puddles and rubber flip-flops were not a good combination.

"Mind if I go barefoot?" I asked, leaving a trail of watery footprints on Mitch's hardwood floors.

"Fine by me," he answered, and took my flip-flops into the kitchen, where he placed them in the dish rack to dry. He had tremendous confidence in the cleanliness of my footwear.

"I didn't know people still used drafting tables," I commented, picking up a mechanical pencil and resisting the temptation to write my name in bubble letters on the open pad of tracing paper. "Isn't everything done on a computer these days?

"Pretty much, but I still like to begin drawing by hand. Call me old-fashioned."

I moved over to the fireplace mantel and picked up a picture frame reclining next to Snoopy. "Is this the famed milkman?"

"The one and only."

The man in the photo had Mitch's brown hair and the crinkles around his eyes, even if his face was rounder and he wore flannel. "A little shorter than Superman."

"It didn't matter; I thought he was invincible. He used to claim he really was Superman, almost had me convinced it was cool to wear tights and a leotard. A poorly selected Halloween costume, and the taunts of a bus full of third graders, taught me otherwise."

"I think your mother deserves some of the blame for that one." I placed the frame back on the mantel. "Isn't lesson one in mother school 'Don't Let Your Boys Out of the House Wearing Nylons and Danskin'?"

"So where do you want to go?" Mitch asked, just as a giant clap of thunder shook the walls and a bolt of lightning shot across the sky.

The lights flickered once, twice, and then the room went black.

I heard Mitch clap his hands. "Guess you need a Clapper for that to work," he said, and I saw what looked like his shadow walking toward me. "Here." Mitch reached for my hand and led me toward the window. I willingly followed.

"So much for dinner. Looks like we're not the only ones in the dark." He let my hand drop.

Outside the open windows we could hear every footstep, every slamming car door and flags snapping in the wind. The smell of wet blacktop floated up to us, as if the street was exhaling the heat that had been trapped inside.

We stood there listening and watching as pockets of light burst through the blackness. Generators. "That's pretty cool," Mitch said.

"Do you have any candles?" I asked.

"Candles?"

I nodded. "Guess not."

"Does this count?" Mitch walked into the kitchen, where he pulled a wand from the drawer and cocked the trigger like a gun. A perfect yellow flame appeared from the barrel.

"Not exactly a vanilla-scented pillar from Pottery Barn, but it will work." Mitch stood there holding the flame, and the only thing I could think of was the Statue of Liberty.

"At least we can still eat. I have some leftover burgers in the refrigerator, I think."

"I think the weather will rain on our barbecue parade."

Mitch bent down and returned holding the flame in one hand and a frying pan in the other. "Gas stove. I guess there'll be no flame broiling tonight."

He looked so cute standing there, his face flickering in the reflec-

tion of the frying pan. Could it be that Mitch's greatest flaw was that
he didn't own any candles?

"And you call yourself the king."

Twenty minutes later dinner was ready. Hamburgers and potato chips
and the glow of the flashlight powered by a Duracell Mitch found in
the hall closet.

Mitch piled the burgers up on the spatula. "Pass me your plate."

He turned a shoulder to his mouth and sneezed.

I instinctively offered a *bless you.*

"Thank—" Mitch barely got the word out before sneezing a second time.

I watched him, waiting for a third. A moment later, it arrived.

Sneezing? A candlelit dinner? The cozy sound of rain hitting the
pavement outside Mitch's apartment? So the dinner consisted of leftover burger meat on English muffins. (Mitch didn't have any leftover
buns.) He was sneezing. More than once. Maybe it was the candlelit
dinner, the darkened city around us. Whatever it was, I knew what
those sneezes meant. And it didn't require reading the abstract Claudia
had printed out.

As Mitch had so eloquently pointed out several times, I'd turned
him down at Elliott's. But that was before. Before I knew him and his
trick knee and the Snoopy trophy that sat in the dark across the room
from us. Before I learned he hoarded parking tickets in his glove compartment. And maybe, because he knew me now, too, Mitch had decided that he'd try again. Maybe he'd decided I was worth the trouble.

"Are you okay?" I asked, my bare knee grazing the cuff of his
shorts. "Is there anything I can do?"

Like lean over and let you kiss me, I thought.

"No, I'll be okay. It's allergies."

"Allergies?"

"If it's green and alive, I'm allergic to it."

"But you were fine the other day on the Cape," I reminded him. "And at my dad's house." Funny how with other women a sneeze meant he was horny. With me it meant he needed to take Claritin.

"They're always worse when it rains, and my doctor put me on this new medication. I've pretty much tried every over-the-counter and prescription medicine out there. You should see my medicine cabinet."

I almost told him I already had.

I watched as Mitch squeezed a stream of ketchup onto his patty, and I could swear there were two eyes and a mouth. A happy face.

"You didn't exactly pick the best profession for a guy with allergies, did you?"

"Probably not, but I can't imagine doing anything else. What about you? Did you pick the best profession for someone who likes to mitigate risk?"

"Actually, I've been considering a career change."

"Elliott finally get to you?"

"No, it's not Elliott. I'm just feeling restless, you know what I mean? Like it's time to do something different." Thankfully he didn't ask what.

"That's the great thing about what I do; it's always different—a different location, a different season that requires a different way of looking at something."

Actually, it did sound great. "You're lucky you figured out what you wanted to do."

"I guess I am." Mitch stood up. "Sorry I can't offer you any dessert, unless you think beer qualifies as dessert."

"It does in my book."

Mitch brought the plates into the kitchen and returned carrying a deck of cards and two cold beers.

"Do you play?" He held up the cards.

"Sorry, I'm not much of a card player."

"Not even a little poker, twenty-one?"

I shook my head.

"Gin rummy? Crazy eights?"

"You're quite the gambler, aren't you?" I asked.

"Just trying to make sure you're entertained."

"Go fish?" I offered.

"Maybe we'll put the cards away for later."

Here we'd dined by flashlight while the rain beat against the pavement outside, and yet there was nothing. Not a sideways glance, not an accidental brushing of his hand against my thigh. Mitch hadn't even held my hand any longer than it took to lead me to the window. Nada. I guess I wasn't worth the trouble after all.

Mitch placed his beer on the table and picked up the cards, which he started to shuffle.

"Hey, I have a question for you."

Maybe this was it. Maybe he just needed to work up to it. "What's your question?"

Mitch put down the cards and picked up the flashlight. He started making animal shapes in the shadows against the wall. Not exactly a prelude to romance, but perhaps a shadow-puppet show was his icebreaker.

"I have a problem. There's this woman I like and I wanted to ask her out," he started, and I sat back, waiting for my moment.

"Go on."

Mitch laughed. "I feel like an idiot: *Dear Abby, I asked a girl out, and she stood me up. Should I take it personally or persevere? Sincerely, Bewildered in Boston.*"

"I don't get it. She stood you up?"

"Yeah. We were supposed to meet for dinner Wednesday night and she just never showed up. Didn't call, nothing."

Oh. Wasn't expecting that one.

My own version: *Dear Mitch, What the hell is wrong with the woman sitting right in front of you?*

"Dear Bewildered," I began. *"Don't take it personally. Maybe she had a change of plans and couldn't reach you. Or maybe she objected to your choice of restaurant. Find yourself a nice girl who will appreciate a Value Meal—nothing says true love like supersizing fries. Better luck next time, Abby."*

"Excellent advice. If you're serious about leaving Verity, I think there might be a future for you as a relationship counselor." Mitch laughed. "Either that, or a food writer for the *Herald.*"

A bolt of lightning lit up the sky and I got a quick flash of Mitch smiling at me. "Do you think this rain is ever going to stop?" I asked, continuing to watch the shadow of his face even after the light was gone.

"I hope so. My sister's baby shower is tomorrow."

"And you're invited?"

"We're *all* invited—my brothers and me." I didn't have to see him to know he was rolling his eyes. "It's one of those coed showers. You know, I'm all for equality, but when it comes to things like baby showers, I'm perfectly content being excluded."

Alex and I didn't talk about children, or when we did it was in a vague *someday when we charter a boat and sail around the Greek islands* kind of way.

We were invited to one of those couples baby showers, where both men and women are expected to spend two hours playing pink and blue games in a gender-neutral environment. We guessed the number of pink and blue and white jelly beans in a two-foot-tall baby bottle. We memorized baby supplies that the hostess passed around on a platter. We raced to see who could diaper a doll the fastest.

At least you don't have kids. Ninety-nine percent of the time, that's what people were thinking when I told them Alex and I split up. Most people didn't say the words out loud, but it was so obvious. The way they tipped their heads to the side and nodded a few times while they observed the obligatory moment of silence. Then they'd express their sorrow and offer to take me to dinner or mumble something about how I could always call them if I needed to talk. After the expression of condolences they'd touch me lightly, either on the shoulder or on the forearm, or sometimes, in a bold move, they'd even reach for my hand and squeeze it for a second like I was some invalid in a nursing home who needed that human touch to keep my heart pumping one more day.

At least you don't have kids, they'd offer up much in way someone would tell an amputee, *At least you have your other leg.* In other words—*It could be worse.*

And they were right. We didn't have kids or a dog or another living creature that would become a bed wetter or a thumb sucker or be otherwise traumatized by the dissolution of our marriage (I didn't count). And this was supposed to make me feel better, how? They may just as well have said, *You have nothing to show for your two years together except a nice set of Pottery Barn plates and a joint membership to Blockbuster.* And they'd be right, yet again. We created nothing that couldn't be divided with a quick round of *rock, paper, scissors.* The closest we came was a frozen fish.

That day of the baby shower, I knew. When the invitation arrived, a pale yellow background with a genderless cartoon baby's head poking out the top of a green pea pod, I knew. Alex and I had been married for a year and I'd started watching other couples, trying to figure out whether they were happy, attempting to discern how Alex and I were different. Did other people hold hands when we didn't? Did the silences that settled around them while they ate dinner mean they'd achieved a level of comfort we hadn't, or that they'd simply run out of things to say? Because that was how I'd been feeling. I'd run out of things to say, or maybe the things I wanted to say weren't the words I wanted to admit to—to admit that maybe I was in over my head, that I didn't know how to be a wife or love Alex like I was supposed to. And I was sure there was a way I was supposed to, a right way, a way that didn't involve the constant fear that at any moment it would end. Was it normal to lack any faith in your relationship, your husband, even yourself?

"I can't imagine ever wanting to do that." Alex shook his head and started walking to the car. As we passed the pink and blue balloons tied to the mailbox, he punched at the balloon bouquet.

I walked beside him, holding our consolation prize for losing the diapering contest—a stork-shaped chocolate bar. Was Alex talking about the coed shower or the games or creating something with me that would last a lifetime? I had no idea. Still, I agreed.

"Me neither."

That night in bed I wanted to ask Alex what he meant. But even more, I wanted him to ask me what I meant when I'd agreed. I wanted to be able to tell Alex that I didn't trust him not to hurt me, that I didn't trust he'd still love me once the shiny newness of us wore off, if not this year, then the next or the next. It took my father almost fifteen years, but he still got there. I wasn't sure it would take Alex that long.

I thought once we were married I wouldn't be afraid. It would finally be safe to be myself around Alex. I knew he'd make me better, fuller. I just knew it. Two are better than one. I'd be me squared, and that would make all the difference. It was the new math. The multiplicative value of marriage.

If he'd asked that night, I might have finally told Alex the truth, just to see whether I'd get the same frightened look I'd glimpsed that Halloween from behind the bedroom door. Only he didn't raise the question, and I didn't offer the answer. And that night I slept as close to the edge of the mattress as possible, as far away from him as I could get, just to see whether he'd notice.

"How long has your sister been married?" I asked Mitch.

"Four years," he told me. "How long were you married?"

As if on cue, a bolt of lightning cut through the sky and lit up the living room. Mitch was watching me, waiting for an answer.

I waited for the room to go black again. Some things are just easier in the dark. Oral sex. Dancing with abandon. Flashlight tag. Explaining your failed marriage. "Two years."

Mitch paused, probably deciding whether or not to continue this line of questioning. "Was it a surprise?"

I shook my head, even though I knew he couldn't see me. "In retrospect, not at all."

"If you don't want to talk about it, we don't have to," Mitch offered.

"It's okay," I told him, almost meaning it.

"It's just that you never mention it, or him," he added.

"There's just not much to say. It sucked. It's not something I'd recommend, in case you were looking for an endorsement."

"Still, you seem to have survived."

"No worse for the wear, right?" I reached for the deck of cards and fanned them out in my hand.

"I didn't say that." Mitch reached across the table, slipped a card out of my hand and laid it facedown on the table. "Red or black?" he asked.

"Black."

He turned the card over. The seven of diamonds.

"Better luck next time," he told me, and reached for another card.

I stared at the card, but didn't venture a guess. "There won't be a next time."

"Are you giving up already?"

"I guess I am," I admitted.

"Why do I get the feeling we're not talking about a game of cards here?" Mitch turned the card over—the six of clubs. "See, this time you would have won."

I laid the rest of the cards on the table and sat there in the dark. "I guess I don't think it's possible—to win, I mean."

"I hate to take this card metaphor to new levels of corniness, but you've only played one hand. Not every guy is your ex-husband." Mitch took the pile of cards and turned it over, exposing their faces. "See, there's only one joker in the bunch. One!"

He laughed at himself, and I let myself laugh at him, too.

I reached for the flashlight and picked it up. "What about you? What secrets are you hiding?" I shined the light at Mitch's chest: *Tag, you're it.* "Tell me something you've never told anyone before—ever cheat on your taxes, shoplift, plant a weed in a client's garden?"

"Never done the weed thing, but you certainly have a wicked mind." In the white glow of the flashlight's beam, Mitch grinned. "Let's see, I used my roommate's brother's birth certificate to get a fake ID when I was nineteen. Never cheated on my taxes, but I didn't declare the tips I got mowing lawns in high school. And once I threw my nephew's Chuck E. Cheese tokens in the toll basket when I didn't have any change. You're not going to report me, are you?"

"No, but I think you should invest in a Fast Lane pass."

"Consider it done."

"What's the worst thing you ever did to a woman?"

Mitch's grin dissolved and he hesitated before answering. "Told her I loved her when I didn't."

He reached across the table for the flashlight and took it from me, turning the spotlight in my direction. "And you?"

Even with the glare of the light on me, I didn't hesitate. "Not telling him I loved him when I did."

Mitch placed the flashlight back on the table, standing it up so the beam of light hit the ceiling. "Are we talking about the ex-husband here?"

"We are."

I waited for him to say something, to point a finger and say no wonder my husband left.

Instead he sat quietly across from me and let the words dissipate in the darkness. "So we both lied," he finally said. "But I bet you at least have a Fast Lane pass, right?"

"I do," I admitted.

"See, you're not all bad."

chapter twenty

"What are you doing here?"

"Just getting a little work done." I turned my laptop away from Maggie, shielding the screen with my hand.

"New computer?"

I gave her a look that said, *What, this old thing?* even though the over-size screen, ultrathin case and brand-spanking-new exterior screamed *tax write-off.* "What are you doing here?"

"Getting my morning coffee. Why aren't you downtown? Don't even tell me you took the day off to work on the database."

"As long as we're here, I could always check on your paramedic," I reminded her. It was easier than answering her question.

"We're not checking on my paramedic. Besides, he's told me every-thing. And he's not even my paramedic. We've only had six dates."

I didn't point out that six was five more than she'd had the last time I'd offered up my services.

Maggie pushed my hand out of the way. "Besides, it looks like you're already checking on somebody else." She smirked when she read Mitch's name at the top of the screen.

"Just making sure nothing happened to the data when the power went out the other night." I turned the laptop away from Maggie. "So why are you hiding this guy from us? And can't you even tell us his first name, or will that spoil all the cloak-and-dagger stuff?"

"His name is Curtis."

"So he has a name."

"Yes, and he also has an ex-wife. And she still lives in Charlestown." Maggie pulled out a chair and sat down. "Hey, I'm sorry about the other night at your place. I didn't mean to get you all defensive."

"You don't have to apologize," I assured her, even though I was glad she did.

"It's just that I know how you get about divorce, and I didn't want to hear you say all sorts of negative things about the guy."

"Curtis."

"Yeah, Curtis."

"I wouldn't do that to someone you liked. So, he's divorced?"

Maggie nodded.

"Maybe the divorce wasn't even his fault."

"Oh, no, he's the one who asked for it," she told me. "Supposedly she's a real handful, and for all I know you have eighty-two entries all about him in there. I guess his ex was really difficult, a total bitch who did nothing but nag and put him down. As far as I can tell, he should have left her sooner." Maggie pointed to the computer, where Mitch's profile was still displayed. "I'd just rather find things out for myself than read the ramblings of a crazy ex-wife."

"Suit yourself, but don't ever say I didn't offer."

Maggie leaned over and tapped a finger on the screen. "What's that?"

I tried to close the laptop, but she wouldn't move her hand. "Nothing."

"That's not *nothing.*" Her finger trailed down the screen, leaving a smudge across seven fields of data.

"I just wanted to see if any of the information got corrupted." If Maggie wasn't going to move her hand, I was left with only one option. I maneuvered the mouse with my index finger and clicked a few times to shut down.

"That can't be right." Maggie kneeled down next to me as the computer asked me whether I was sure I wanted to quit. Hell, yeah, I was sure.

"Mitch is a fugitive under investigation by the Boston Police Department?" Maggie read from the screen. "He dresses up in tights and thinks he's Superman? Addiction to over-the-counter medication? A gambling habit? Defrauding the Massachusetts Turnpike Authority?"

"I'll fix it later," I told her, just as the screen flashed a royal blue and went blank.

"That stuff can't be true." Maggie reached for the POWER button, but I moved the computer out of her reach. "Something's going on, Abby. What is it?"

I gave her a vacant look that conveyed not only my innocence but my complete and absolute befuddlement. "I have no idea."

Maggie wasn't going to let it drop. "That information for Mitch has nothing to do with the power going out. So who put that in there?"

"They have great blueberry muffins here." I rubbed my stomach and made an *mmm* sound. "Yummy."

"Abby," she warned, "who did that?"

"Me."

"You?"

"Yeah, me. I put it in there."

"Is any of it true?"

I shook my head.

"So you're skewing his data? On purpose?" Maggie smacked my leg under the table. "You can't do that."

"I only did it for Mitch, so if any members pulled up his information he wouldn't look so attractive."

"And how exactly does that benefit your members?" she asked. "Or Mitch?"

"You make it sound so bad. It's not, really." Even I had trouble believing me. "It's just that all his data was just so normal, like there was nothing wrong with him. I just wanted to keep members away until I uncovered the truth."

"The truth?"

"Yeah, that he's not perfect."

"And have you? Come to the conclusion that he's not perfect?"

"Well, yeah," I admitted. "He's not perfect, but that doesn't mean he's bad, either."

"And you're just realizing this?" Maggie shook her head at me, disgusted. "Are you kidding me?"

I didn't answer.

"So fix the guy's data!" she practically shouted. "Why are you continuing to screw with him?"

I reached for my muffin, but Maggie grabbed my hand before I could tear off a piece. "You're not doing this to help your members, Abby; you're doing this to help yourself. Do you really think that keeping every other woman away from Mitch will make him want you?"

What could I say? *Yes? You're right? You caught me?*

"You don't understand," I told her, only she understood exactly.

"You have to stop this, Abby. All of it. Ditch this database thing before it blows up in your face. Now."

"I can't."

"Of course you can."

"No. I can't," I repeated. "I quit my job."

"You what? When?"

"About two hours ago. You are now sitting in my official virtual office."

"There's no way you're going to continue doing this."

"I couldn't keep up with the business and do my job. Besides, womenknowbetter.com is doing so well, I had to hire Claudia's students back just to keep up with the data monitoring." My explanation was not eliciting any sympathy from Maggie. "I couldn't do it all myself. I barely have time to assign user IDs to all the referrals coming in."

"You better hope members don't find out what you're doing, or this business of yours is over." She stood up, broke off a chunk of my muffin and stuffed it in her mouth. "And you're right. That's one damn good muffin."

Maggie walked out of the coffee shop and left me alone with my database. I pushed the POWER button and watched my new laptop come to life.

"I was stood up again." Mitch was helping me pick out bushes for my dad's house. Susan had decided to hire him to redesign the garden out back. "The third time in three weeks."

"Who was she?" I asked, and pointed to a purple azalea bush.

Mitch shook his head. "Needs too much sun. Over here."

I followed him over to a row of hydrangeas. "So, are you going to tell me who she is?"

"It doesn't matter at this point. I met her through a client—you remember Bruce; we went to his house. Everything seemed great, we made plans to go to a Red Sox game and then she never showed up. I was left standing outside Fenway with an extra ticket that nobody wanted because the Sox suck these days."

"You could have called me," I reminded him. "I don't care if they suck."

Mitch didn't answer. Instead he crouched down next to a hydrangea bush and inspected its root-ball. "I just don't get it. You know me. Is there something I'm doing wrong?"

"This looks good." I crouched down next to him and pretended to knowingly approve his selection. "Can I ask you a question?"

"Sure. Shoot."

"Why haven't you ever asked me out?" I blurted. Yes, I was not only a woman who asked a man why he wasn't infatuated with her, I was also someone who blurts while crouching beside a root-ball.

"I thought I asked you to come to the nursery with me," he reminded me, winning on a technicality.

"I meant, why haven't you asked me on a date? Why do we just hang out?"

"Are you complaining?" Mitch stood up and turned to face me. "Is there something wrong with just hanging out and having fun?"

"No." *Yes.*

"Can I be honest?" he asked.

Not if it meant I was about to hear something I didn't want him to say. "Of course."

"I've never asked you on a date because I don't want to date you."

Oh.

"Besides," Mitch continued, "I did ask, sort of, when we were at Elliott's. You said no. Don't you remember?"

Now I stood up, only I wasn't quite ready to face Mitch, so I fixed my eyes on a green thorny shrub. "Okay, well, thanks for not beating around the bush."

"No pun intended, I'm sure." Mitch laughed, but I didn't join him. "Don't get me wrong. You're great and we have fun, but I don't think I could handle it."

By *it* I knew he meant me. All of a sudden I had a mental picture of Mitch handling me. And it was pretty damn enjoyable.

"That's fine. I was just wondering. You seem to ask out every other single woman in Boston. I was just wondering if you ever planned on getting to me."

"I wasn't planning to."

"Super."

"It's not—"

I held up my hand to deflect his explanation. I didn't need another explanation. I'd finally discovered Mitch's fatal flaw. He didn't want me.

"Please, don't say *It's not you, it's me.*"

"I wasn't going to," he assured me. "It's definitely you."

"It's me?"

He nodded.

"It's me?" I repeated, as if hearing it said twice wasn't enough to make me feel terribly desperate and pathetic. I needed to say it one more time just in case the woman browsing the perennial aisle didn't hear it the first two times. "What exactly is there to handle?"

"I couldn't handle you having no faith in me."

"Why wouldn't I have faith in you?"

"Because you don't seem to have too much faith in anything."

"Maybe you have *too* much faith," I shot back, a thirty-one-year-old woman's version of *I'm rubber, you're glue.*

Mitch smiled. "And maybe that's why we won't be going on a date."

"There are worse things you know."

"It's not just the lack of faith that's hard to handle. It's the expectation that you'll be disappointed. You're just waiting for it."

Mitch had no idea. If he even knew about the database, the way I'd skewed his data, he'd realize that having faith in someone just puts you at their mercy. Because he'd had faith in me, and look what I'd done. And he had no idea. He had no idea.

But I did. And what I was quickly learning was that sometimes being the one in control didn't mean you avoided getting hurt. It only meant you had a choice to make. And the ramifications of that choice sat squarely on your shoulders, whether you liked it or not. And the weight of that choice didn't feel anything like the triumph I'd antici-pated.

"That's so not true," I told him, resisting the urge to flip him off—a thirty-one-year-old woman's version of sticking her tongue out. "Be-sides, don't tell me you've never gone out with anyone who didn't do anything wrong."

"I did have a girlfriend who folded my underwear."

"And this was wrong because?"

"They wouldn't fit in my drawer when they were all folded. They'd get stuck and then I couldn't get the drawer open, and when I did, half of them would be pushed to the back where they'd fall behind the drawer and I'd have to empty the whole dresser out to find them."

"So did you ask her to stop doing it?"

"Yep."

"And did she?"

"Nope."

I pictured the great underwear battle that ensued.

"So what'd you do?"

"I moved all my underwear to a bigger drawer."

"Didn't it bother you that you had to change?"

"Not really. I wasn't about to go to the mat over underwear."

"So why aren't you dating her anymore?"

"My underwear wasn't the problem. It was hers. And her inability to keep them on when I wasn't around."

"She cheated on you?"

"With her landlord. I think they ended up getting married. She's probably living in the suburbs somewhere folding underwear all day."

Mitch bent down and picked up the hydrangea and then placed it back on the ground. "If we're getting six of these, we need a wagon." He tipped his head toward the front of the nursery and led the way.

"So aren't you going to ask the burning question?"

I thought I already had. "Which question would that be?"

"Boxers or briefs."

"That would be a big no."

"Okay."

Of course, after he brought it up, that was all I could think about. And I really hoped it was boxers.

"Is that your phone, or are you just happy to see me?" Mitch pointed to the vibrating noise coming from my pocket.

I took it out and saw Claudia's number flash on my screen. "It's Claudia."

"You take it. I'll go back and get the bushes and meet you up front at the register."

Mitch walked off, wheeling his little red wagon behind him, and I flipped my phone open.

"What's up?"

"We have a problem." Claudia was using her PhD voice, which sounded exactly like that of a narrator of a PBS documentary.

"What's this *we* stuff?" I joked.

"This isn't funny, Abby. Your little *project* is about to get me fired."

chapter twenty-one

"Look, she's pissed. She found her brother in the database and started asking all sorts of questions. She wants to know what the hell she's been working on for two months."

"Shit. I knew I shouldn't have handed the monitoring over to them." I paced around Claudia's office, which took only a few seconds and didn't have the dramatic effect I was hoping for. "I should have assigned them the user ID numbers."

"That's what you're worried about? That you didn't allocate work appropriately?" Claudia shook her head at me. "I could lose my job over this, Abby. Do you not understand that?"

"Where is she?" I asked. It was already two o'clock, and Deep Throat, otherwise known as Veronica, was supposed to have met us a half hour ago.

Before Claudia could venture a guess, the elusive Veronica walked in. She looked like she should be working in the Gap, not programming databases.

"I'm Abby Dunn." I held out my hand, but she didn't shake it.

"I want my brother's name out of there."

"That's fine. Consider it done."

Veronica moved over to Claudia's desk and leaned her bell-bottomed ass against the corner. "So, it's you, not Professor Johnson, who started all this?"

"It's me."

"How do I know you're not just saying that to cover for her?" Veronica certainly talked tough for someone wearing a T-shirt that covered less skin than a Band-Aid.

"Do you really think Claudia has time to do this? Besides, she wouldn't need you to create the database; she could do it herself."

"So, how's it work?" Veronica wanted to know.

"You programmed the database; you already know how it works," I reminded her.

"I know how it's coded, but I don't know what you've been doing with it."

So I told her about the site and how members can refer friends. I explained that the database fields were used to share information that the members submitted. I even told her about the PayPal account.

"I want them to know. The members." Veronica stood in the doorway. "I want them to know who's behind this."

"That's not really necessary, is it?"

Veronica looked over at Claudia, who hadn't said a word the entire time. This girl meant business. What the hell did one of the members write about her brother anyway?

"Fine, let me talk to Claudia and we'll get back to you."

Veronica seemed satisfied and turned to leave us alone to discuss the situation. "By the way, my brother does not build toy soldiers with his ear wax. He stopped doing that ages ago." She slammed the door behind her, leaving me and Claudia alone.

"What do you mean it's not necessary?" Claudia practically yelled. "My ass is on the line, Abby. You bet it's necessary."

"But I can't."

"Why? What's the big deal? They're your members; it doesn't matter."

"But I'm supposed to be the one they can trust."

"You are. Telling them who you are doesn't change that."

"It does if I've done something that makes me as bad as all the investments the database is supposed to help them avoid."

Claudia hung her head in her hands. I thought she'd had just about enough of me for one day. "What are you talking about?"

"I cheated on Alex."

Her head popped up. "You did what?"

"I cheated on Alex. I slept with someone. Right before he left."

"What do you mean you slept with someone?" The head was fully upright now.

"Do you want the play-by-play?"

"You slept with someone," she repeated, as if trying to wrap her hands around the words. "Who was he?"

"Mike Martin? Dave Douglas? I don't know, there was some sort of alliteration going on. I tried to avoid looking at his name tag."

"Where was this?"

"A conference in New York. He works for another mutual fund company—Vanguard, Janus, American Century, I don't remember which one. It wasn't like it was a job interview, I wasn't exactly interested in his credentials. The only thing that mattered was that he didn't live anywhere near Boston."

"Jesus, Abby, what were you thinking?"

"I don't know, Claudia. I obviously wasn't thinking."

Claudia stood up, went over to her whiteboard and began furiously erasing an equation. She was obviously in damage-control mode, and designing methodologies for synthesis of multivariable feedback control systems wasn't going to take place anytime soon.

"Okay, so what do companies do when they need to do a little damage control without setting off a wave of speculation?"

"Maybe they hold a shareholder meeting," I suggested, almost feeling like I should have raised my hand first.

"Then that's exactly what you have to do," Claudia told me. "I'll call Veronica and tell her it's all taken care off. Your job is to set this up. And fast."

Fast meant that I had to compose e-mails to the members, coordinate a place to host the meeting and come up with a way to satisfy Veronica's demands without freaking anyone out—all within a week. But I couldn't say no. I was in no position to bargain with a girl who had a sterling silver ring through her nose. I'd already given up one job; I couldn't afford to lose the only one I had left.

By Saturday morning I had the Four Seasons' ballroom reserved, thanks to Maggie's connections with a meeting planner, I'd e-mailed the invitations to the members and the only thing left was to figure out what I was going to say.

I took my laptop back to the coffee shop and downed three hot chocolates—in the middle of August, mind you—before I even had a word beyond: *Welcome to womenknowbetter.com's first annual shareholder meeting.* It sounded good, even if it was a total lie. There was no way I was making this an annual event.

"Abby?" I felt a tap on my shoulder and I was convinced it had to be the owner telling me to either pony up for a muffin or take a hike. But when I looked up, it was Sarah.

"Sarah!"

"Hey, we miss you—okay, I miss you. It's been depressing walking past your office and seeing the light off and the desk bare."

"I miss you, too," I told her, and it was the truth. I missed her. But I didn't really miss Verity. Or the research I'd done.

"You know, they've finally hired your replacement. He starts next week and we were going to take him out for drinks on Friday. Why don't you come?"

"Wish I could."

"Hot date?"

"Not exactly. Just promised I'd meet a friend after work."

"So, what are you doing? Everyone thinks you're going to go work for Elliott, but I keep telling them that you don't have the stomach for it."

"No, not working for Elliott. I'm doing a little independent consulting right now."

"Well, it's too bad you can't meet us on Friday. I talked to a friend over at Janus and she said the new guy is supposed to be pretty hot—and not just because he was their golden-boy analyst."

"I'll have to take a rain check."

Sarah turned to go.

"Hey, are you still seeing Duncan?" I asked.

She nodded. "Almost three months. Why?"

"Just checking," I told her. At least Sarah wouldn't be there on Sunday. At least there was one person who wouldn't learn my secret.

chapter twenty-two

My mother's shower went off without a hitch. I'd invited five of her friends and Maggie and Claudia, and we'd spent a lovely two hours drinking tea in the Park Plaza's Swan's Café. I'd had no idea when I booked the party that a mere two hours after I'd kiss my mother and her friends good-bye, Claudia and I would be heading down the street to the Four Seasons, where I'd kick off womenknow better.com's first shareholder meeting.

But that's where we were at one o'clock, in the ballroom preparing to introduce members to the Web site's founder. Me.

As much effort as I'd put into the database, I put even more into the shareholder meeting. Because once I stood at the podium and explained how the site worked, there were no passwords to protect me, no black screens I could hide behind. That's why Claudia and I devised the next best thing. A rigorous check-in process that required each member to show ID at the door along with her member number.

"I can't wait for this to be over," I told Claudia as we stood to the side and watched members check in.

"It will be soon enough," a voice called out, and we turned to find Maggie standing behind us.

"What are you doing here? I thought you left after the tea."

"I may not agree with what you're doing, but I'm here to support you. Besides"—she handed me a gorgeous arrangement of magenta and pink peonies clustered in a low vase—"I thought these would look nice on the podium."

"How'd you get past the check-in table? Your name wasn't on the list."

"I told them I was your best friend."

"And they let you in? Not exactly the most stringent security going, is it?"

"Actually, I think these did more for my cause than our friendship." Maggie held up the shiny metal pruning shears she kept in her purse. "Who's going to argue with a woman carrying these?"

Claudia checked her watch and gave me the signal. "It's time. Let's go."

I took the arrangement from Maggie. "Thanks."

"Good luck!" she said.

"Thanks. I'll need it."

Up on the podium I looked out at the women who wanted me to be right, who *needed* me to be right. They wanted to believe that the woman behind the black home page, the person approving passwords and developing indexes and graphs and charting data points, had figured it out. But I wasn't nearly as stout as the wizard behind the curtain, and there were no levers or pulleys, no deep voice of authority booming over the speaker. There was just me up at a podium, getting ready to address my members. And I was someone a lot like them, someone who hoped a database had all the answers.

It took me all of five minutes to read my speech, and in the end Veronica got exactly what she wanted: full disclosure about how the service worked. A few members were surprised that it was just me, someone like them, and not a division of one of the big dating Web sites looking to branch out. But all in all, there was no mass exodus, not a single request for a refund. I even seemed to have gained a few fans.

"I just wanted to tell you how great it's been being a member." A redhead was waiting beside the stage, holding out her hand and waiting for me to shake it. "When my friend referred me, I was so excited—only I couldn't tell anyone! This is the closest I've come to being in a sorority."

"I'm glad it's been helpful," I answered, and shook her hand.

"My name is—"

I cut her off before she could tell me. "I don't need to know, really. The idea here is that we're all anonymous—or at least we used to be."

"Well, I'm your most satisfied customer; I can just about guarantee that. I don't make a move anymore without logging on first to see what the deal is with a guy. I've cut my dating in half, but the ones I go on are so much better. I know exactly what to expect. I know what he's going to dress like, his favorite restaurant, what he'll order when we sit down. Nothing's left to chance anymore."

She smiled a big, toothy grin, even though what she'd just described didn't sound all that great once she put it like that. Knowing everything there is to know about a person. Never being surprised. The redhead seemed happy about it, though.

"The last date I went on I even knew he was going to take a bottle of Purell out of his pocket and rinse his hands after he paid the cab driver."

Too much information. Maybe there was such a thing.

My most satisfied customer went on to regale me with stories of her most successful dates, but I'd stopped listening. Maggie was across the room talking with a group of women. After a minute she grabbed the arm of a blonde to her left and laughed so hard I thought she was going to take the woman down to the ground. Maybe the women had convinced Maggie that this wasn't such a bad idea after all. Maybe she'd finally understand why I was doing this, even if she couldn't understand why I'd fabricate Mitch's data.

"I've blown off three guys in the past two weeks," the redhead boasted. "And it's all because of what I learned on womenknowbetter .com."

"I don't know that blowing off men was exactly what I had in mind when I started the site, but, well, if that's what works for you," I started to tell the redhead, when suddenly a hand grabbed my shoulder and spun me around. "We need to go after Maggie."

"What do you mean, we need to go after her?" I asked Claudia. "Where'd she go?"

"She ran out."

"But she was just over there laughing." I pointed to the spot where the blonde now stood talking to another woman.

"Well, she wasn't laughing when she left. That woman she was talking to—she's Curtis's ex-wife."

The blonde was Curtis's ex-wife? The attractive woman covering her mouth so a stuffed mushroom wouldn't go flying out as she laughed—that was the arch bitch Maggie's boyfriend had married?

"I've got to go," I told the redhead. "It was nice meeting you."

I grabbed Claudia's hand and together we went to find our friend.

The Flower Carte was only a few blocks away, and as long as Maggie was running instead of hopping in a cab, it was the logical first stop.

A CLOSED sign hung limply in the window, but there was a light on inside, and we could see Maggie sitting at the small wrought-iron garden table, a glass of wine in her hand.

"Should we knock?" I asked, and not a second later Claudia was rapping on the glass door.

Maggie looked up at the noise, but she didn't move. Instead she waved a hand at us, the universal sign for *Go the hell away.*

"We're not going anywhere," Claudia shouted, cupping her hands around her mouth so Maggie could hear us through the glass. "You may as well let us in."

Maggie swirled the red wine in the bottom of her glass like someone evaluating the bouquet, and then downed the remaining liquid like someone who needed to get drunk.

"Let us in," I called, and slapped my own hand against the glass. "We can stand here all night if we have to."

Maggie placed the glass on the table, grabbed the neck of the wine bottle and came over to let us in.

"What happened?" Claudia asked.

Maggie was already on her way back to the table. "I told you. I just met Curtis's lovely ex-wife." This time she didn't bother filling the glass and instead drank straight from the bottle.

"I'm so sorry." I reached for Maggie's hand, but she pulled it away.

"He lied. He fucking lied to me."

"I didn't want to be right."

The wine bottle came down hard on the table, knocking the empty wineglass on its side. "You weren't right, Abby! God, why is that all you care about?"

If I wasn't right about Curtis having some hidden flaws that Maggie should discover sooner rather than later, then what was the problem here? I obviously was not understanding the situation.

"So, then, what's wrong?"

"What's wrong, *Abby*"—she spoke my name with about as much contempt as she could muster given that she was talking into the open end of a near-empty wine bottle—"is that she was nice. She wasn't some arch bitch. She was sweet and poised and funny—the woman was funny! I was laughing with her!"

"That's a good thing, right?" Claudia asked, and Maggie let out an exasperated sigh.

"No! It is not a good thing. You know what she was telling me? How hard it's been on her ex-husband since she left him—she left him! Not the other way around. He didn't leave her because she was a bitch; she left him! All along he was telling me how horrible this woman was, how miserable she made him, how she made his life hell—and I felt bad for him. Poor Curtis with the mean ex-wife. Why'd he have to do that? Why couldn't he just say she was this nice, smart, articulate woman who just happened to leave his ass?"

"Maybe he was embarrassed," I suggested. "Maybe he thought you'd think he was a loser."

"I guess if anyone would know about a liar, it would be a liar, right, Abby?" Maggie narrowed her eyes at me in what was obviously supposed to be a menacing look but, due to the merlot mustache along her upper lip, only made her look ridiculous.

"What is going on here?" Claudia asked, standing between us.

Maggie had the opening she'd been waiting for. "Abby's been populating the database with lies about Mitch so no one else will date him."

"Look, we're not here to talk about me," I told Claudia. "I'm not the one who ran out of the Four Seasons like a crazy person."

"I'd be very interested to see what Mitch would think of all this," Maggie continued, ignoring me. "What would he do if he got a little glance at your profile, Abby?"

The store fell silent, the only noise coming from the fan behind the refrigerated cooler.

I couldn't even look at Maggie and instead watched as the little wine left in the overturned glass dribbled out onto the wrought-iron table and fell onto the tiled floor below.

"Is there another bottle of wine somewhere?" Claudia wanted to know. Obviously we were going to need it.

Maggie pointed back toward her office.

"That's not fair," I said.

"Yeah, well life isn't fair, Abby. Only you think running an algorithm or a regression analysis or whatever the hell it is you're doing will change all that."

"I don't need to listen to this," I told her. "I came after you because I felt bad about Curtis."

"You feel bad for me? What I just experienced will be nothing compared to what's going to happen when Mitch finds out what you've been doing." Maggie stood up, grabbed a pair of shears and started snipping violently at a miniature rosebush. "Do you really think that the women there today won't tell anyone?"

Mini red rosebuds and green foliage flew across the floor tiles as Maggie whittled away.

"It's only a matter of time before Mitch hears it from someone, Abby. You better make sure it's you."

As much as I wished Edward Scissorhands over there wasn't right, I knew she was. I had to tell Mitch about the Web site before he found out from anyone else. I owed it to him. I only hoped that my status as a Fast Lane pass holder would make up for this, too.

chapter twenty-three

On Friday I was late. And Mitch was early. And that added up to one very drunk man waiting for me at the bar.

"Want to get a table?" I suggested. "You look hungry." Actually, he looked bombed, but hungry came in a close second.

"You know, Abby, I just don't get it. What the hell is wrong with me? I mean, do I smell?" He lifted his arm and stuck his nose right into his armpit. "See, I'm fine—smells like Speed Stick. Here." He moved over so I could partake in the fresh scent myself.

"Why don't we get a table and talk about it." I placed my hand on his arm and tried to get him to move away from the bar, but Mitch wasn't moving.

"It just doesn't make sense," he continued, and then reached across the bar and tapped a guy on the shoulder. "Mind sharing a Marlboro?"

"It's illegal to smoke in bars now," I reminded him. "Besides, Mitch, you don't smoke."

"I don't do a lot of things. For instance, I don't gamble. And I'm not a cross-dresser, either, but for some reason that's what women seem to think."

Suddenly, Mitch stood up. So suddenly, he had to catch his balance by grabbing onto the head of the guy standing next to him like a banister. "There she is! Hey!" he screamed toward someone I couldn't even see through the crowd.

"That's her," he told me. "That's the woman who blew me off last week without a phone call or anything. Nothing."

Dealing with a drunk Mitch was not part of the plan. We were supposed to sit down to a lovely meal, during which I'd explain ever so cleverly how my new career change had resulted in a slowdown for his social life. Or something like that. The term *computer glitch* might come up once or twenty times if things didn't seem to be going my way.

Mitch kneeled on the stool, trying to get the woman to notice him. "Hey, you! Over here!"

I reached out to pull Mitch down, to tell him that yelling *Hey, you* at a woman wasn't the best way to get her attention, but I was too late. He'd already jumped off the seat, pushed the stool aside and disappeared into the crowd.

"Abby!" A voice called my name from the far end of the bar. When I turned around, there was Sarah, standing next to Jason and a few other portfolio managers and analysts clustered together. She held up a finger indicating she'd be a minute, and then ordered a drink from the bartender.

I waved, then quickly turned my attention back to the crowd in hopes Mitch hadn't been swallowed up.

And that's when I saw Mitch coming toward me, and he was leading a woman by her elbow. Not just the woman Mitch had asked out a month ago. Not simply the woman who didn't return his call and never provided an explanation after he left numerous voice mails.

No.

It was the none other than womenknowbetter.com's most satisfied customer.

"Tell her, Abby," Mitch demanded when he reached me. "Tell her I'm not a bad guy. Tell her she could have just told me she didn't want to go out for dinner. I'm a big boy; I can take it."

And all I could think was *Oh. My. God.* Only I'd renounced God in tenth grade when being an atheist seemed a lot more convenient than going to five o'clock mass with my mom. And this was where I got my payback for pretending to be asleep so she wouldn't make me go. God was getting even with me. And it was too late to change his mind.

The woman looked from me to Mitch, and Mitch to me, like this was some sort of joke.

"I don't get it," she said, feigning a laugh that didn't fool any of us. "What's going on?"

"Mitch, let her go; we need to talk." I tried to release his grip on her elbow, but he pushed me away.

"Just tell her, will you?" Mitch implored, his eyes wide and pleading with me. "Tell her I'm not an asshole."

"He's not an asshole," I told her, and meant it. "He's a really good guy."

"Thanks, Abby." Mitch loosened his grip and smiled at me. "I really appreciate that."

"This is too weird," the redhead told us, finally shaking her elbow loose.

"Just tell me why," Mitch demanded of her. "Why'd you blow me off?"

The woman held out a perfectly red nail that matched her perfectly red hair and pointed it matter-of-factly at my thumping chest. "Her."

"Abby!" Sarah was now standing next to me holding a beer in one hand and an introduction in the other. She pushed her way between Mitch and the redhead. "Abby, this is Duncan; Duncan, this is Abby." *White French tulips,* she mouthed behind his back.

Before I could say *Nice to meet you* or *Abby who? My name is Mildred*, Sarah pulled another arm through the crowd until the entire body stood facing me.

"And this is Chris Collins; he's the new analyst replacing you."

I looked up at the familiar blond hair, the perfectly straight nose with the prep-school attitude, and said the first thing I could think of: "I have to go."

Chris Collins. So that was his name.

"Where the hell are you going?" Mitch yelled, pushing Chris Collins aside. "And what the hell are you talking about?" he asked the redhead before pointing to me. "Do you know Abby?"

It didn't take very long for my most satisfied member to spill the beans to Mitch, which just goes to prove that maybe the only thing more exciting than keeping a secret is being the one who lets the cat out of the bag. In public. Where sixty people, including a guy named Chris Collins, can witness one very freaked-out woman attempting to slink away from one very irate man, and all the obscenities such a scene requires.

The only thing missing from this train wreck was a conductor in a striped hat calling *All aboard*.

Needless to say, Mitch didn't take the news very well. He didn't appreciate the irony that *this* woman would choose to visit *this* bar on exactly *this* night, the night I was going to tell him the truth. And it was ironic, no? I mean, sure, he probably would have been pissed when I told him that all those women weren't exactly rejecting Mitch the Guy so much as they were rejecting Mitch the Freaky Dude in the Database I'd Created to Scare Them Off. Quite successfully, too. But it turns out the best way to scare off a man is to reveal yourself as the crazy psycho chick who started an underground service to share information on guys.

"You?" Mitch looked around like he was waiting for someone to tell him this was all a big mistake. "You were telling people not to go out with me?"

"Well, not *telling* them, really," I started to explain. "It was all in a database."

"So the service was all a bunch of lies?" interrupted the redhead, whose name I still didn't know.

"I can't believe it was you," Sarah muttered, only I couldn't hear her above Mitch's next round of questions, so I had to read her lips.

"How could you do that to me?" Mitch was asking, his disbelief almost palpable. "What'd I ever do to you?"

I was surrounded by people with questions, people who had just discovered I wasn't exactly who they thought I was—the benevolent Web site founder, the coworker who couldn't stomach the unpredictable, the woman who'd cheat on her husband, the friend who turned out to be someone else entirely. And it was the person I knew Mitch saw that wrenched my stomach. Because the friend he'd thought was on his side, the woman who saw beyond the fields on a database to the good guy standing before her, that was who I wanted to be— even if she'd done some things in the past that she wasn't exactly proud of.

It had all started because I wanted answers. I wanted explanations. I wanted penance. Only sometimes even having the answer doesn't change anything; it doesn't make everything all right. Sometimes the answer is so unpalatable, so unpleasant and painful, it's easier to just walk away.

Maggie was right. Karma is a bitch.

There was no use trying to answer Mitch. Or the redhead. Or Sarah.

So instead I apologized. Again and again.

"I'm sorry," I told Mitch. "I'm so, so sorry."

As I pushed my way through the crowd, I looked back one last time at the people I'd left in my wake—one irate data point, one pissed member, one thoroughly confused former coworker, a guy who sent French tulips and Chris Collins. I might not have remembered his name, but at least I got the alliteration part right.

chapter twenty-four

speed walked a block and then hailed a cab home. "Can you turn up the music, please?" I requested from the backseat, and the cabbie obliged.

Noise. It was the only way I could think of to drown out the conversation in my head. I could already hear what transpired after my hasty exit.

Sarah to Mitch: *How do you know Abby?*
Mitch to Sarah: *She's the* [insert appropriate expletive here] *who's been telling everyone I'm a* [insert appropriate expletive here].
Mitch to Chris: *How do you know Abby?*
Chris: *I fucked her last year in New York.*

"Louder," I shouted to the cab driver, and then hunkered down in the backseat, closed my eyes and tried to think happy pine-scented thoughts while listening to Yanni.

"So, what happened?" We'd decided to meet at Maggie's store first thing the next morning. Claudia's office was obviously not the place to discuss last night, and the thought of being in the same room as the computer that had taken on a life of its own gave me the cold sweats. It had become my own personal Pandora's box.

Even though the CLOSED sign was still hanging in the window when I showed up, Maggie and Claudia were inside waiting for me.

"Ever see *Titanic*?"

"That bad?" Claudia handed me a cup of tea.

"Worse. At least in *Titanic* the girl got some jewelry."

"Well, what did you expect? That Mitch would laugh it off, congratulate you for really pulling one over on him?"

"Oh, and Mitch yelling at me isn't even the best part of the night."

"It gets better? What'd he do, get you in a headlock and give you noogies?"

"*He* was there."

"He who?" Maggie looked from me to Claudia. "Who is he?"

I felt like the fat man who finally got tired of sucking in his gut and lets it all hang out. "He is the man I slept with right before Alex and I separated."

Maggie sat there watching me, her mouth open and a cranberry scone poised in her hand.

"And yet, it gets better!"

"What? Somebody jumped out and announced that you were on *Candid Camera*?"

"Are you ready?" I shook my head and let out a sad, pathetic excuse for a laugh. "I don't know if I should be humiliated by this or relieved. The guy didn't remember me!"

"No!" they shouted in unison.

"Oh, yeah. Apparently he had no idea who I was. Sarah called me when I got home and when I asked if Chris—that's him name, Chris Collins—had anything to say, she had no idea what I was talking about. Apparently he thought I was just some crazed woman fighting with her boyfriend."

Chris Collins had no idea who I was. None. To him I was simply the woman who had occupied his new office for four years. And yet to me, he was a culmination.

"OK, enough with the tea." Claudia stood up and took my cup off the table. "Where's the booze? The flower cooler out back?"

"It's ten o'clock in the morning," Maggie pointed out, but she also pointed the way for Claudia, who returned holding a bottle of champagne and a carton of Tropicana.

"Mimosas, anyone?"

Maggie reached over and handed Claudia a vase. "Use this to mix them; I don't have any pitchers. Or champagne glasses, for that matter."

Luckily, Maggie did have the ability to improvise, and five minutes later the three of us were drinking mimosas out of blue-tinted bud vases. It reminded me so much of that night, more than a year ago, when I'd sent them an SOS for help. And they deserved to know the truth.

"Alex wasn't seeing anyone else when he left me," I told them, and then took a long sip of my mimosa before adding a final, "He never cheated on me."

Maggie's eyes slid in Claudia's direction, then back to me. "We know."

"You know?"

"Well, we didn't know for sure, but we didn't think he did."

"So, why'd you let me believe that you thought he was a cheating prick?"

"Because it seemed to help and we didn't see any harm in it at the time."

"You knew all along?"

They both nodded.

"Well, if you're so smart, tell me what I should do about Mitch."

"If I'm so smart, I'd know what to do about Curtis." Maggie reached to refill her bud vase. "He keeps calling me, wanting to explain, asking for me to just listen to him. Am I supposed to just forget that he lied to me?"

"He didn't lie to you," I told her, and she stopped midpour to roll her eyes at me.

"Okay, so he lied. But in the grand scheme of things, it wasn't the worst thing in the world. And you like him. So give him the benefit of the doubt."

Maggie frowned. "This sage advice from a woman who thought a database was the cure-all for a broken heart."

"Can you at least tell us his name now? If he's going to be on our shit list, at least we should know his last name."

"McWilliams," she conceded. "Curtis McWilliams."

"I have some news," Claudia announced, sitting up straight and raising her bud vase in a toast. "I was offered tenure."

"That's fantastic." I reached across the table and hugged her. "Congratulations."

"We never doubted you for a minute," Maggie added.

Claudia gave us a weak smile. "Thanks."

"What's the problem?" I asked. "You have exactly what you wanted; shouldn't you be happy?"

"Well, I was happy," Claudia started to explain. "And then it occurred to me."

"What occurred to you?"

"That I had tenure. I really had it. I proved I could do it. Only, now what?" Claudia asked.

I proved I could do it, too. I proved I wouldn't let Alex leave me for no reason at all. I proved I could act like I didn't care.

"Now what?" I repeated.

"Yeah, now what the hell do I look forward to every day?"

"Shouldn't a thirty-one-year-old with freckles be a little more care-free? Why don't you learn to jump rope or skip rocks or make those macramé friendship bracelets?" Maggie teased.

"I always wished I knew how to make those," I told them. "All I could ever do was braid."

They both looked at me, and I knew I wasn't helping the situation.

"Why don't you just start working toward something else?" I suggested.

"Like what?"

"You are asking the wrong person. Did you not just hear me tell you that the database has fucked up my life? That after word gets out that I was inputting false data, I won't have a single member paying their monthly dues? I don't think I'm someone you should be asking for help."

"I was just asking for advice," Claudia said. "I didn't say I'd follow it."

"You can always go work with Elliott," Maggie suggested. "He'd have you in a minute."

She was right, of course. I just wasn't sure I was ready to take the leap, to be the person who took the risk on the small chance it would pay off. It was so much easier to be the analyst who evaluates the facts and then hands it over to someone else to decide what to do. As far as my ability to make good decisions, I didn't think what happened last night with Mitch would instill a lot of confidence in Elliott.

"I just want to be over it. I want to be over everything that's happened in the past year."

"I thought you were," Maggie said.

Even I rolled my eyes at that. "I just want to move on. It's time."

"Okay, we thought *you* thought you were over it."

I didn't just *want* to be over it—I was ready, too. Really ready. My experience with Alex had changed me, but I didn't have to let that be a bad thing. It didn't have to be a good thing, either. There didn't have to be a silver lining to all this, a pot of gold at the end of the rainbow. Maybe it just made me into the person I was meant to be. Maybe I was better off for it. Because right now, if I had a chance to go back and make things turn out differently, it wasn't my marriage I'd salvage.

"I must be one hell of an actress," I told them.

Maggie disagreed. "Actually, you suck. We're just really good friends."

chapter twenty-five

loved *Laverne and Shirley*. I even renamed my Ken doll the Big Ragu. Tuesday was my favorite night of the week because my mom and I would lie on the couch and watch Laverne and Shirley's latest escapades, my head on her lap as she stroked my hair and tucked wispy strands behind my ears. I always felt sorry for my friends who had to share toys with their brothers, or got stuck wearing hand-me-downs from older sisters. I had my parents all to myself for the first thirteen years of my life, and I didn't want it any other way.

But when my parents told me they were getting divorced, I felt outnumbered for the first time. It was two against one. In the equation that was our family, there was a huge less-than arrow pointed in my direction. Maybe if there'd been a brother or a sister it would have been harder to end it. Maybe my father would have tried to stick it out, or my mother would have fought harder to make him stay. As it was, with just one kid, it seemed too easy for him to walk away.

I once told Maggie and Claudia that I didn't cry when my parents broke the news, and they didn't believe me. And as much as I'd insisted they were wrong, they were right. It was simply a matter of definition.

For so long I'd thought that if nobody saw the tears, if nobody saw the pain, it didn't exist.

But I did cry, into my pillow at night, my head buried deep inside the open ends of the pillowcase, pressing my face into the soggy foam filling. Why I thought the extra layer of floral cotton made a difference is beyond me. I only know that this way my parents would never see the water marks my tears left on my pillowcase. It didn't occur to me until much later, after we'd moved out of our house, that my mother changed my sheets on my bed and there was no way she could miss the darkened stains on my pillow.

Sylvia Bartlett wasn't my first therapist. After they made the announcement, my parents had hugged me and explained that there was a woman, Ms. Castagno, who I could talk to if I wanted.

But I didn't need Ms. Castagno; I had DeBeers commercials, and they taught me all I needed to know—a diamond may be forever, but love doesn't last.

"So, what do you think?" My mom patted down the satin A-line skirt, careful not to ruffle the floor-length hem that the seamstress was currently pinning into place. "Do you like it?"

I thought she'd decided on the pearly gray dress that afternoon we were shopping. But I was obviously wrong. "It's white."

"Well, more like off-white. A creamy ivory. What do you call this?" she asked the seamstress kneeling on the floor.

"Sand," she mumbled through lips that remained clenched around a straight pin.

"It's beautiful," I told my mom, and reached over to lay a hand against the simple band of alençon lace around her waist. "And I like the way it shows off your shoulders."

"So you approve?"

"Completely. I guess I just wasn't expecting you to wear white."

"Sand," the seamstress corrected.

"Sand," my mom repeated, and winked at me. "I just loved it and figured, why not, you only get married once, right?"

I laughed and my mom did, too, as soon as she realized what she'd said. "Let's change that to *You only stay married once.* Does that work?"

"Yes, that works."

When the seamstress finished pinning the sides of the bodice into place, my mom spun around the dressing-area platform as if on a pedestal. She looked amazing—from every angle, if the images reflected on the walls in three-by-three mirrored panels were any indication.

Next week my mother would be married to Roger. In eight days my mom would take a new last name and for the first time she and I would no longer share Dunn. And before that happened, there was something I needed to know.

"Here, let me help." I extended my hand and guided my mother off the platform. She held the hair off her neck as I carefully pulled the zipper down her back, the wiry gray strands coming loose from her grasp and falling against her freckled shoulders. The brown spots dotted her back and I attempted to make sense of them, like I used to when my dad would point to the starry sky over the ocean and call out constellations I couldn't quite make out. All those summers going to the Cape with my dad and me had left their indelible mark on my mother, only instead of standing out they simply became part of who she was.

"Do you know why Dad left?" I asked, and my mom let her hair fall around her face and turned around to look at me.

"That was ages ago, Abby."

"So you don't remember?"

"So it doesn't matter."

"I know it doesn't," I agreed. "But it does. To me. I'd just like to understand."

"Why?" she asked, turning around again and letting me help her step out of the dress.

"Because maybe if I understand why Dad left, I'll understand why Alex left, too."

My mother stood there in a strapless bra and a white slip shaking her head at me. "It's not going to bring him back, Abby. Is that what you want?"

I shook my head. "No," I told her. "I can honestly say that now." I said it again, just because it felt so good to mean it. "I don't want Alex."

"Then why?"

Losing Alex was easy, almost effortless. We never looked into each other's eyes and said it out loud—*You're not making me happy*. I know, no one can *make* you happy. I've read Stephen Covey, done the *Cosmo* quizzes, been to Oprah.com. Maybe what I really meant was that neither of us spoke the truth—*I'm not happier with you than I was alone. In fact, loving you is harder.* I took the easy way out by letting him go.

"Because if I understood, then maybe it won't happen again."

"I don't think having an answer will change that, but I'm not the one you need to ask."

I knew she was right.

"Why'd you wait so long to say yes to Roger?" I asked.

"I guess I never thought it was necessary." She slipped into her clothes and sat down on the platform in the center of the room. "Things were good between us the way they were."

"So it wasn't because you were afraid of making another mistake?" The first mistake, of course, being my father.

"Your dad wasn't a mistake, Abby. The only mistake was not dealing with our problems before they became so big we couldn't see past them." She patted the platform and I sat down beside her. "Is that what you thought? That I was *afraid* to say yes?"

"Maybe not afraid; maybe a little leery?"

"Maybe. Probably the first time he asked, I'll give you that," she admitted. "But at that point I didn't expect to ever get remarried. I figured I'd had my chance."

"So why now? Why'd you say yes?"

"I just couldn't imagine saying no." She bit her lip and distorted a smile that made its way all the way up to her eyes. "I finally realized that we get more than one chance, and I didn't want to miss mine."

She didn't have to elaborate. I understood completely. Because I didn't want to miss mine either.

"I did something completely stupid," I said, and then before I could stop myself, I was crying on my mother's shoulder. Crying the way I should have cried when my family fell apart, sobbing the way people are supposed to sob when the dream they'd had for their marriage shatters and they realize they were the one who cast the first stone.

I told her everything, about cheating on Alex and making the database and Mitch, how I'd lied to him and how now he wouldn't even take my phone calls.

The tears fell fast and furious, soaking my mother's shirt as she rubbed my head and pulled me close.

Wasn't love supposed to make you feel perfect? That's what I always thought. But the only thing Alex's love did was make me feel more flawed, a defective woman who could be returned without a receipt for store credit. I never believed he could love me the way I loved him.

I didn't know how to keep a marriage together because I'd been preparing to get divorced my entire life. It was the only way I could be the one who decided what would happen, the only way to avoid getting hurt. To be the one who inflicted the pain, or at the very least, became impenetrable to it.

Even the remains of what I once felt I had are hard to let go, and I'm not really talking about Alex and me here. Just me. It's hard to let go of the idea that there was no way that I, the shitty Abby, who'd cheat on her husband, the one who could keep secrets and who has a left breast that's slightly smaller than her right (and a right breast with a nipple growing a long blond hair, no less) could be loved just because I'm lovable. Maybe there is something that's better than being right. And that's allowing yourself to be loved even if love itself is no guarantee that love will treat you right.

Whatever Alex could have done, it would never have been enough. Never enough to convince me it wouldn't end someday. That one day he wouldn't walk in and discover me lathering blueberry-scented Nair in the crack of my ass, and that would be the end of it. I asked more from our relationship than it could possibly deliver. I never trusted myself and, as a result, I never let myself trust Alex. That, ultimately, was what I'd missed out on: not discovering what we could have been together, but discovering who I could have become. It wasn't Alex I needed to have faith in. It was me.

Is it possible to believe in something and still fail to live up to it? Because I believed I loved Alex. And it was love; that I'm sure of. I'll go to my grave believing that in the deepest place inside me. But it stopped being love and transformed into something else. And toward the end, there was no denying what it was. Plain and simple. It was fear.

"How did I get here?" I sniffled, and my mom dabbed at my eyes with her sleeve.

"The T?" she answered, and despite myself I smiled. "A cab?"

"Actually," I told her, "I drove."

chapter twenty-six

"What did you do, kiddo?" Elliott asked.

For a minute I thought it might be Mitch calling, that he'd finally decided to return the eleven messages I'd left on his voice mail.

"Did Mitch call you?" I laid facedown on my couch and waited for it to swallow me up.

"He did. Is it true?"

I had no idea what Mitch told him, but I couldn't imagine he had to stretch the truth to make it sound bad. I didn't believe it could get worse than it was.

"It's true." I reached under the cushion and felt around for stray Doritos and Cheez Doodles. As long as I was lying there, I figured I may as well clean.

"Jesus, Abby, what were you thinking?" I heard Caroline in the background playing with her Barbie laptop.

"That's the million-dollar question, Elliott, isn't it?"

"Well, I sure as hell hope you're going to fix this."

"I tried. He wants nothing to do with me." I dug my hand farther down into the couch until I hit something hard and round, and then I pulled out a heads-up penny. "I want to fix this, but what else can I do?"

"How should I know?" he answered. "I can't even work an iPod."

"So are you going to tell me what he told you?" I asked. "Or do I not want to even know?"

"Why don't you come over and we can talk about it. I have the Van Morrison all cued up and ready to go."

I stuffed my new lucky penny in my shorts pocket and told him I was on my way.

I was the first person to know that Elliott was leaving Verity. He asked me to lunch on a Tuesday and told me he'd decided to start his own hedge fund.

"You can't just leave," I'd told him. "People spend their entire careers trying to get where you are."

"Then let them have my job," Elliott replied, and then grabbed his knife and pretended to plant it into the tablecloth like a flag. "I'm striking out on my own."

I still didn't think he was serious. "Oh, really?"

"Really. And I'd like to take you with me."

Now, Elliott Cohen asking you to go work for him is like George Steinbrenner asking whether you ever considered wearing a Yankee uniform (very bad analogy for someone who lives in Boston, but it serves my point). Most people who know anything would jump at the offer. But I can't hit a curveball, and I certainly wasn't about to try.

"No way. Do you have any idea how many hedge funds fold each year?" At the time I didn't really have any idea, so, being the researcher I was, I went back to the office and looked it up. And the answer was *a lot*. "The odds of this working out are like a billion to one." They're not, I learned; more like two to one.

"I'm fifty-nine years old," he told me. "What have I got to lose?"

His house, his car, his retirement, his reputation. Did I need to go on?

I picked up the menu and started reading the specials. "I can't do it; I'm sorry."

Elliott picked up his own menu and shrugged as if he'd given it his best shot and now it was time to chow down. "Well, if you ever decide you're willing to take the chance, just let me know."

I found Elliott and Caroline down by the tennis court. In tennis whites! Elliot was actually dressed to play.

"What's with the white shorts?" I asked, walking out to the net just as Elliott smacked a forehand into it.

"Caroline decided she wants to learn to play." Elliott wiped his forehead with the sweatband around his wrist and came over to me. "I'm not the best person to do this, you know."

"You have the outfit."

"I figured I had to start somewhere. Buying the clothes was the easy part; getting the ball over the net, not so easy."

"Hey, Caroline," I called out. She stopped bouncing the ball on the baseline and looked up at me. "What do you say you and I take on your dad?"

"Yeah!" she shrieked, and jumped up and down until her ponytails followed her lead. "Get the extra racket out of the pool house."

"Is that okay?" I asked Elliott. "You both look like you can use the help."

"Great idea," Elliott agreed, "only there's no way we can play a game. You'll kill me."

"We don't have to keep score, nobody has to win. Let's just volley."

"Won't you get bored?"

"I think I'll be just fine," I told him, and then, before I could chicken out, I added, "So, I hear you're hiring, and, lucky you, I just happen to be in the market for a job."

"Are you doing this because you've exhausted all other possibilities?" he wanted to know. "Am I your last resort?"

"Nope. I'm just ready," I said. "I can't promise I'll always pick a winner or that I'll increase your returns every time."

"Me neither," he agreed. "But that's the nice thing about it. You don't have to be right every time. Just when it counts."

"So does that mean I have a job?"

Elliott laughed. "See you on Tuesday."

I smiled to myself and turned to get the racket from the pool house when Elliott said my name. "And Abby?"

"Yeah?"

"You might want to bring breakfast for the boss. I hear he's an eccentric old man who likes sesame bagels with chive cream cheese."

"Got it."

I don't know when I decided to tell Elliott I was ready; maybe on the drive over or maybe after drowning my mother in the dressing room after her fitting. Whenever it was, I'd realized that sometimes you need to go out on a limb even if the odds are against you. Because after a while, you just have to take that chance. You have to just believe that a heads-up penny means more than that you're a horrible housekeeper. It just may mean you're ready for some good luck.

chapter twenty-seven

took my mom's advice and invited my dad to lunch. We picked a place downtown and made plans to meet at one o'clock, after the lunch rush. We had a lot to talk about and I didn't want some hostess giving me the evil eye because we were holding up a table for two. After what happened that night at the bar, I also didn't want to run into anyone from Verity. I was sure Chris Collins had filled everyone in on the psychopath who used to occupy his office.

We were seated along the front window, and I picked the chair facing the sidewalk. It felt like ages since I worked downtown, and I wanted to see the people rushing by on their way to meetings, testing myself to see whether I missed the security of working in a glass high-rise where all I had to do was provide information and let other people decide what to do with it. And while my dad and I talked about our summers and the week he and Susan just spent with her sister in Washington, DC, I can honestly say I didn't miss it at all. Well, maybe just a tiny bit.

My membership had already begun declining and was down to half of the number I had registered when I held the shareholder meeting. That whole thing about one member referring a friend and that person referring a friend, and so on and so on? Well, it worked in reverse, too. In a few days womenknowbetter.com would probably be history.

"I'm stuffed, but do you want dessert?" my dad asked after our plates were cleared away.

"I'll have a piece of cheesecake, please," I told the waitress, and then looked over at my dad, who had never seen a cheesecake he didn't like. "With two forks."

When the waitress brought out the cheesecake, we both wielded our utensils and set about making our way down to the graham cracker crust. "You never eat the crust, do you?" I pointed out.

"And neither do you," he answered.

"I wanted to ask you a question before we leave," I started, and then pushed the plate to the edge of the table so there was nothing standing between us. "I wanted to know why you left."

My dad pulled the plate toward him and tapped his fork against the crust until there was nothing left but crumbs floating in strawberry sauce.

"Abby, I would never condone what I did, but I also can't live my life punishing myself," he told me before answering my question. "I left because I didn't know any other way to fix it. Your mom didn't know how to fix it either."

I swallowed hard and waited for the lump to form in my throat. "But she wanted to."

He tipped his head in a way that meant *Maybe, maybe not.*

"I made a mistake, but probably not the one you think I made."

Swallow, swallow. "And what would that be?"

"You think I had an affair and left you and your mom for Susan."

Give the man a cigar. "So what was your real mistake?"

"My real mistake was falling out of love with your mom and not realizing it until too late. I know everyone says life isn't fair, but it wasn't fair, to your mom or me, to be in a marriage like that. It wasn't fair to you. I wanted you to grow up knowing what it's like to love someone, Abby."

Funny, I wanted to grow up to know what it was like to be loved. "Alex wasn't fair."

"Were you fair to him?" he asked.

I didn't answer.

"I stayed because I didn't want to leave you," my dad continued. "I didn't want to be one of those men who leaves. So I stayed too long."

"Are you're telling me that your mistake was that you didn't leave sooner?"

"My mistake was not leaving when I could have explained it to you, before it became too complicated."

"You mean before you fell in love with Susan."

He nodded. "Look, Abby. I'm not perfect, but I've always loved you."

"I know that," I told him, and I did.

"I loved your mom for a long time, Abby. And then I didn't," he admitted. "But don't be afraid of making my mistake. You're not me."

I shook my head no. Not because I wasn't afraid of making his mistake, but because I was afraid of making my own.

"I loved Alex." Once I said it I realized I'd used the past tense. I *loved* Alex. And I did. But I didn't anymore. And maybe that's what really sucked. That in the end my mom and dad ended up with different people. That in the end, maybe I'd end up with someone besides Alex. Because I could no longer end up with him. Love isn't enough for very long. Maybe in the beginning, but not for the long haul. Maybe that's why it had taken me so long to get over him, so long to allow myself to get over him. Because I thought that if I got over it quickly and painlessly, it would have meant it had never really mattered. So I wanted it to hurt, to be painful, as if somehow that proved it was real.

Maybe Alex just wanted to be happy. And maybe, because even on some level I'd like to believe he still remembered the person he fell in love with, he actually wanted me to be happy. And maybe that's all there is to it. He knew that the only way for us to find happiness was to do it on our own.

"If today was a color, which one would it be?" I asked my dad after the waitress placed the check on our table.

He rubbed his chin and thought for a moment. "Pink. What about you?"

"Green."

"And why is that?"

I pointed over his left shoulder toward the street. "Because that's the color of the Love Bug that's parked right outside the window."

chapter twenty-eight

My dad picked up the tab, which was a nice gesture and totally appreciated considering I'd spent a bunch of money on a Web site and database that were losing members by the minute.

"Is there anything you want me to tell Mom?" I asked as we stood on the sidewalk waiting to say good-bye.

He shook is head and I realized that it wasn't his place any longer. It hadn't been for a long time. "You just enjoy yourself," he told me, and leaned in to kiss me on the cheek. Instead of letting him step back away from me, I reached for his hand and pulled him toward me again, wrapping my arms around him as tight as I could get them. And instead of waiting to see whether he'd hug me back, or thinking about whether he was ready to let go, I squeezed my eyes shut and held on.

"Back to work?" I asked when my grip finally loosened and we pulled apart.

"Back to work," he told me. "Have fun on the Vineyard. I'll be thinking of you."

I stood there on the sidewalk and watched my father walk away down the street until I lost him in the dwindling lunchtime crowd.

I had turned to walk the other way, toward home, when I saw him, no more than twenty yards away on the other side of the street. Alex. Standing on the corner diagonally across from me, staring up at the walk sign, waiting for the blinking red light to turn green.

A surge ran through my body, and I stood there, my feet immobile, while I attempted to figure out what it was that kept me from moving forward. What kept me from continuing toward Alex as if nothing had happened. As if I was the same person I was before we met. A person who wouldn't be standing outside a restaurant watching a familiar man across the street check his watch while a UPS truck idled next to him at the crosswalk.

But I wasn't that person. And I wasn't the person Alex left. Or the person who prepared for our inevitable meeting one day by making sure her legs were shaved and her eyebrows plucked.

In the beginning, which was really the end, I saw Alex everywhere. Or I thought I did. I was on the lookout, on high alert. A pair of shoes, a laugh, an overcoat. The things that I'd thought made Alex unique weren't unique at all. They were perfectly common.

Running into Alex in a restaurant, at a bar, a store, a Red Sox game—that I'd always imagined. That I'd prepared for. But simply finding him staring up at a red blinking sign of a stick-figure pedestrian with a line through him—that wasn't exactly what I'd envisioned.

He looked exactly the same. The brown hair with the slight cowlick he was always attempting to tame with the palm of his hand. A blue oxford he'd probably purchased at Brooks Brothers after receiving the catalog announcing a sale. I even recognized the pants.

For the first time in a long time, instead of wondering what I'd look like to Alex, I thought about how I looked to myself.

And I looked a lot like Alex. The same, and yet entirely different.

You are who you are, even if over time you tilt a little like a carnival ride. You, but viewed from a different perspective, a different angle. If you'd asked me when I was younger, I would have told you there was no way I would ever cheat on my husband. If you'd asked me when we got married, I'd have told you there was no way I'd ever cheat on Alex. Never. Amazing what time can do; just a little tilt and you become an altered version of yourself. The *you* you were afraid existed. The *you* you never wanted to become.

I started out being the sort of woman who wanted real love. The kind of love that consumes you, envelops you body and soul in a sort of mist that you think makes you invincible. Instead I ended up being the sort of woman who wanted to be good at watching her husband leave.

Alex left, and possibly not because he didn't really love me, but maybe because he came to realize I didn't really love him. At least not the way I was supposed to. Not the way he deserved.

Maybe it wasn't the best kind of love, but it was all I was capable of at the time. I had to believe that. And I had to believe that now I was capable of more. Maybe in the end, getting over the failure of my marriage wasn't about wanting Alex to be happy. Maybe it was about wanting me to be happy.

The light changed and I watched as Alex joined the rush of people crossing the street. I didn't make a move to go toward him, to say hello and ask how he was doing, and I didn't go out of my way to avoid him. I'd probably never have another chance to say what I should have said: *I'm sorry.*

Alex left me because he had to, and now I had to leave him. Not in anger or resentment, but in the hope and belief that there was happiness out there. And in me.

And that's why, instead of going over to him or calling out his name, I let Alex walk away. Then I stepped to the curb, held my hand in the air and hailed a cab.

* * *

I gave the cab driver Mitch's office address, and ten minutes later I was sitting outside his office on the ground floor of a gray stone on a residential stretch of Commonwealth Avenue.

"This is it," the cabbie told me. For the second time. Then he tapped the meter just in case I didn't get the hint.

I managed to extract a ten-dollar bill from my purse, stretching what should have taken a few seconds into what felt like a slow motion sequence from *The Six Million Dollar Man*.

When the cab drove away I didn't ring the bell. Instead I stood outside and tried to catch a glimpse of Mitch through the large bay windows. Once I got the angle right, which required standing on the edge of a flower box lining the front steps, I spotted him. I found exactly who I was looking for, standing over a drafting table under the white glow of pendant lights dangling from the exposed-beam ceiling.

I could have stayed there hoping he'd glance out the front window and see me. I could have waited for his reaction and adjusted mine accordingly, letting my fight-or-flight instinct kick in. Because that's what it had become. Instinct. Or maybe more like a learned response. It had been so long, I could hardly tell the difference anymore. Only I didn't want to fight anymore, and I didn't want to flee, no matter how afraid I was to face Mitch and risk hearing that I'd finally crossed a line that couldn't be forgiven.

I stepped down from the flower box and went to ring the bell. A minute later, there he was, standing on the other side of the glass door, hesitating before reaching for the handle.

"What are you doing here?" he asked, his body filling the space between the doorframe and the door, and leaving little room for me to push myself in. And that's exactly what I should have done. In the movies that's what I would have done, pushed him aside and staked out my ground before pleading my case.

"I need to talk to you," I told him.

"I'm not sure I need to talk to you."

"Give me five minutes. That's all."

Mitch inhaled loudly and then stepped aside, this time giving me enough room to pass by without even having to come close to touching him.

I waited for the sound of the front door clicking shut, and let him lead me to his office.

I sort of expected the place to look like the Flower Carte, with plants and shrubs lined up against the wall. But there was only one plant, and it was seated inside an old brick fireplace that had been painted white. There were a few square samples of granite resting against a fireplace, some stone bricks lined up on the mantel and a scale model of someone's backyard on a table toward the back.

"Look, you've seen me at my worst. I was paranoid and stupid, and not thinking clearly." I stood in the center of the studio, my voice echoing off the hardwood floors before bouncing off the stark white walls. Just what I needed: fabulous acoustics.

"You forgot dishonest and manipulative," he added.

"Yeah, that, too," I conceded. "But I realized what I did was wrong and I was about to tell you."

"Too little, too late, Abby." Mitch walked over to the drafting table and leaned back against it, his fingers curling around the edge as if he was holding on. "You know, I have no idea what else you put into that database of yours, what other malicious information you were spreading around the city."

"It was nothing that horrible," I told him. "Really."

Mitch shook his head at me. "Nothing that horrible. Well, gee, thanks, Abby. As long as it was nothing *that* horrible."

"Fine, I'm horrible. I deserve it."

Something turned up the corners of Mitch's mouth, something that looked vaguely like he was trying not to smile.

I found myself smiling back.

He instantly frowned. "This isn't funny."

"I know," I told him. "But it's over. I shut the whole thing down. I'm out of business."

"I hope you don't expect me to feel bad for you."

Okay, maybe a little. "No."

"Look, Abby. I don't know what you expect me to say. What do you want?"

What did I want? I'd known for a while now, probably ever since I noticed Snoopy on his bookshelf. Only now I had to say it out loud, here, in Mitch's office where the words would reverberate around me, around us, and I'd have no idea where they'd land.

"Say you forgive me," I said, and then added something I never could have imagined saying a year ago, or two, even though I probably should have. Only this time, I wasn't going to make the same mistake. "Say you're willing to give me a chance."

Mitch hesitated for a minute, letting my answer settle around him before turning and reaching for a mechanical pencil resting on the drafting table. "I've got a lot of work to do before the long weekend, Abby."

"Sure." The word tripped over the lump taking root in my throat. "I understand." I turned to leave.

"Tell your mom I said congratulations," he called after me, although he didn't look up from the table or the pencil in his hand.

He couldn't forgive me, but he could remember that my mother was getting married.

Before the door closed behind me, I glanced over my shoulder one more time. Mitch had the T square in his hand, his fingers pulling a pencil along the straightedge. I paused, waiting for him to look up at me, waiting for him to say something. But he never looked up. And I let the door close behind me.

chapter twenty-nine

When I got home I had refunds to process. A database to purge. There were eight voice mails on my office phone complaining that the Web site was down. I deleted every single one of them and sat down to write my last e-mail as the founder of womenknowbetter.com.

There was no way I'd get through all of this, not with everything I had to do. I called the Whitney Inn and left a message for my mom telling her that I wouldn't be on the ferry tonight. I had too many things I needed to take care of.

Dear Members, I began, and then stopped. There was no good way to spin what really happened. I blew it. Instead of ensuring that women invested wisely, I'd given them an excuse to hedge their bets, to play it safe.

Luckily, the phone rang and I didn't have to type that. "Hello?"

"Hi there, I'm a member, my ID number is 412 and something seems to be wrong with the site."

Here it was, one less e-mail I'd have to send. "The site is no longer working," I told Member 412.

"So, when will it be up and running again?"

"It won't."

"But I need to access it. Now. I'm supposed to have a date tomorrow night and I need to know what I'm in for."

"I'm sorry, I can't help you."

"Can't you just look him up for me? His name is Alex Madden."

I inhaled sharply, and Member 412 must have thought I'd had the wind knocked out of me.

"Alex Madden?" I repeated.

"Yeah, can you see if he's in the database?"

See, this was why I stopped believing in God. Because if I believed in the Almighty, I'd have to believe that I was being set up for some sort of test. That this *member* wasn't simply a woman checking up on a prospective date, but rather was part of some greater cosmic design. As if, in his limited time, the Creator of All Things decided to spend a few minutes on Abby Dunn, and see whether she was worth saving.

Because I could look up Member 412's prospective date. All it would take was a click of a mouse. Better yet, I didn't even have to exert the energy. I knew everything she could ever want to know. Or I could save us both the time and simply tell this woman to stay away from Alex, that he hid his horns and tail under the navy pinstriped suits. And three months ago, when the database was merely an idea, when the thought of avoiding potentially painful relationships was the holy grail, that's probably exactly what I would have done.

"I can't do that," I told her instead. "The service is no longer available. You'll find a refund for the remaining fee on your credit card next month."

"What am I supposed to do now?" she practically wailed.

"Well, I guess you could go out with him and decide for yourself what you think." I spoke slowly, letting the words imprint themselves on my brain. I was telling a strange woman to go on a date with my ex-husband. And I didn't do it to prove I could pass a test or to garner some sort of positive goodwill from the powers that be.

I did it because the woman needed to take the risk, just like me.

There was only one last purpose the database had to serve. I'd be damned if at least one good thing didn't come out of this. I typed in the name of one final data point and took down the information that popped up on his screen.

I finished writing my letter, e-mailed it to my members, and then logged on to the home page and posted one last message: *This web site is no longer in service.*

Then one by one I purged the database files, not even looking up Member 412 to see who she was, to see whom Alex would be having dinner with tomorrow night. It no longer mattered.

By eight o'clock, every file, every index and fund, had been wiped clean. And considering how long it had taken me to get here, I figured at least a clap of thunder or bolt of lightning was the least I could expect. But all I got was a beep from my computer and a pop-up box telling me that the process of deleting the selected files was complete.

I shut down the computer one last time, grabbed the paper with the handwritten address off my desk and headed out the door.

Curtis McWilliams lived in the North End surrounded by bakeries and Italian restaurants that filled the narrow streets with the smell of roasted garlic. I probably should have called first, but I wasn't sure Curtis would see me, considering he'd never met me and I was Maggie's best friend. I wasn't even positive Maggie had told him who I was.

When he answered the door, Curtis looked like a normal guy, average in every way. Not tall, not short. Not too fat, not too thin. He didn't look like a liar, or an ex-husband or someone who went around telling unsuspecting women his ex-wife was a bitch. He seemed perfectly normal, which I thought was a good thing considering the alternative.

"Can I help you?"

"I'm Abby, a friend of Maggie's."

Curtis stepped back into the brick foyer, bristling a bit.

"I know what happened, and I know she was pissed, but you shouldn't give up."

"I think it's out of my hands now," he told me, moving toward the doorway again. "I tried to talk to her."

"Well, keep trying. She's worth the effort, I promise. Don't give up."

Curtis crossed his arms over his chest and examined me. "Did she tell you to come here?"

I shook my head, and Curtis smirked at me. "Then why are you here?"

"Maggie didn't tell me to come, but that doesn't mean she's ready to cut you loose."

"So what should I do?"

"Go see her at the store. Make her listen to you, and she will. Maggie's not unreasonable."

"And you think that will work?"

"Do you really like her?" I asked.

"I really do. I did, anyway."

"Then you've got nothing to lose. But you'll have to wait until Tuesday. She'll be gone all weekend."

"I'll give it a try if you think she'll talk to me."

I smiled at Curtis, and he gave me a hopeful smile in return. For a normal guy, he had a great smile.

I stepped back onto the sidewalk, figuring I'd done what I came to do. "Can I ask you something?"

He shrugged.

"Why didn't you just tell Maggie the truth?"

"I don't know. It seems stupid now, but at the time I thought if she knew the truth she might think there was something wrong with me."

I nodded. He was right; it seemed stupid now. "Can I ask you one more thing? Which bakery has the best chocolate chip cannolis?"

My fingers clutching the red and white string tied around the bakery box, I walked up Charles Street toward Mitch's place. It was Friday night and he was probably already out, but I wanted to take the chance. Worst-case scenario, he'd be home and wouldn't even let me in. Best-case scenario, he'd not only let me in; he'd offer to share his cannolis as well.

As I approached his building, I could see the light on in his apartment window. The same window we'd sat next to for fried hamburgers and a shadow puppet show.

"Who is it?" he asked through the intercom, answering the buzzer so fast, it was almost as if he was waiting for me.

"It's Abby."

No buzz to let me in.

"I have something for you."

Still no buzz.

"I brought you something."

Silence.

"Cannolis from Mike's Pastry."

The front door buzzed to life and I pushed my way in. Only five floors to go.

Mitch was waiting for me in the hallway, and so for a second I thought maybe he'd just come out to take the cannolis and send me on my way.

"Hi." I smiled at him and he returned a polite *hello*. "I thought you'd like these." I passed him the box and he took it.

"How'd you know these were my favorite?" he asked, and then shook his head at me and turned to walk into the apartment. "Forget it, I know how you knew."

Mitch had left me standing alone in the hallway, but he'd also left the door open, so I followed him inside.

"Aren't cannolis the patron pastry of repentant women everywhere?" I joked, but Mitch wasn't having any of it—my joke, my attempt to apologize, even my cannolis.

He placed the box on the breakfast bar and turned to face me, but I wasn't about to give Mitch an opportunity to tell me to leave.

"You never told me about the baby shower."

"Is that why you're here, Abby? To see if I took home the prize for guessing the number of jelly beans in the baby bottle?"

I shook my head no.

"I've heard your messages. I know you've apologized. I just don't know what else it is that you want from me."

My chest tightened as I told him exactly what it was I wanted. "I want you to say you don't hate me."

"Anything else?" he wanted to know, as if my first request was so out of the realm of possibility, it didn't even warrant a response.

"I want you to know that even if I made some bad choices, did some not very wise things, I didn't intend to hurt you," I continued. "I really didn't."

"Then what were you trying to do?"

I could go through the whole thing again, the idea that I'd be the savior of all damaged women everywhere, but I didn't. Because that wasn't the reason I'd continued changing Mitch's data. "I guess I just didn't want to share you with the redheads of the world."

"Her name was Sophia," he deadpanned. "And, if I remember, you were the one who told me you weren't interested, Abby. From the get-go you let that be known."

I wanted to look away, at my feet, or the wall, or out the window toward Cambridge. I wanted to turn around and walk out the door before he could ask me to leave, before he decided this entire conversation was more trouble than it was worth. Instead I made myself look at Mitch and hold his gaze without turning away. "I was wrong. I changed my mind. Now I realize I went about it the wrong way, but I'm trying to correct that, Mitch. At least I'm trying."

He didn't deny that. "I don't know that it's that easy," he told me.

"I don't expect it to be easy, but at least I'm trying. At least now you know." I pointed to the bakery box. "I hope you enjoy them, I've got to go. There's an early ferry to Martha's Vineyard with my name on it."

Mitch didn't stop me from leaving, but as I pulled the door closed behind me, he called out, "Thanks for the cannolis."

By the time I got back to my apartment it was past eleven and there was only one more thing left for me to do: pack for my mother's wedding.

I removed the navy blue strapless dress from its hanger, threw in some shorts and a bathing suit, and zipped up my bag. Claudia and Maggie were picking me up at the ferry in Vineyard Haven tomorrow morning—a mere seven hours away. It had been a long night and I was ready to fall into bed.

Sleeping in my T-shirt required less effort than finding a clean nightgown, and sleeping in my makeup, while guaranteed to result in a whitehead that would make me regret my choice in the morning, was easier than washing it off. I was about to shut off the light when I remembered one more thing. And, while sleeping in a T-shirt I'd worn all day and waking up with broken eyelashes on my pillow weren't exactly the best decisions, I couldn't go to bed without taking care of something that should have been taken care of a long time ago.

I got out of bed and walked over to my dresser. From inside my underwear drawer I pulled out the small plastic bag and tossed it into my suitcase. I fell asleep before I could contemplate the state of my karma, or wonder whether what goes around really does, eventually, come around.

chapter thirty

We're expected to remember our *first*. Only what we sometimes forget in the wistful moments of longing for our *first* is the enduring significance of our *last*. The last Sunday morning you saw your parents holding hands on the porch, their fingers intertwined as they watched you doing cartwheels on the front lawn. The instant you realize that, even though you never believed it could really happen, you've said good-bye to someone for the last time. The last person who made you feel like you'd spontaneously combust if you didn't kiss him right then and there.

Only I never got to kiss Mitch, and yet I still hadn't exploded all over the passenger deck of the Martha's Vineyard ferry. A few seagulls had, however, which is why, instead of standing at the rail looking for Claudia and Maggie waiting for me at the dock, I watched the seagulls floating over me and prepared to take cover if they decided I made an easy mark.

"The bed-and-breakfast is gorgeous!" Claudia and Maggie were waiting for me at the ferry dock in Vineyard Haven. "Wait until you see the porch and the garden out back. And it's right on the main street. If

I'd known it would be this great, I would have told your mom to get married years ago."

"What have you guys been doing?"

Maggie ran down the list of activities. "You name it, we've done it. The beach, shopping, bike riding."

"There's a great bookstore on Main Street," Claudia added. "And it's always nice and cool inside."

"How's my mom doing? Is the stress getting to her?"

"Stress, are you kidding me? Who do you think led us on the bike ride?"

Maggie squeezed my shoulder before reaching for my suitcase and tossing it in the backseat of her car. "How are you doing?"

"Hanging in there. I'm officially out of business and public enemy number one among the landscape architect community."

"Ooh." Maggie feigned a good cringe. "And I hear they're a tough crowd."

"The worst."

I'd tried calling Mitch one last time before I left for the ferry. Seven o'clock in the morning and he didn't answer. He was either avoiding me, as he had the other times I'd left voice mails, or he had spent the night somewhere and hadn't made it home. As much as I hoped he wasn't lying in bed with a pillow over his head so he wouldn't hear me leave another message on his answering machine, I hoped even more that he wasn't lying in bed with a pillow over his head in some woman's apartment.

"So, what do you want to do first? Check out the beach? Hit the stores?" Maggie slowed down as we entered Main Street. We all kept our eyes open for a parking space, which, as it was August and Labor Day weekend and Martha's Vineyard, verged on utter futility. Not to mention insanity.

"I'll drop you guys off and drive around," Maggie offered, and, being the person she is, Claudia offered to stay in the car and keep her company.

Being the person I am, which is someone who had pretty much alienated almost every single woman in Boston and even a few of their friends in Providence, Rhode Island, who'd managed to convince me I should let them join due to the short commute, not to mention a landscape architect who was probably at this moment being served eggs Benedict in bed by a woman named Willie, I got out of the car and headed for the front door of the Whitney Inn.

"You must be Abby Dunn." The man at the front desk appeared to be waiting for me.

"Don't tell me you were in the database, too."

He shook his head, confused. "Aren't you here for your mom's wedding?"

"Yep, that's me."

"She's out back in the garden waiting for you." He suggested he take my bags up to my room and I accepted the offer.

The garden was actually a nice-size backyard with a slate patio and about fifty oversize hydrangea bushes circling the perimeter. There was obviously nothing wrong with the soil here.

I found my mom reclining on an Adirondack chair, an iced tea in her hand.

"Yeah!" She tried to clap, and the tea splashed on her shorts. "I've been waiting for you to get here."

She looked so relaxed with her feet up on the footrest and her hair pushed off her face with a pair of sunglasses. This was not a woman on the verge of a breakdown because in less than seven hours she'd pledge to love and honor the same man for the rest of her life.

I walked over, bent down and kissed my mom on the cheek, only instead of letting me get away, she reached up and pulled me down into a full-on hug that felt like it lasted longer than the ferry ride over.

"I'm sorry I couldn't come sooner," I apologized, but she just squeezed harder.

"Roger's a mess," she told me, letting go. "He went into town to try and walk it off. At least that's what he told me. I think he probably went to Mad Martha's for a mint chocolate chip ice cream cone."

I smiled at the idea that my mom knew exactly which flavor Roger would order.

"Ice cream sounds good right now." I swiped a trickle of sweat from my forehead. "Actually, I was thinking of walking into town myself."

"Go ahead." She waved me away. "Enjoy yourself. As long as you're back in time to get dressed for the ceremony, you can go anywhere you want."

"In that case, do you think I could borrow Roger's car? I have an errand I want to run."

"The keys are at the front desk, and it's parked around the corner by the church." My mom reached for my hand and held it. "But before you go, are things any better with Mitch?" she asked.

I shook my head.

"Why don't you give him a call and invite him to come out and join you?" she suggested. "Nothing says truce like a wedding invitation."

"I can't do that. It's your day."

"I know that, and if the blushing bride is telling you to invite him, you better make sure you listen."

"I've tried."

"Then keep trying," she instructed. "Call him. He has to answer eventually, right?"

I nodded, but I wasn't so sure. Isn't that why they invented answering machines in the first place?

* * *

The streets of Edgartown were packed with tourists eager to order ice cream and lobster and submarine sandwiches for twice what they'd pay at home. And I was one of them. With my double scoop of chocolate with rainbow sprinkles, I wandered down Main Street like everyone else, searching the window displays looking for what they'd bring home, what they'd remember—sunsets over Menemsha Harbor, the steamed lobsters that made their chins glisten with melted butter. They'd forget about the jellyfish and the ants in the cupboard and incessantly driving around Edgartown's narrow streets in search of a parking space. Instead they'd tell their friends about the huge waves at South Beach.

I obeyed the signs warning me to keep my food and drink outside, so I didn't wind up with a new T-shirt or a pair of pink and green flip-flops. But by the time I reached the sundry shop on the corner, I'd finished my ice cream and was willing to pay whatever they wanted for a bottle of cold water.

When my parents split up, there must have also been a sort of implicit arrangement to divide every other part of their life down the middle. And in the settlement, my dad somehow got Cape Cod. The first summer they were apart, my dad took me down to the Cape by himself. He didn't even bring Susan, which surprised me and delighted me at the same time. What didn't delight me, but also didn't surprise me, was that my mom didn't go anywhere that summer. She'd stayed in Newton by herself for one week and with me for the eleven others.

The next summer, she decided it was time to claim her own summer vacation, to start making some new memories to replace the old ones—not to mention the Cape Cod magnets we kept on our refrigerator. And that's when she started coming to the Vineyard. That's also when she replaced the Cape Cod magnets with new ones of the Edgartown lighthouse and miniature lobster traps and refrigerator-magnet-size replicas of yellow and blue buoys.

As I waited in line to pay for my water I noticed the magnets on display and wondered how many times my mother stood in line at the sundry shop before she decided that her refrigerator could use an update. And that's when I noticed the display of Christmas ornaments on a small carousel beside the magnets. Instead of red stockings and candy canes, there were wooden sailboats and shellacked shells and carved scenes of Main Street dangling by satin ribbons.

I reached for my favorite, a snowman in a yellow fisherman's slicker with a fishing pole dangling over his shoulder. There weren't any fish attached to the hook, only a set of Christmas lights, which made me think that the snowman wasn't the best fisherman out there. But from the looks of his black rubber boots and the weathered beard under his carrot nose, at least he was willing to keep trying.

"Will that be all?" the girl behind the counter asked, pointing to my bottled water.

"One Lucky Roll," I said, picking the scratch card with the pair of dice tumbling toward me. A little wedding present for my mom.

"Anything else?"

I handed over the ornament. "This, too, please," I told her, thinking my snowman would make a perfect replacement for a wooden moon in a Santa hat.

After my shopping trip, I went back to the inn and dropped the ornament in my room, where my suitcase was waiting. I reached into the case's side pocket and then headed downstairs to the front desk to get Roger's keys.

I had one more errand to run.

❊ ❊ ❊

When I got to South Beach, it was almost three o'clock. The parking lot wasn't nearly as crowded as Main Street, and the lifeguards wore their Santa red sweatshirts with SOUTH BEACH emblazoned across the front—just in case the young girls couldn't tell whom they were supposed to be gawking at.

I walked barefoot onto the beach, dropped my cell phone and Roger's keys onto the sand, and headed straight down to the water. The tide was going out, but I followed it until the salt water rose above my ankles. And then I kept on going, even until I could no longer see my toes. And even though I was sure there were all sorts of creatures down there just waiting to feast on the flesh of a thirty-one-year-old woman, I didn't stop.

"Shouldn't you have a bathing suit on?" a little girl asked me when I finally walked out of the water and took a seat on the sand.

"Probably," I told her, wringing out the hem of my shorts. "But sometimes you can't wait, so you just have to dive right in."

I turned over onto my stomach to let the sun dry me off, and picked up my cell phone, ready to dial.

"It's me." I waited for Mitch to say something. Anything. I wasn't exactly expecting a friendly *Hey there*, but I definitely wasn't prepared for complete silence. At least he picked up the phone; that had to be a good sign, right? Or maybe I'd just decided to utilize the knowledge that pressing *69 blocked caller ID. "Look, I'm sorry. I could say it a million more times and it wouldn't make what I did any less horrible. But I am sorry. Really."

More silence, and then finally, "I know you are."

I dug my toes into the sand and then kicked them into the wind.

He knew. If I was a butterfly, I'd begin flapping my wings; if I was a dog, I'd wag my tail. But I was a woman on decidedly shaky ground, so instead I took a deep breath of salt air and charged on. "I was wondering if you'd like to come join me on the Vineyard for the weekend. There's a ferry every hour from Woods Hole," I added, ready to recite the entire schedule if that's what it would take to get him on a boat over here. Shit, I'd stand on the ferry dock holding a boom box over my head while Peter Gabriel songs played, if that was what it would take to change his mind.

Only it didn't sound like he'd changed his mind. "Your mom is getting married, Abby."

"So maybe you can catch the bouquet; Maggie says it's beautiful."

I thought I heard Mitch smile. "I doubt she wants a total stranger at her wedding."

"Actually, she's the one who told me to invite you. I guess she heard through the grapevine that you do a mean chicken dance." As soon as I said it I knew I'd left myself open. There was no grapevine, only a database. "Or was it the electric slide?" I asked, hoping he'd laugh.

But he didn't laugh. Instead he asked, "Can I bring my peg leg and eye patch, or is it semiformal?"

It was almost four o'clock and I had a wedding to get to. There was just one more thing I had to do. And my shorts weren't totally dry yet, so it wasn't exactly an easy task. But finally I managed to get my hand into my pocket and remove the crumpled plastic sandwich bag. The platinum and diamond rings were wedged deep into the corner, and I had to shake the rings loose from the plastic stretched across the prongs.

I looked out at the dark blue ocean and the whitecaps of foam as they welled up on the surface. Maggie had once suggested I toss my rings into Boston Harbor, but what were a bunch of fish supposed to do with a couple of platinum bands? So instead of winding up like I was on the mound at Fenway Park, I kneeled down and dug a little hole in the sand, deep enough to hit the damp, dark layer under the surface, but not so deep that its contents couldn't be found by someone with a metal detector. Or someone who just felt like digging and was lucky enough to discover an emerald-cut diamond that once belonged to someone who didn't need it any longer.

I glanced down at my hands, ready to wipe away the grainy bits of sand clinging to my damp skin, and for the first time in months I didn't see what was missing. Instead I noticed how much they resembled my mother's hands.

It wasn't Nantucket, and I didn't have two point five kids tugging on my Lilly Pulitzer skirt, but at that moment, life was feeling pretty damn good.

Roger was standing on the front porch already dressed in his white pants and blue oxford. A navy blazer was draped over the back of the Adirondack chair to his left.

"Don't you look nice," I called to him. "But a little early, aren't you?"

"Maybe. White pants, what was I thinking?" He tapped his fingers on the porch railing like he was playing the piano. "I can't even sit down."

From the way he was pacing back and forth, I didn't think it mattered what color his pants were. This man couldn't stay still long enough to sit anywhere.

"Where's Mom?"

"Upstairs. I think she's waiting for you."

Before I went into my room to take a shower and slip into my navy strapless dress, I needed to see my mom.

"Hello?" I tapped lightly on the door to her suite and then let myself in.

There she was, seated at the vanity, looking at her reflection as she painted on lipstick with a slim gold brush.

I held up the large-barreled curling iron on the tabletop, its tip still warm. "What, no hot rollers?" I joked.

"Can you explain to me why a ceramic curling iron is better for me than any other curling iron?"

I shook my head. "Sorry. I gave up curling irons after the singed-ear fiasco of 1993."

"I remember that," she told me. "I don't blame you."

"I better go get ready. Roger's downstairs pacing on the porch."

"Is your friend going to be coming?"

I nodded. "But he probably won't be here until the reception."

"That's fine. There's no rush, right? He'll be here when he gets here."

You can take the risk of setting yourself up for happiness, or spend your life avoiding the possibility of losing it. I'd regretted it, everything I ever let Alex see in me—the weakness, the insecurity, the neediness. But what I regretted most of all now was that I was afraid to let him see more.

Will Alex ever be reduced to simply *the man by the door* or *that man getting into the cab* or *the guy on the escalator at the airport*? Maybe. Possibly. I hoped so; at least a part of me did. Another part imagined that if we ever ran into each other, I'd look at him in an entirely new way, see him, maybe for the first time, for the person he was. Someone who always ordered cheese on his burgers but asked for salad dressing on the side. Someone who listened to my *Phantom of the Opera* CD and never suggested I not sing along. A person who could love me and still hurt me. A person with flaws. A person not unlike me.

"Are you ready?" My mother poked her head into my room and then came toward me, her satin dress swishing around her ankles.

I stood up, twirled around in my dress and watched her smile. "You look beautiful."

I smiled back. "You stole my line."

"Here, before I forget." I reached for the lottery ticket on the dresser. "I figured today was your lucky day, so why not?"

I handed over the Lucky Roll, but my mom didn't take the ticket. "Why don't you keep it? I think I have all the luck I need today."

I took back the ticket.

"Are you feeling lucky?" she asked.

"I do believe I am."

"Then, shall we?" She reached for the loose change in a pile on the dresser and handed me a quarter. "Start scratching."

One by one I uncovered the images beneath the purple coating.

"Oh, well," my mom said, after I'd revealed that the card was a total loser. "There's always next time."

"You're right," I told her. "There's always next time."